GEMINI COVEN

SEVEN

Gemini Coven
Zodiac Rising Series Book #2
Copyright © 2022 Seven / House of Seven Publishing

Internal illustration by Seven
Formatting by Seven

This book is licensed for your personal enjoyment. This book may NOT be reproduced or copied in any way. Any form of copying this book is plagiarism and theft. Thank you for respecting the hard work of this author.
All Rights Reserved.
This is a work of fiction. Names, characters, places, brands, media, and incidents are either the product of the author's imagination or are used fictitiously.

Gemini Coven as told by Seven, Published by House of Seven.
First Edition 2022
ISBN: 9798372354395

*In loving Memory of
Daniel Joseph Denigris.*

The only father I ever had, who was also a Gemini.

PLEAIDES

PANTHEON

METOS

POIDS

Old Gemini Coven

OUTLIERS

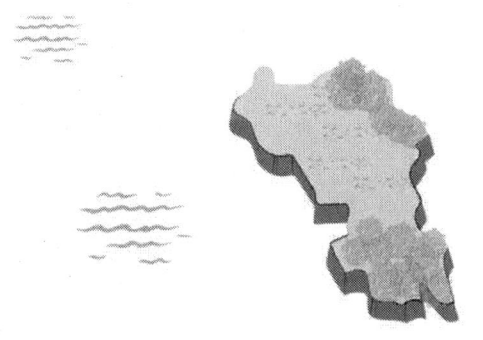

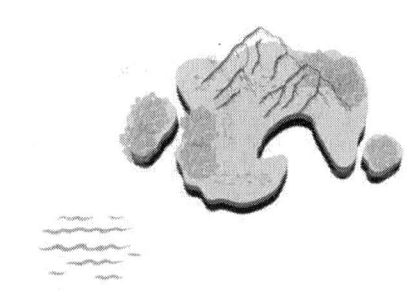

META

Twin Seouls

Gemini Coven Hideout

Nobility

For My husband and children, who without, I would be nothing.
or my family who raised me.

For my best friend who supports me and encourages me every single day.

For my arc team, who without, I would have many errors.

For my street team who keep me sane and have watched me cry and want to quit, but have never let me.

For my team, my right hand three.
Without you guys, I'd be bald and drunk.

For the Baddies in Booktok Baddies.

All my love to you many beautiful and wonderful humans, shifters and witches, who've helped me form the world we love.

An ode to my reader:

Here we are again, on the second installment of Zodiac Rising. It's because of you giving me this chance that we are here.

You care about me. I care about you. This book, like the first, has trigger warnings- as will all books in this series.

This series comes from my own experience and practices growing up, as well as a love of science and an extreme past. I, like many others out there, possibly even you, suffer from anxiety, C-PTSD and panic disorder. I have ADHD and Autism and I've struggled all my life with being able to verbalize what's in my mind.

I am a SURVIVOR of DV, SA, and many other things that no one should ever have to experience. On the next page, you will find my list of trigger warnings. Some are there because the theme is evident. Some are there as a precaution. You may think the list is extensive. I think it's necessary because you never know what one word can do to someone else. Words are so, so powerful.

So, to you, my dear reader, I say this: Please love yourself the way you should. Take care of you and know that you providing me the chance to live out my greatest dream of being an author means everything to me and even that isn't worth risking YOU and YOUR MENTAL HEALTH.

If you find that the trigger warnings are too much, and you don't want to risk reading, please email Seven at its7theauthor@aol.com if you've purchased this copy. This applies to all copies from my author website as well as Amazon and B+N.

You are important.
You matter.

Always,

Seven

Trigger Warnings:

-Mental Health
-Body Dysmorphia
-Horror
-Demons
-Blood
-Murder

Gemini Coven Playlist:

- Darkside - Alan Walker, Au/Ra, Tomine Harket
- Devil Doens't Bargain - Alec Benjamin
- STAY - Kid Laroi
- Pompeii - Bastille
- Freaks - Jordan Clarke
- Crash and Burn - Maggie Lindemann
- Witching Hour - Rezz
- Someone To You - Banners
- Under the Influence - Chris Brown
- Frozen - Madonna, Sickick
- Golden Hour - JVKE
- Villain - K/DA
- Play with Fire - Sam Tinnez, Yacht Money
- Viliante Shit - Taylor Swift
- Breakfast - Dove Cameron

Find the playlist on Spotify at
https://open.spotify.com/playlist/6ntkdL37V3ILSrzkCUBylt?si=iupCuABUTVyDdmzariy9Tg

Character Pronunciation Guide:
(In no particular order)

Riley - Rye-lee
Riot - Rye-uht
Locke - Lok
Kaz - Ca-z
Vertez - Vur-te-z
Arabia - Uh-ray-be-uh
Tambo - Tam-bow
Madame Deveraux - Mad-ame Day-vou-roux
Arnoldous - Are-nul-dew-us
Cordelia - Core-dee-lia
Sideon - Sid-Ee-On
Martino - Mar-teen-oh
Phaedra - Fay-dra
Posh - Posh
Amira - Ah-meer-ah
Aene - Ay-uen (Aye-n)
Quincy - Quinn-see
Bayldonite - Bale-don-ite
Mordechai - More-de-kai
Elliot - El-li-ot
Sterling - Stir-ling
Ophiuchus - Oh-few-kus
Suche - Sue-ch-ay
Charitha - Char-ee-tha
Marcella - Mar-sell-uh
Staler - Stat-lur
Kodjo - Ko-jo
Rori - Roar-we
Jira - Here-uh

PROLOGUE

"Suche, please. You have to stop this nonsense. You're going to cause an all-out war and for what? Some meaningless throne!"

"Meaningless? Are you mad, woman?"

"Then for what?"

"A place of belonging for our daughter! A chance to free her of a life like this!"

My wife was everything to me, but she was ignorant. Ignorant and beautiful. She had a life of luxury in Pantheon while the rest of us rotted away in the Outliers, subjected to crime and disease. I want to make it better. No, I *need* to make it better. I needed to create a world where we could separate the vile humans from those of us who were civilized. Those without magic were animals.

It isn't their fault, I can sympathize with that notion, but it's in their nature and there's nothing that can be done about it. Even still, their mortality and selfish ailments are a sickness, one I refuse to raise my daughter around.

"Charitha, please. Please just understand that this is for the best."

She looks at me, blue eyes sad and sparkling.

"Our daughter deserves a free life. Right now, she isn't showing any sign of magic beyond shifting."

"Eclectic shifting! That's not even a faction, Suche. Pantheon will never accept her. They will never deem her worthy of luxury. Of immortality, even if she fights for it. If she were to even fight, she'd be doing it for all her life."

My wife's face is paled, and the lines etched deep into her porcelain skin from years before were now sunken and sad. The laughter we had shared to create those were long gone, thanks to the deities and their broken promises.

"We can't go on like this. If not for our daughter, then for us."

"You're not even supposed to speak to the Cardinals, much less the way that you do. If you're caught, there will be deadly consequences." She sits now, grief taking hold of her delicate body.

Kneeling before her, I take her small hands in mine. She's always been so fragile, so helpless. Looking at her now, I know deep down that she's my reason for being alive. For fighting through the challenges being born in the Outliers possessed. When I'd met her, she was just a small Basilisk. I was so much larger than she, both in size and in stature.

She liked to hide back then, so I'd taken my time with her, going to visit her hiding space in Corset Forest every single day. When she finally showed me her human self, I was enchanted. I find myself evermore enchanted with her every day, even now.

"I promise, my queen, that when this is all over, we will have everything you've ever wanted not just for ourselves, but for all factions."

She nods and I plant a kiss right on her forehead. Leaving her behind clawed at my heart every single time I had to do it, but it wasn't safe for her to be out in the factions. It was tense, everyone was on edge, and no one trusted anyone else. The less I had her out there, the better.

I made my way through the heavily armored Loyalists guarding the gates to Pantheon by showing them my access chip.

"You, Outlander, where are you going?" A heavily armored guard carrying a long weapon I've not seen before approaching me demands with great purpose.

"I'm visiting the Sovereigns. They have beckoned me to a meeting with them." I show him my access chip, given to me the last time I'd snuck to Pantheon to see the Cardinals a few days ago.

He eyes me wearily then turns to his comrade and speaks in a language I don't know.

"Glo jy hom?"

"Hy is 'n vuil Outlander, wat sal?" Responds his comrade as he turns, walking away from me and back across the wrought iron gate that separates the Zodiac Covens from the rest of us.

The gates were just another reminder that we were seen as less than them instead of equal to them. The gods and the Zodiac covens had it all wrong. We were better than the humans.

"I'll take you," he said, gesturing to a cart that was now pulling up next to us.

I tried not to show how nervous I was as I climbed into the cart, taking the seat on the bench that had my back facing forwards. The guard took the seat across from me, looking in the onward direction, looking directly at me.

I kept my face and demeanor calm and passive as the cart took off through the gates and along the guarded bridge. The guards' eyes didn't leave my face for a moment as we traveled. I stared right back, not trusting the guard just as much as he clearly didn't trust me.

We pull up to the Zodiac Coven's lands. Pantheon had since been walled into a circle with twelve equal sections, each one a home to a Zodiac Coven. The center was a smaller circle that hosted three large castles where the modality leaders lived. We traveled through the designated travelers' routes until we reached them. The Cardinals lived in the center and biggest castle. The Mutables in the left, the Fixed in the right.

The cart pulls to a stop in front of the Cardinals Castle and the guard watches me as I stumble out of the cart, the energy here being almost too much to handle. It took time to adjust to like I was suddenly breathing in lots of thin air at once, but I quickly found my ground and waited as the guard got his bearings as well.

He accompanied me to the looming front doors.

"We will see now if you tell the truth, Outlander."

The doors open and Statler, Leader of Capricorn Coven, answers it.

"My Lord," the guard bows low.

"This Outlander indicated he was on his way to see you," He breathes, holding his bow.

"Yes, thank you. You may come in, Suche. Your prompt response is much appreciated," his voice like wine.

The guard looks gob smacked as I shoot him a mocking glance as if to say, *see*? He quickly fixes his posture, still in the presence of the Lord, until the door closes.

Wordlessly, Statler guides me through the castle. We can't risk anyone knowing I'm here just yet. I'd never been in the main parts of the castle before. We hurried through the main entrance which was flooded with intricate details. The walls were etched to the ceiling with filigree, gold trim and hand painted scenes of the gods and covens.

When we finally got to the detached cathedral building, Statler offered me a seat at the half moon table. Around the outside were twelve seats, one for each coven leader. On the inside, one for the person they were meeting with. An intimidating seat. One that sent a message.

I took it as he took his in the center. We were now across from one another. He threw a formation over us and covered the shield with the elements.

"No one can hear us now. As per usual, I placed a silencing formation over us. I should start off telling you that I have given specific instructions for the Fixed and Mutable signs to arrive here in that order. We have moments to speak."

I nod, adrenaline coursing through my veins. All my whispering to Statler, to the Cardinals, came down to this. For months I had been speaking to Statler so that he would speak to the other Cardinals. They were clearly above the other signs as would be expected for natural leaders; and it was time for them to take control.

I'd taken my time to learn about the Sovereigns from my wife when we were younger. When she chose to leave Pantheon to be with me, she gave up the title her father had given her. I used her knowledge. I took years to ask her everything I needed to know, and it all came down to this, right here. This moment.

"I'm ready. We've done all we can do to prepare. The Cardinals deserve to be at the top. We need real change for the betterment of Meta."

Statler eyes me, his black horns glinting light off the shimmering water over his shields. He was in all sense of the word, breathtaking. He was every bit a man and every bit a goat, like he stayed in a constant state of in between, rather than full shifted as a human or his true self. Hopefully, he'd done his job properly and was going to be the goat of change.

"Agreed. We have company. Please stand."

I felt like he had sized me up one last time, to see if I was worth all of this. He decided correctly, lucky for him. With a wave of his hand, he diminished the swirling elements and shield, and I stood, stepping aside, my back now to him. The rest of the Cardinals entered the room.

A fiery red and orange haired woman who I knew immediately was the Aries Lordess followed by a man with green and cerulean hair entered the space first. Last to enter the room was a woman with long silver hair and a crown made of pearl light.

Her skin was glowing from beneath its surface on her cheeks, shoulders and around her head like a halo. She was undoubtedly the Libra Lordess. Libra was the first to speak, her throat lighting up in its center with that orange-golden glow.

"Statler, who is this? Why have we been summoned?"

"Please, Adonia, take your seat. We only have moments to discuss as the Fixed and Mutables will be joining us soon."

They each stood behind their seats, not taking them.

"What is the meaning of an Outlander in our royal cathedral?" the other male asked.

"Moon, Adonia, Burn, thank you for coming. This," he gestures towards me. Their eyes were already plastered to my face.

"This is Suche, a shifter from the Outliers."

"Yes, Statler, that is clearly evident. *Why* is it *here*?" Burn said through gritted teeth.

Her amber skin glowed similar to Libra's, but her glow was deep reds and oranges. The halo around her head looked like flitting embers, playfully dancing around her. Her horns curled back on either side of her head, unlike Statler's, who's veered up and back towards the sky.

"This is the confidant who has been giving me information. The information that you all have agreed to."

They look at me now with different eyes.

"You? You think the world of the Cardinals?" Adonia speaks now, her face questioning, but her tone lit with excitement.

I nod. They must have thought me strange for this, in my long black coat and dirty demeanor whilst they were all so flawless.

"It's now or never, my Lordess, and my Lords. You should be the reigning powers. Humans are vile. The rest of the magical beings who aren't witches are different than the Humans."

"You dare challenge the decisions of the gods?" Moon asks now, his sparkly skin reflecting an array of colors, lit by Burn's embers.

"I do. We have great power and could be essential to Pantheon. To Meta."

"We could sanction new lands for those who are magical to live. A place separated from the Humans. Then, a ground of similarity between them and all of us. To show that we still see them as valuable, but not on the same level as we are." Statler speaks now.

They consider his words. They've been told this before by him, it's apparent on their faces, but now, this matter was here, in the form of myself, and they couldn't look away.

Just then, the chamber doors swung open, and the four fixed Sovereigns entered the space.

The Taurus Lordess led them, her long green hair flowing like vines down her broad back from two short brown horns. Her long arms looked like they were etched with glowing vines.

Following her was the Leo Lord who looked almost like a twin to Adonia. His long golden locks curling around his shoulders. A crown of golden sunbursts starting on his third eye and rounding his head.

The Aquarius Lord following him closely. His short curly hair was stark white, and he looked relatively normal, with a black halo of night surrounding his head.

Finally, the Scorpio Lordess entered the chambers, everyone looking to her as she commanded the room with nothing more than her presence. Her long inky hair falling like waves, cascading to just below her supple breasts.

Under her bright green eyes were two pointed drops of silver. Her tiny stature no match for the weight of her influence, she was the first to speak. Her raspy voice tearing through the room.

"Statler, what you are looking for, is war. "

The room stiffened, as if that word hung in the air, staring them in the face, but until this moment, they had chosen to ignore it. They looked to one another, waiting for who would speak first. The fixed signs didn't even acknowledge my presence.

"Marcella, please. Just hear the Cardinals out."

"It's always been you verses the rest of us. You're always so quick to define that the four of you are Cardinal and we are not!" Marcella lashes out.

"Marcella! It is how it is. We can not change the stars!" Adonia cries.

Marcella turns wicked green eyes on her, and she shrinks back behind Burn.

"Don't lash out at us. Marcella tells the truth. You'd all jump at a chance to be throned above the rest of us. This is against the gods!" the Taurus Lordess steps forward, placing herself in front of Marcella protectively.

I slink back into the shadows slowly, below their radar. If they choose to fight, I do *not* want to be caught up in the middle of it.

"Oh, that's rich, Rhea, coming from the one who's trying to constantly climb the ladder to Cardinal status!" Moon spits at her.

The Mutable Sovereigns entered the chambers now, all looking equally confused. Marcella ran to link hands with the Virgo Lordess.

"Please, Avani, please tell them that this is asking for war!" Marcella pleaded her.

Avani, the Virgo Lordess was a blast of color. Her pink and blue hair mimicked the sun setting in the sky, flowers sprinkled like stars all throughout it. Her skin had the same coloring, softening her already soft features. She bit her full lips and looked worriedly into the eyes of Marcella.

The Gemini Lordess stepped forward. When she walked, she seemed like she split in two, her entire body followed in a translucent copy behind her. When she stopped, her translucent self seeped back into her. I'd never seen anything like it in all my time. Her blue-black pin straight hair barely moving as she did.

"This is outrageous!" She declared, her voice echoing through the chamber.

The Pisces Lord stepped up beside her, slowly forming a wall of Mutables as they did so. I could tell from here they were the most united.

"I stand by Constance and Avani," he said.

"I stand by my fellow Mutable Sovereigns," the Sagittarius Lord said, standing next to his comrades.

Statler took a step between the Fixed signs towards the Mutables.

"I would have thought you Enold, and even you, Bevan would have had enough sense to see what mattered here and speak some sense into your Lordess counterparts," he chimed.

Bevan, the Sagittarius Lord, stepped forward, the fiery red hair on his head almost taking on a life of its own.

"Don't ever try to form a wedge between my fellow Mutables and I. This will cause a war, and as such, we can not stand for it!" he eyes the room.

"On *either* side." He clarifies.

They all stare at one another. Statler turns to the Fixed Sovereigns now, his face blank.

"And do you, the Fixed Sovereigns, agree with the Mutable declaration?"

They look to one another as if sending messages no one else could hear. Marcella is the one to speak.

"We can not stand by the Mutable declaration," she says.

That was it, she created the divide between Mutable and non. My plan could be falling apart, but I held my breath, pressing myself hard against the cold stone wall, shrinking into the shadows.

Statler's shoulders relaxed ever so slightly but tensed again when she spoke.

"Nor can we stand by yours. I stand by what we said. The Cardinals are not better than the Fixed signs. Nor the Mutables, even if they *have* taken themselves out of the argument." She shoots a look at them, still standing in a solid protest.

"Then it is war you are declaring and not between them and us, but amongst ourselves." Statler warned, Adonia verbally wincing from behind Burn.

Marcella stood tall, unwavering and firm. She held out her hand and Staler took it.

"Then, war, it shall be." she declared.

RIOT

Lightning struck a tree somewhere outside my window, rattling it in its steel frame. I sat with my shoulder pressed against it and could feel its power as it shook the night, lighting the sea floor. Kaz had moved Locke and I to his family's unused cave somewhere in the mountains of Metos after my father declared war on me. I don't regret attacking him, even if it did lead to this. At least I'm able to be honest with myself. Eventually, this is where we would have ended up.

While I told them both about what had happened with my father the night we went into hiding, Kaz made the inference that my father could possibly have some connection via a link to my mind that I wasn't aware of. Just to be safe, they placed confusion formations on me, drugged me, and culled us there.

An interesting ability it is to be able to cull. Starting off in one place and appearing somewhere else- *anywhere* else. Kaz's ability to cull has been an unknown blessing to our mission. He was able to cover for me in other places while simultaneously erasing our tracks from the weeks before.

My father and I had our differences, but offering up his entire fortune and estate- *everything* he had worked so hard for, in exchange for my life? It was a new level; a low one, even for him. To get ahead of the game, we left Pleaides for now, the one place he expected me to be.

We took Simmer, Kilo and surprisingly, Faustus with us. Simmer assured us of Faustus' dedication to my movement. He revealed that my father had killed Faustus' entire family and kidnapped him, forcing him to work for Stone Castle. Unsurprisingly, this turned out to be the reality for most of the new staff that had come to Stone Castle once it was in my father's hands.

I regret not talking to them more; seeing them as below me.

"You good, brother?" Locke appeared in my doorway.

I guess the water refraction and lightning gave away the fact that I was fighting adrenaline and nightmares. Ever since waking up, all I've had are nightmares. Locke sits across from me in the same position as me, against the window.

"I'm fine."

"Don't look it, but, you don't have to spill your deepest thoughts to me or anything. I can't sleep either."

I smile, my muscles feathering as I squeeze my left wrist, my elbows resting on my knees.

"How many days has it been? Since the confusion magic?"

He counts on his fingers while looking at me. We both chuckled.

"Too many. I'm happy you're back." He says.

Locke and Kaz have been together doing gods knows what since they got here. I'm a bit uncomfortable around them, knowing they have a bond and knowing how Kaz feels about me.

"What do your tattoos mean?" I realize I've never really asked him about his past. From day one, Locke had been all about me and I've treated him like nothing but an annoyance. To be fair, though, he is a lot to handle.

"It's a long story, but since neither of us are sleeping, I could tell it." he smiles. He was pure of heart in that way. Asking him something so simple, you could see the entirety of his emotions splayed across his tan face.

"Tell me. I could use the distraction." I assure him, thankful for his presence. My mind has always teetered on the darker side of things, but lately, it's been so much worse.

"So, all the ones on my back and torso were earned at different stages of my life through things I did for my family. For my people. " he begins.

I can see from here the dark lines that twisted and turned, displaying depictions of a mighty brute of a Minotaur. The art was broken into quadrants, each a story of their own yet somehow still cohesive.

"The ones on my left arm represent my family, who you've met. My right arm has been a canvas for the gods. They change all the time on their own."

"Wait, you're telling me all of these are done by the gods?"

He nods, excitement crossing his features.

"I'm so close to my deities that they bless me this way. My life story, sprawled across my skin. "

Anyone who works with deities have blessings. One of the things I loved most about it is that everyone is blessed differently based on their relationship with them.

"And here I thought you just never wore a shirt to be an ass," I chuckle.

"I mean... there are more... in other places. If you wanna see them, I can show you?" he offers, a grin crossing his face.

"Gross, no. Leave that for the ladies."

He bellows a laugh. It's hearty. It's real and full of life just like him.

"I have to be honest, when I first met you at Stone Castle, I didn't know how this would go. Im pleasantly surprised that you've become a brother to me, Riot."

The lightning strikes again, lighting the room again. I can that he means what he's saying in my core. Like a tiny fairy, a feeling I can't quite name flits around in my stomach. It was odd not being angry all of the time. I feel like I can relax a bit, the tension not so evident within me.

"You too," I say. I think I really mean it, but I don't have a chance to say more because there's light tapping at my door. Kaz.

"It's rude to chill and not invite your host," he jokes, inviting himself in.

"Well actually, I was trying to be alone and watch the storm surge from this awesome underwater window, when Locke here rudely interrupted."

"I can leave!"

We all laughed. I mean, really laughed. Something I'd not done in a while. Since Kaz brought us here, leaving Pleaides behind us, I've felt freedom for the first time in my life.

"So, I have a proposition," Kaz announced once the laughter died down.

I've barely left my room as I recovered from the magic induced amnesia. I barely ate. I was paler, my muscles weaker. Honestly, a sense of lost and unfeeling hit me hard after my father declared his war on me.

It was nice.

It was nice being no one for a while. No responsibilities or expectations. No electrocution treatments from my father. No one watching me out of malice. Kaz hadn't so much as bat an eye when Locke asked him for this favor. It's taken a bit to get used to not being in control for once, but now that I have, I've found peace in it.

In my father's eyes, he had done me a favor- he'd done me a kindness *allowing* me to leave the castle, announcing it as a head start.

"We have a week until the Royal Dragnet, that's what my sources say your father has decided to call it," Kaz informs us.

Locke scoffs at that, rolling his eyes.

"He's broadened his offer, since you last heard as well."

Locke and Kaz eye me.

"He's opened the offer to all men in all of Meta; royal or not."

"Ah, come off it no one's gonna fall for that," Locke assures me.

"Oh, but they will. The king has offered ten million stone if they die to the family left behind, and if they win, a place in Pantheon."

This development is huge. It would take the winning family out of the poverty and constant struggle to make it.

"Oh that's rich, so he's even casting doubt on his Royalists' sons?" I snap, trying not to let the excitement over my father's fear of my power overtake me. It's a bit hard to ignore though.

"According to my source, it's to light a fire under the Royalists' Sons asses. So, I have a proposition, as I was saying."

Locke and I look at one another and then back at Kaz. I secretly hope that this won't get much worse, but knowing my father, it will. He would start an all out war to make sure I was punished for my actions. The longer I don't step forward, the worse it will be. I know this, but I'm not sure they do.

"I was reading some of my parents research and talking with some of the other Alpha leaders, and they said there's a type of magic called Connection Formations."

Locke stares at Kaz like he just spoke another language and threatened to steal his life away.

"What the hell are connection formations?"

"We can basically learn how to borrow magic from one another and combine it to our own, making us connected, powerful and unstoppable."

"That sounds dangerous and unhinged," Locke breathes.

"That sounds perfect," I counter.

Kaz's face lights up as he starts telling us the ins and outs of his discovery. He explained that the magic was new to him, but other wolves have been successfully using it for quite some time and there were ways for us to safely try it. If it went wrong, it sounded like you could die, which would completely negate everything we had done up until this point.

The possibility of these formations working though brought excitement. We didn't bother trying to sleep again since none of us could, and instead elected to start trying it right away. Kaz led us from my room to a new part of the hideout.

"My parents are Alpha Locks, meaning they travel and train other Alpha wolves. They make sure that the powers needed both mentally and physically exist in a packs elected alpha."

"You mean you're the most stable one they could find for yours?" Locke teases.

Kaz shoots daggers with his eyes as he swings open a massive stone door to reveal a wide, open area. Everything was smooth grey stone. I stepped into the cold arena, noting that it wasn't climate controlled like the rest of the hideout. Weapons lined the walls near where we entered, but beyond a short stone barrier there was nothing. It was a long, grey football field of stone and nothingness.

"This is the arena," Kaz gestures to the open space in front of us.

"That's it? That's the big scary name?" Locke's voice booms.

"Not everything has to have an ominous name in order for it to be feared or respected, Locke. I'd think you'd know that considering what you look like shifted versus your unassuming name."

Locke stopped laughing and lunged for Kaz, catching him around his neck and pulling his head down into a headlock.

"They call me Locke 'cause I put necks in locks and then break 'em,"

"Okay, okay, I'm sorry!" Kaz laughs, pulling his head out of Locke's grip.

Although so much has changed, it's not been long since things were more stiff. Watching them be able to joke and play around struck up envy in my core. Once free, Kaz walks over to the other side of the barricade and runs about a mile down.

"I'll demonstrate the arena," he shouts from his place down the way. I could imagine he was merely talking, and his voice just traveled, bouncing off the walls back to us.

Before anyone could answer, he made a formation, shooting bright blue light into the ceiling. Like a living thing, it jumps to life, shifting the space in front of us. The stone shifts in every direction, morphing to reveal an open field. Green grass stretched in every direction, the air warm. Even where Locke and I stood was transformed.

"Stay where you are, behind that rock." Kaz's voice travelled to us.

I could feel the dirt beneath my bare feet, the sun on my shoulders. I could feel the light breeze that trickled across my forearms. There were even crickets somewhere off in the distance. Kaz stood in the middle of the sprawling green, the barrier we stood behind now a wall of rocks. We watched as Kaz made new formations and almost instantly, a beast appeared in front of him.

The large reptilian figure had horns that shot forward off its massive scaly head. It thrashed its head around, standing on two legs, towering stories above Kaz. I caught a glimpse of its face as it tilted its head side to side, listening. The angle provided me a better look, showing he had no eyes.

A sickening grin crossed Kaz's face as he shifted, his skin turning into fur. He became the large wolf that lived within him, the one I last saw on faction night.

This is the true identity of his soul.

Maybe it's the confusion formations I'm still recovering from or maybe it's because no one expected me to attack and overpower him, but from here, Kaz is every bit as fierce as I am when I shift, just different.

His fur is thick and protective. His blue eyes piercing from the dark contrast of it on his face. As he paced, he growled, his lips displaying sharp canines situated to kill in his salivating mouth.

Flawlessly and quickly, he took down the beast. Once it was dead, ripped to shreds before us, he shifted back to the Viking I was starting to respect.

Even worse, he was the Viking I was beginning to *like*.

LOCKE

Kaz and I struggled getting Riot up to the Alpha mountains the day we decided to hide. Riot had never been up there as they were prime lands for wolf shifters and his father absolutely has never allowed Riot out there. The struggle wasn't so much knowing where to take him once he'd told us what his father had done, that was a no brainer for us. The real struggle it was physically getting him there.

Even with Kay's ability to cull, we needed to be sure the king couldn't see us. So, we decided on confusion magic. At first, I wanted to take him to my lands, but Kaz had made the valid point that his father knew them all too well, and that would probably be the first place he'd expect us to go.

I try not to think about my lands much these days, but hope my family is safe. I've not heard from them in so long, but deep down I know where my father stands. On the wrong side of the crown.

Kaz has become our secret weapon, in a way. Someone Arnoldous Blair probably never expected us to run with. I wasn't even sure that the king knew of Kaz or his connection to Riot, but we couldn't chance anything.

"I can cull us in and out of anywhere that's not protected from cull magic. Some places have barriers against it, but I can get everything we need without risking going out. You and Riot should stay here as this is probably the safest place for him."

I look at the list Kaz slid over to me from across the table. It has five items scrawled so small I could barely read it. I take it in my massive hand and hold it to the light.

"You expect me to read this, man?"

He snatched it from my hands, patting the furs on his shoulders back down into place when he hops off the table.

"I'll handle the list," he says, shooting me with daggers for eyes.

"Okay, fine but what's on it?"

"Stuff we need."

"So, is this connection magic stuff a spell or is this like a permanent thing?"

Kaz writes a few more things down and shoves the list in his pocket. The whole place is made of smooth stone with minimalistic furnishings. Clearly the taste of his parents. I wondered how much he'd told his parents about why we were using this place; about us. I watch as he thinks about whether or not what he's about to say is going to upset me.

"It would be permanent unless I can help it," His voice just above a whisper.

Raising a finger, he goes to Riot's door, peering in for only a second. He keeps checking on him like a worried mother.

"Why would it matter? It could be beneficial to link all of our powers especially if his father is going around building armies to kill us."

"It matters because it'll sever the connection I have to my mate. It could make you and even him unable to ever connect to your mates if you were to find them." He whispers, watching Riot.

"I don't have a mate. I never will. I'm meant to be shared," I joke. He doesn't look at me as he smiles, but it doesn't reach his eyes.

I haven't considered what Kaz could have been giving up to help Riot. To help me. All because I simply asked him to. I can see the melancholy of his soul in his eyes now and wonder what he's been going through. We'd lost contact awhile back and throughout our lives, but we always connected as though we had never lost it in the first place.

"He's fine brother, he always makes that sound." I try to ease his mind.

"He always makes that sound, and you think that means your friend is fine?"

Riot is complicated. I don't babysit him or pay attention to what's normal or not for him. I shrug as Kaz returned to the island in the kitchen.

"I don't know what you consider normal, but that's not it." He sighs.

"Look he's been through a lot and although he can't tell you now, he will be ever grateful for this and what you've done already for him. Even if it's the only thing you ever do for him."

Kaz smiles halfheartedly at me. I know the two of them have had bad blood; by nature they were enemies, but I truly believe that if they gave one another a chance they could be really great friends.

Wolves are protectors of their kind and love helping other species, but the Basilisks had made many deals with them and then turned their backs on their agreements. Basilisks have never been ones to keep their promises, nor have they ever watched anyone's backs but their own.

"I know he's rough around the edges and he probably won't say thank you, so I'm doing it for him."

"How long will you do it for him?"

I shoulder that response with a sigh. If I'm being honest with myself, I would do it for the rest of my life. My family hated the Blairs, even after my father got us to Pantheon. But then, when I met Riot, I saw deeper than what everyone else saw. I saw myself in him. He just went about it differently than most do.

I know he has potential to be so much more than everyone expects him to be. If he could truly do this and change Meta for the better, I know he will do right by the factions. Personally, I believe that he should make everyone equal, but I have time to convince him that's how it should be.

"You're a good man, Locke. I can only hope to be half as good as you. If I don't deserve your friendship, that snake doesn't either. " Kaz says, letting it go when I don't answer.

I know he doesn't mean anything by it. He has to get to know Riot. Even the wolves had issues that Riot could fix. Kaz and Riot are smart; more alike than they probably want to admit. There has to be a way to make this work.

The days passed while Riot slept. Kaz showing me the ins and outs of the security system and the hidden tunnels, watching every news outlet in Meta for information we could use. Apparently, part of the hideout was above ground and Riot was in the lowest section under water behind a hidden waterfall. He took the time to teach Simmer, Kilo and Faustus all the emergency exits, back doors, dead end caves and regular entryways. He taught them about all the illusion magic set in place to protect it as well.

He sat around tiny crackling fires in the fireplace making plans and back up plans with them. Simmer delivered information from his position at Stone Castle, but it wasn't much. We had to guess and assume all possibilities of what Arnoldous could or would do and even with the many scenarios we'd laid out to possibility, there were probably hundreds more we weren't even considering.

After about three days, Riot finally woke up. He seemed normal to me. Sure, he was nicer than usual, but he remembered who we were and why he'd been essentially drugged still. I silently prayed to Hades that he would stay this way. I loved him like a brother, but he could be heartless.

We'd decided to only tell him what was necessary. During all of our meetings, Simmer confirmed that Arnoldous had information he'd only have if he'd been watching us or had direct connection to Riot.

"He knows that Riot is no longer at Pleaides, and he assumes Riot has gone into hiding." Simmer says, sitting perched on the edge of his seat.

I sit next to Kaz who's leaned forward writing out notes on everything Simmer says. I watch Simmer's black eyes as they dart between Kaz and myself, telling his story along with his mouth. His face is young. He looks like he's carved from marble, but his long black hair almost looks like plastic, it's so shiny.

"Not good information, but not bad either. It would have been better if he'd taken longer to figure out that Riot has disappeared."

"He assumes Locke is with him," Simmer adds.

I look at the floor.

"Naturally." Kaz agrees.

I hoped that my family would be safe. I'd assumed my father had chosen his side, although it was never a conversation we had. I had started out on the same side as him, and now, I stand as his adversary if the king is truly where his loyalty lies.

"He has no idea about you but he assumes Riot is trying to coerce those who follow the crown to side with him, so he's broadcasting Riot's disappearance as a betrayal to the crown. He's giving details about the fight and he's using Memorials to prove it."

"Memorials?" Kaz questions.

"He's put his memory from the fight up for everyone to see. He had someone on his team of Royalist Loyalist bullshit whatever pull the memories out so he could show the world."

"I can't follow what's what and my father's on his panel of idiots." I note.

They all look at me. Kilo looks like I've wounded him, but no one says anything. I never have the pity of anyone, and if this is what it feels like, I never want it again.

Simmer continues with Kaz, their voices fading into the back of my mind as I walk to Riot's room and lean on the doorframe.

Come on, Riot. Wake up. We need you.

Days later, after Riot had awoken, Kaz brought us to his training arena. We watched as Kaz tore apart a monster I know I'd never seen before. I had to assume by the look on Riot's face that he hadn't either. The beast now in shreds, Kaz approaches us.

"So, this is your murder practice cave, essentially?" Riot said, sitting on the stone divider.

"It was built, as I've said, by my parents to train other wolves."

We watch as Kaz pulls on a fresh shirt that complimented his toned arms and torso.

"For practicing murder," Riot mumbles under his breath. Kaz shoots daggers at him with his eyes.

"As if you're any stranger to killing things for fun? For me, it's survival. For you, it's murder." Kaz sneers.

Riot looks like he wants to rip Kaz's throat out.

"So, what was that thing out there?" I ask, stepping over the barrier and looking around. I need to break the tension before something happens.

"It's a monster my parents have fought. Every single one they come across, they log it and replicate it here to train other Alphas and packs on how to fight them."

"That's fucking brilliant!" I exclaim.

Riot follows me onto the stone field, looking around for what I assume are seams as well. Kaz must have known what we were doing since he chuckled as he approached holding three long staffs. Each looked as thought it were made of copper with intricate filigree running along its surface.

One on end, it had a flat edge and on the other, a thick purple crystal. It was wrapped with wire and leather cords, beads and feathers hanging from its base.

"Are we about to have a drum circle?" Riot sneers.

I guess he wasn't going to stay nice for much longer.

"These are direction staffs," Kaz bellowed, ignoring Riot.

He handed me one and threw the other in Riot's direction, stiffening when he caught it flawlessly.

"These direct energy where you want it to go. They are incredibly powerful and can backfire, taking energy from their wielder instead of providing more, so you will have to learn how to use them. Be careful. It can deplete you to dangerous levels, but I thought these were a great tool to start with. Not only will they help us to feel what it's like to share energy with another person, but we will learn how to direct that energy, interrupting its natural flow. "

Kaz walked further down the field before turning to us, holding his staff in front of him like a mighty wizard.

"Alright, Riot. Hit me with your best shot."

RIOT

It's not often that someone you don't particularly enjoy the company of offers you to go at them with all your force. Kaz asking me to hit him with my best shot makes me feel like what I assumed most kids felt at Yule. I have never had those pleasures, since my father despises me. The thought brings up rage like bile to the back of my throat.

Free shot.

I focus my energy on the staff in my hands, trying to force everything I have into it as fast and as I can when I start to feel the swirl of emotions swelling within me. They start in my core, building up my strong back and into my thick biceps. I can feel the heat as it rolls down my veins like lava. When it gets to my palms, it spreads like wildfire to my fingers, blasting out of the tips and sending the staff flying out of my hands with such force that pain actually tore at my muscles.

It hits the ceiling and then a wall before dead weighting to the ground. Kaz and Locke both watch it before looking back at me, while laughing. I fight the smile trying to break across my face and stare back, not daring to break in front of them.

"This is going to be a lot of work," Kaz sighed.

Locke howled with laughter as I went to retrieve the staff, feeling annoyance build in my core. My mind was still so jumbled from the confusion magic. I probably could have done without, but Kaz convinced Locke that my father was able to track me. Never had he been in my mind enough to do something like that, but when I'd made that argument, they countered with, "that you know of." It was a valid point.

We'd been here over a month already, but the effects hadn't fully worn off.

I picked up the direction staff, turning towards Kaz once more. I tried again, funneling my energy into it, but the same thing happened. Kaz ducked just in time to avoid being hit by the flying staff.

"Argh! Help me!" I bellowed.

"Calm down or I won't."

I hated being at the disposal of others, but I focused, trying to stop the anger that coursed through me.

"Great. Now ask nicely," Kaz sneered.

"Please," it comes through gritted teeth but sounds nicer than I'd anticipated.

Kaz bows his head and turns on his heel. He retrieved the staff from the floor and sprinted back over to us as Locke took a seat on the floor, his staff in his lap as he watched us, clearly amused.

"First, you need to focus," Kaz began, placing the staff back into my hands.

"I am focused but this stupid tool keeps bouncing the energy back off me,"

"There's your first mistake. You're thinking of the staff as a *tool*."

I look at him and then the copper weapon in my hands. It was truly a work of art.

"If it's *not* a tool, then what is it?"

"Think of it as an extension of you. Like an extra arm. Imagine that the fire is traveling along its core and out one end."

I nod. This time, Kaz backs up and steadying himself, shouts,

"Whenever you're ready. Breathe. Focus. Then, take your shot!"

I breathe in deep. I can feel the fire swelling within me again like it normally does. It follows the same path within me. I try to breathe but it's rolling down my veins much too fast for me to stop it. When it gets to my hands, it pools for a moment before shooting out the end of the staff and then in every direction from where my hands connect with it. The explosion of green fire was erratic and unlike me.

"This is pointless!" I yell, frustration building inside of me.

"It's not. You did better that time. What did you *feel*, Riot?" Kaz asks, not leaving his stance like I might attack him at any moment.

I think on it for a moment. I felt the anger well up, but as it traveled down my arms, I think I'd felt something different than I ever had. It was like some part of me was missing. A part I'd not experienced yet, but that I knew about. I couldn't quite place it as I thought about the other feeling that trickled beneath it.

I hadn't known where my element was going or what it would do. I was unable to stop it, losing control as always. This time though, I felt something about it. Maybe it was uncertainty.

"I felt... uncertain," I try.

Kaz nods slowly and then more quickly as he processes what I've said.

"Good. Yeah, good! That's a start. Is it a feeling you can find again? Your goal is to take familiarity and soften it with something else, so you have control. Your power should pool in your epicenter."

"My what?"

"Your epicenter. Wherever it is you normally feel your magic before you release it," he clarifies.

"Normally it's in my core. I release it from there, but it has never been too stable. Which makes me dangerous."

"Right but better than being dangerous is being precise. Acting with not only reason, but with purpose," he counters.

"That takes time which makes you vulnerable and weak,"

He shakes his head like he's disappointed.

"No, it makes you better than dangerous,"

"What could be better than being dangerous?"

He narrows his icy blue eyes at me.

"Being lethal."

We spend every waking hour in that arena, day after day, taking turns mastering directing our elements into the direction staffs. Kaz counsels us, allowing us to use him as a target. Over and over again, we fail.

The staffs fly in every direction as Locke, and I take turns trying and failing to direct our energies into them.

"It's been three days of this shit, Kaz." I groan.

My muscles are sore and I'm exhausted. The plus side is that I have been finally sleeping without interruptions. Since we got to the cave, my dreams have been interrupted by visions of places I'd never been. A sweet scent like bourbon, strawberry, and vanilla infiltrating my nose and my mind.

"And it'll be more if you don't get this down," he counters.

He's made it a lagoon. Locke and I stand on the grassy shore, dark blue water spanning miles before us with a rock in the center that currently hosted a shirtless Kaz on it. He took his usual stance and wiggled his four fingers at me, signaling he was ready.

The staff is hot in my hands from all the energy I've tried and failed to put into it. I adjust them, taking on a firmer grip. I breathe in and then out, looking deep within myself for the feeling of uncertainty. I try and mash it with anger, controlling it.

It's okay to be angry.
It's okay not to know what will happen.
Take control.

I feel the fire start bubbling within my core. This time, instead of waiting to feel it move, I tell it to. I direct it around my waist and up my chest this time, feeling it move through my abs and up into my arms. I reel it back when it hits my elbows, relaxing my shoulders and concentrating.

"Good! You've got this, Riot! Now, imagine you are one with the staff!"

I can hear Kaz yell in the distance and I do my best to listen, but scenes from my dreams come to me. That smell of bourbon, strawberry and vanilla filling my nose again. I relax more.

I release my hold on the swirling heat in my forearms and it trickles like falling glitter down my veins and into the staff that warms in my massive hands. I feel it pool for a moment before slipping calmly into the staff and waiting there for further instruction. I can feel myself within the copper, as if *I'm* made of the stuff. I feel like me but armored.

Ready.

I open my eyes, slowly.

The staff has a weird shift hovering just above it, the crystal on the end pulsing the same beat as my unruly heart. The purple lighting from within. It looked alive. It looked powerful.

"You're doing it! Holy fuck, you're actually doing it!" Kaz yelled.

Locke let out a whoop somewhere behind me as I lifted my eyes to Kaz. He spun his staff expertly in front of him like a windmill.

"When you're ready, aim at me and let it go. Let it all go," he calls over.

Holding the staff like this has me in a state of content. I'm suddenly able to feel so many things at once that it's almost as if I can't feel anything at all. It's like for the first time, I'm just me. Just Riot. I'm not a pit bull, I'm not a pawn. I'm not even a Blair.

I squeeze my eyes shut as my breath catches in my throat, and I demand the staff listen to *me* now. I can imagine the elements, the feelings, and the energy flowing from the staff in a powerful but calm torrent towards Kaz.

When I opened my eyes again to look at him, there were two glowing streams of light flowing from the end of my staff. One was green- my element. The second was purple, I assumed from the crystal. They twirled around one another, connecting over the lagoon water to an icy blue beam. I followed the magics water-like movements back to their source- Kaz's staff.

We locked eyes and I could feel his energy through the connection of the beams. I could see and feel his thoughts, opening like a gateway before me. Suddenly, the power amped up and his mind opened like a flood gate that had just broken. Without warning, I was subjected to all his private thoughts and emotions.

His secret wedding to Amira, meeting her, even his secret visits to the Forest of Broken Dreams. His pack didn't want him there. I saw him fighting, locked jaws with a wolf almost twice his size, his fur the color of coal. I could feel the pain between my shoulder blades and on the nape of my neck as he ripped fur from Kaz's sensitive scruff.

I studied Kaz who just stared back at me, horrified. I couldn't tell if he knew what I was seeing or if he was seeing into my mind, but it had to be stopped. His first kiss, their first time, all their sweet nothings flooded into my head. My skull started pounding as all of his memories were forced into mine against my will.

    With nothing else to do, I dropped the staff, tears rolling down my face, looking up just in time to see Kaz falling to his knees as I heard Locke running to my side, as I too, hit the ground.

LOCKE

Riot and Kaz fell to the ground as their magic became unstable. I tried so hard to get to them before that point, but Riot had formed a wall of energy behind him and despite all my attempts at storming my way past it, I couldn't. I almost dislocated my shoulder trying to get past, but when that magic finally bounced off every surface in the arena, I dodged it, running to my friend's side.

"Riot! Are you okay brother?"

"Kaz," he choked out.

I looked down at the already shifting arena and saw Kaz, face first on the floor. I ran to his side rolling him onto his back. In seconds, he was coughing up liquid. I guess he'd gone into the water as the arena shifted. I pulled him to a sitting position as he caught his breath.

"Are you alright, man? That was wild! It was like real Merlin type shit!"

Kaz smiled, still coughing and nodding his head. I pulled him to his feet just as Riot made it to us.

"What the fuck was that?" he demanded.

When Kaz finally stopped coughing, I helped him up.

"That was too much success. Clearly, we have to find a way to block our minds or else anyone can enter them. Something I should have known."

He looks a bit embarrassed, and Riot shuffles a bit while looking the other direction.

"Wait are you telling me you guys entered each other's minds?"

"Sort of? I could feel Kaz's emotions like they were my own."

Kaz's eyes widened as the realization of what Riot is saying hit him.

"What did you see?" he questioned; his face worried.

"Not much… just you and Amira. A wolf fight,"

Kaz's jaw feathers as he looks at the floor.

"I think that's enough for today. We made great progress. We should rest."

Riot nods before turning on his heel and sprinting from the arena. When the heavy armored door closes, I watch as Kaz tries to contain his emotions. He busies himself collecting his staff and then ours from the floor.

"What did you see?" I try, rushing to grab the armory door as Kaz struggles to open it with his hands full.

He exhales deeply as he places each staff back in its proper place.

"I saw a lot of things I don't think I was supposed to see, as he did with me."

"Like what?"

Kaz shakes his head as he pulls some large leather duffel bags from the armory shelves. I watch him as he slams them onto one of the long tables that line the stone walls behind the barrier.

"Now isn't the time to discuss it and I'm not sure I can at the moment," he mutters, throwing me a bag.

"Be useful if you're going to stand there and help me pack these."

Before I can even ask with what, he presses a paw to the wall, popping open a large door about three feet tall that hadn't been there previously. He pulled on the top, opening it to reveal something I'd never seen before.

Silver and gold disks piled high almost completely filling the secret space. Kaz began grabbing stacks and loading his two duffels. As he pulled one full bag out, I dipped in behind him and got to work. They were cold in my hands as I packed them tightly into my own duffel.

"Kaz, what are we doing?"

"Getting ready,"

He didn't look at me as he continued packing and moving duffels. We worked until all the coins were gone and once he'd finished with his and had sealed the door again, I tried to find out more.

"What are we getting ready for?"

"Amira has sent word that there will be an attack. I'm preparing to run. These are being sent with Faustus, Kilo and Simmer who will then disperse them around chosen locations for us. We are no longer safe here. The Royal Dragnet is upon us."

"I thought we had at least a few more days!" I exclaim.

"As did I, but Amira's word has never been compromised. She has many valuable sources and some of the royal sons have already approached King Blair, ready to find Riot and rip him limb from limb. He's offering them free room and board while they travel all around Meta at any of his estates and hotels. He even bought out old buildings in the Outliers, fixed them up and is offering them as safe houses as well."

I stare at him with my mouth open.

"Don't look at me like that. This has gotten dangerous fast."

"What about training?"

Kaz pulls the bags to the armored door now. I help by throwing two over my back. As we exited, he listened for Riot, and signaled me towards one of the illusioned exits. He didn't speak until we were out of the main part of the hideaway and walking down a long poorly lit walkway. It sloped down and smelled strongly of water. I guessed we had to be nearing the hidden waterfall clearing as we went.

After a few minutes, Kaz spoke again.

"We will train on the move. We don't have an option, Locke."

We arrive at a large opening in the cave. There's indeed a gorgeous waterfall spanning miles above us into the sky. The small circular area is obscure from up above by the billowing mist of the waterfall. I can taste the air it's so thick, cool and humid.

Simmer and Faustus cull into the area in front of us, grinning and greeting us with a hug.

"You didn't bring more to help?" Kaz asked, passing them each a bag.

"No, it's looking very grim if I'm to be honest."

I looked to Faustus who had dark circles under his eyes. I could tell they were worn out, but their spirits were strong.

"What do you mean? Have you encountered trouble?"

"Some, but only in the way that Arnoldous has sent all the original butlers to new posts outside the castle. He's brought on new ones to protect him and the Queen inside and no one has been allowed near the castle since Riot's disappearance." Simmer huffs.

Faustus moves forward to grab two more bags. He bows shortly to us before culling away leaving us alone with Simmer.

"What's really going on out there?" I ask.

He looks between us before sighing and visibly giving up. His tense stature now growing slack as he inhales deeply.

"They are saying he's created creatures that he can control. He wants Riot's head on a golden platter."

"He said this? Like he actually admitted it to people?" I asked completely baffled.

"It's the word on the street. He's opened the pool to anyone who is a son, and the stakes are higher and higher every time he adds something. Soon, every man will be looking for Riot. There's not a place in Meta he won't be hunted."

I run my hands through my hair. It's been growing out since coming here, the sides coming in, covering the tattoos that decorated my scalp. I felt fear for my friend.

"There has to be something we can do?"

Kaz and Simmer exchange looks.

"There are other islands that aren't participating in the Royal Dragnet. In fact, there's one in particular who doesn't even follow the rule of any leader."

"What? Then how do they know who's the best?"

"They are all the same. They exist purely on one concept." Kaz says, following up Simmer's train of thought.

"What's the concept?"

"Nobility."

I have to keep myself from scoffing. This couldn't be real. I'd never heard of such a place and even if it did exist, Arnoldous Blair would have made sure it didn't.

"Then why hasn't King Blair found a way to take it? To destroy it?"

Simmer looks to me now, breaking his eye contact with Kaz.

"He can't see it."

I scrunch up my features.

"He has eyes, why can't he see it?"

"Only those with pure intentions can see it. Only those with honesty and nobility in their core can step foot into their lands."

I bark a laugh.

"Then it's a no go for Riot and I."

I quickly stop laughing when I notice they aren't joking. They aren't laughing. They were really going to try this.

Faustus culled back in, grabbing what was left of the bags and

44

disappearing again before anyone could move.

"Well, *fuck*."

RIOT

Locke and Kaz told me to pack up. They never gave me a direct answer as to why, but I was beginning to feel less and less like myself as I did what I was told. I packed clothes that weren't mine in a room that wasn't mine.

Ever since the arena and connecting to Kaz's energy, I'd felt this intense shallowness within me. At first, it had been a glimmer of feeling in the arena but now, it was growing, and I was drowning in it. I couldn't talk to Locke about it because he was obsessed with planning our next move with Kaz.

I'd started floating beneath the radar, unbeknownst to them. Every thought that I had that wasn't about training, every time I felt that creeping shallowness, I pushed it out of my head.

"You ready?"

Locke stood at my door now. Something else that wasn't truly mine. I'd grown to like this place, but we had to leave it for an island that may exist, but also it might not. And if it does, I may not even be able to see it.

My psychopath father had declared war on me, putting a hefty price on my head and now, I was a running fugitive. I nodded my head and slung the duffle Kaz provided to me over my shoulder.

They led me out of the hideaway and into a small cave that made me scowl because it was dry and hot. I much preferred the cold and Locke knew that. The space was cramped and soon, with a wave of Kaz's hand, it only had four walls completely blocking us in. The ceiling was just tall enough for me to fit without bending.

"Is this some kind of joke?"

"Just wait. Don't speak."

I wanted to object, but as I opened my mouth to do so, I could hear a loud bang overhead. Some tiny rocks fell from above, making little noise as they fell in the dark at my feet. I could feel a thumping deep within me, and I noticed it wasn't my heart; it was Kaz's.

He must have felt the same because I could feel him looking at me.

"How are you so calm?" he whispered.

I just shrugged, not daring to speak.

He must have gotten the message as he quickly looked up. The silence was deafening as we all strained to listen through the rock. At first there was nothing. Kaz looked at me, holding up a finger, waiting for the most opportune moment.

In a breath's notice, bang after bang came. It sounded like concrete blocks being smashed together.

"Take my arm and don't let go!" Kaz yelled over the sound, extending his arm to us. I grabbed hold of Locke exchanging glances with him. Together, we took hold of Kaz.

The sickening feeling of culling took me over. We folded into one another, becoming everything and nothing all at once. I saw the lights of places passing us until we finally came to a stop on a muddy road in the middle of nowhere.

"Where the fuck are we now?"

Kaz picks up his duffle as Locke gags from the thick rotten air.

"The Outliers by the stench of it," he chokes out.

"Yep. We have to keep moving."

"Hold on, dude what was that back there?" Locke asks, blocking Kaz's path.

"We can talk and walk, but we need to keep moving."

"No, I think Locke is right, Kaz. You need to talk, and you need to do it now. We have been following you. Going where you want us to go. Without question. Without hesitation. Your "super safe" hideaway is no longer safe, so what's going on?"

They both looked at me now, Locke giving me knowing eyes.

"So, you knew? All this time you've been planning with him and leaving me in the dark!" I shouted.

The hurt on Locke's face tells me he's sorry, but I don't care. I can feel another piece of myself chisel away in my core. It falls away from my very being. I'm strangely at peace knowing that I simply do not care.

"Riot, listen, the less you know, the safer it is for you-"

I cut him off, yelling now so that it's echoing off the surrounding trees.

"No! I didn't do this in order to fall under the rule of someone else- much less a *wolf*."

The words are out before I can stop them, and I feel another piece of me falling away. I should be thankful to Kaz for putting aside our differences to help, but even the thought of *that* angers me.

I start off in the opposite direction, throwing the duffel down as I walk.

"Riot!" Locke calls.

I don't stop.

"Follow him," I hear Kaz sigh.

I continue to storm as quickly as I can away from them, hoping they will just stop following me. Glancing over my shoulder, I can see that they are quite a distance from me, even in the dark. There's not one ounce of color around me. In fact, everything feels and looks pretty lifeless here. A creeping feeling crosses my spine as I slow my pace, looking around.

A spot just past the ominous wood catches my attention. I can't see any movement at first, but it's enough to make me stop in my tracks and stare. I don't hear Kaz or Locke yet and I'm suddenly very aware that I'm alone. I hadn't dared take my attention off the spot just yet, but I wanted to see how far they were from me as their words suddenly flooded my mind past the dark inky feeling that was taking up residence there.

The hair on my arms stood on end as I stared. It was becoming harder not to look away. I knew what was going to happen the second I moved my attention from the wooded area, so I braced myself, and shot a glance down the street. Kaz was running now, Locke in tow, towards me as I felt a blast throw me onto my back.

I must have passed out for a while because when I came to, Locke was shifted into a terrifying Minotaur. It was the first time I had seen him in his true form, I realized. He was massive. His arms bulged with muscles and veins. Even his bullring piercing seemed like it got bigger. His eyes were frightened and angry. His horns yellow and rigid as they jutted from his head, turning back in on themselves and then straight up towards the sky.

If he were to put his head down and run at someone, he would easily impale them. His sheer mass and power alone stunned me, and that's rare. Realizing I was still on the ground, I scrambled to get up, looking for Kaz as I did so. He was blasting a figure I couldn't quite make out with a stream of water.

"Riot! Watch out!" Locke screams as he throws a formation my way that acts as a shield from an attack I can't see. I hear a loud thud as whatever it was bounces off it.

I spin around just in time to see there are three figures culling in and out of the area so quickly that it's hard to get a read on their faces or any features. They are covered in black wisps that, before they can dissipate, form again from the strangers' cull.

"What's happening?" Locke shouts.

I can't seem to get my bearings. Everything is blurry and the ground feels like it's going to slide out from under my feet. My stomach starts to swim, and my head follows right behind it, aftermath of the cull, the mix of magic and the connection to Kaz's ever evolving emotions.

"Riot talk to me, what's going on over there?" Locke shouts.

I can hear magic blasting all around me and the taste of dark magic crackles along my tongue. The flavor strengthened the growing lump in my throat. I hear the sickening thud of a body hitting the ground and it's enough to make me empty the contents of my guts right there on the wet soil, causing me to feel another piece of me float away, darkness growing ever closer to the corners of my mind.

"Riot!" Locke screams on the top of his lungs.

From the corner of my eye, I can see him going down as two figures stand over him, a blinding red light forming a seal above him, growing ever bigger as they move in perfect synchronization.

"*You are power,*" a voice seeps in under the blackness.

"*Let him die!*"

Tingles and goosebumps kiss my neck. My friend was in trouble, and I needed to help him. I thrust my hand out feeling my magic was more streamlined within me since using the direction staff. It moved through my core the way I demanded it to instead of uncontrollably as it had before Kaz trained me. The darkness didn't subside this time, maintaining its place at the edges of my mind, instead it backed up, though I didn't have time to dwell on it now. Pushing back on it as best as I could, I forced the magic out. I forced it to be erratic, to take on multiple directions at once.

In a torrent of flames, it split into two, blasting the figures back. Locke jumped to his feet, using vines to grab them, tying them together. He shifted once more, using his powerful horns to ram them, impaling them at the same time.

When the threat was over, he shifted back. Shirtless and covered in blood, he made his way over to Kaz and I. Kaz had already shifted and was assessing the damage to his leg.

"What happened are you okay?" Locke started trying to check me out.

"I'm fine." I clench my jaw.

"Are you sure cause you were out for quite a while and you seemed lost when you finally got up,"

"I said I'm fine." I snap.

I round on Kaz now, unable to hold it in any longer.

"Tell me what's going right now, or I'll destroy you next."

His face doesn't falter. Instead, he looks to Locke who nods, and he begins telling me every detail of what's really been going on over the past few weeks.

LOCKE

Kaz told Riot everything he knew. Everything I knew. He told him about the duffels, the coins, Simmer and Faustus. He even told him about Nobility Island and how we were planning to hide him there.

"So, what? Am I being hunted for the grand Blair prize by every person with a dick?"

I glanced down at the ground.

"Well, clearly not,"

They come closer to me, taking a look at the waterlogged body before us. Her hair was void of luster, her skin pale and bloated. She looked as though she had been underwater for days.

"That's a really big problem," Kaz sighs.

"I couldn't see them long enough to tell one was a girl,"

Kaz nods in agreement with me, as Riot saunters over to the other two bodies still tangled in my vines.

"Useless." He grumbles and delivers a swift kick to their mangled bodies. He grunts as he delivers another and then another. When it's clear he isn't going to stop, I try to grab him.

"Hey! Stop, man."

"Why? They didn't stop. This isn't going to stop!" he yells, gesturing to the space around us. I hang my head.

He was right in a way. It wasn't going to stop until we found a way to stop it. Right now, none of us had any clue as to how we were going to do that, but I had hope in Kaz. I had faith in Amira. Centaurs were good and kind. They were blunt and honest. I had no reason not to take her word for what it was. I hoped Riot would see that the longer we spent time with Kaz.

"Riot, it will end," Kaz tries.

"When?" Riot 's voice was growing now.

"We have to find a way but believe me there are ways,"

Kaz was calmer than I'd ever seen him, despite being yelled at by someone he didn't particularly like.

"There are ways, huh?"

Kaz just nods at him.

Riot spit at his feet, his eyes on fire. I swear that if looks could kill, Kaz would've been dead now.

"If that's how you feel,"

"It is."

With that, Riot started walking away again, but this time in the direction we had originally began. When he was far enough ahead of us and after some time, Kaz started speaking to me, but fully intending for Riot to hear every word this time. I guessed he'd rather avoid any more hostility.

"So, we are going to take the most hidden of paths and try avoiding the Royalists and Loyalists and really all men in Meta. We are being watched and the trees whisper amongst themselves."

"I can hear you," Riot snaps over his shoulder.

"Good. You're meant to hear."

Kaz lets a small smile creep across his features when Riot turns his back on us again, clearly enjoying being the reason for the annoyance in Riot's tone. We walk on in silence. I can see from Riot's posture that whatever's been bothering him is starting to subside. I trot to catch up to him, the gravel crunching beneath my feet as I slap a hand to his shoulder.

"Hey brother, what's going on?" I say, giving him a chance to just speak to me.

"Nothing, I'm fine."

He maintains the same air about him but doesn't seem like his normal self just yet. Deciding it's best to just back off, I slow my pace until I'm in line with Kaz again.

"Let's hope he changes enough by the time we get to Nobility." Kaz whispers.

I don't answer, though.

I'm lost in my thoughts.

RIOT

Kaz made plans for our movements which were typical and if I had been hunting me, I would've been able to find us in a heartbeat. After a few more attempted attacks, he suggested moving only at night was the best move. Of course, no one else was trained like me, so they couldn't have possibly comprehended the gravity of this situation.

They wanted me to see them as honorable or brave or some shit for them choosing to help me, but I saw them as stupid and foolish. Who gives up their freedom to help someone who doesn't even like them?

Over the next few days, I tried my best to push them off me and all it did was make them hover more. I tried demanding they leave my side but that did no good either.

One morning, after a long, rainy night, I was greeted by the river after breakfast by a group of hopeful Outlier boys looking to get the jump on me. They were all dead by the time Locke and Kaz joined up with me. I tried explaining to them what had happened, but the incident only made them trust me even less.

I wasn't frightened by the fact that little by little the anger took over and I could feel pieces of me fading away, crumbling into nothing.

It used to worry me, but at this point, it was a welcomed feeling. I didn't feel the need to explain myself. I didn't even feel the need to talk most of the time. I knew what they were thinking about me, and I knew from their actions that they didn't really want to help me.

We culled into some snowcapped mountains, hoping the thick flurries would conceal us a bit better, but soon, it was too much, and we had to cull back down to an elevation that was warmer, exposing ourselves again. The thoughts trickled in more and more frequently.

So, I stayed to myself. Only speaking when they spoke to me first. I slept when they told me to, I ate and drank when they told me to. After a nightmare one night where I woke up to my hands around Locke's throat, they decided it would be best someone keep watch over two sleeping at a time.

That meant I was being watched around the clock now. Kaz takes night shift and Locke takes day.

I didn't let my guard down that easily though. I could feel them watching me. I could feel them whispering about me.

The darkness seeped into every corner of my existence. It was suffocating at first, but when I would sleep, it would talk to me, reminding me that I am powerful. That I *am* power.

The swirling black provided an endless cold that somehow comforted me. I don't know why I'd tried fighting it before. I had enough pieces of myself left that kissing the darkness wasn't really that dangerous.

"We've been doing a great job making sure to detect danger beforehand,"

Locke was always praising Kaz like a sick and sad puppy. It was disgusting.

"Indeed,"

I turned away, mocking their conversation with my mouth. Listening to them converse made my blood boil. Their fake pleasantries and strategic planning were for nothing.

"*You don't need them, Riot. You are everything you need*," that familiar voice in the void told me.

It was right. I *am* everything I need. Gathering up my clothes into the duffel I was growing to hate as well, I heard a twig snap somewhere in the woods.

Like a dog on watch, Kaz was in front of me, pulling out a bow and stringing it up with arrows, a set he'd made in the forest during his shift.

"Get behind me, Riot." Locke said, shielding me with his massive body.

I scowled.

"I see them, I'm gonna track." Kaz shifted and took off darting between the trees with lightning speed before anyone could respond. I watched him until he was completely out of line sight.

Locke turned to me, opening his mouth to say something, but spotted movement over my shoulder.

"Hold that thought," he said, shifting and taking off in the other direction, leaving me in the heavily wooded space on my own.

With both of them gone, I had a rare minute to myself and could just *think*. The voice made itself known when I was mostly asleep, but over the course of the days, as I accepted its presence within me, it became a never-ending trickle of assurance and compliments.

I packed up all the duffels and sat on a rock, cleaning some tools Kaz had made for sharpening his arrows. I allowed the darkness to consume me just a bit more

"You should be careful with that," a voice like satin entered the clearing.

I probably would have jumped if the edges of my being weren't cracking away inside of me, but I didn't. I hadn't heard anyone approach the area, but there she stood. She had long brown hair that curled at the ends. Full hips. I could just see the dip of her breast behind her square neck dress. She had on a long cloak that only revealed her chest and arms. The massive hood swallowing her beautiful face.

"What do you know?"

"I know a lot, Riot Blair."

Something in the way she stayed away from me, but said my name, tickled in the fractured pieces that were buried somewhere in the abyss that had become me.

"Really. Like what?"

She thought for a moment, then answered.

"I know you're fractured. I know you're suffering."

I clap less than enthusiastically.

"Wow, you have eyes. You're no one special." I mock, turning back to my work.

"Aren't you afraid?"

"Of?"

"Well, aren't you running?"

I scrape the debris from the bone knife, not answering her. Still, she doesn't move. After a moment, I decided to answer her.

"No, I'm acting."

"Acting?"

"Yeah, for the sake of my friends thinking they can stop my father. I am acting."

"What does that mean?"

"Have you really not heard?" I question, getting louder now.

She shakes her head no as I stare at her. Her features become clearer the longer I look and something in me twinges.

"I know you." I breathe. Not a question, but a statement.

A realization.

"Surely not."

"But I do. Somewhere, inside of me. I can feel it, I *know* you," I insist, standing now.

I move to approach her, something in my very core, pushing me towards her. It feels magnetic. It feels propelled by the cosmos and the gods and everything that's in me. In this moment, I feel like there's *more* in me. Like maybe I have a soul and maybe what's left of it is enough.

She doesn't move as I approach her, her features crisp and clear now. The dip in her lips, the brown eyes so deep they remind me of the Earth. They remind me of the mountains and wet tree bark. Of chocolate and of whiskey. Maybe even bourbon.

Bourbon.

I could almost smell it, followed by strawberries and a hint of vanilla. A smell that instantly brought pieces of me back. I perked up. I touched her face. We were so close now; I was sure she could feel my breath and hear my pounding heart. It was filling my ears. I couldn't place her name, even this close to her, but my heart, my *soul*, knew her.

I lifted my hand to touch her face and immediately felt the magnetic rush of two ends that were supposed to touch finally connecting. I was bursting, pieces of me flying to the surface but as quickly as I felt the snap of being in tune, her fiery warmth beneath my palm started going cold.

Her mouth that had been a subtle smile, turned rigid and the light in her eyes went out. She started shaking as blood poured from her left nostril and then the corner of her mouth. Her full weight collapsed into me.

No, this wasn't right. My first time having her in my arms she couldn't be dying. Why was she dying? I could feel the shattered pieces of me fighting to get to the surface, but they were being pulled back, replaced by shards of inky nothing.

I fell back, as she landed on the forest floor in front of me. Stunned I stared. She wasn't breathing anymore, so I scramble to her, flipping her over to see her bloody and bruised, her neck bent at a sickening angle.

No.

No.

NO.

Another piece fell away.

Pulling her to my chest, I wipe her hair away from her face and notice double fang marks. As I take a closer look, I notice mine are out and the sweet taste of blood tinges my tongue.

I did this.

Her black eye, her broken bones. Her spirit gone. Her light was destroyed.

"You did this, Riot Blair," a voice echoes throughout the wood

I rock her body back and forth, shaking her.

I know her.

I know her.

But I can't place her.

Another piece crumbles into the darkness.

I look down at her beautiful face and promptly throw her off of me, backing up as fast as I can as I see her staring at me with wide open black eyes.

"You did this to me, Riot Blair. You are a monster!"

Her voice is guttural now, deep and layered with many others. She gets on all fours approaching me slowly. I try blasting her with my element, but it doesn't come.

The inner parts of my spirit are shattered. I feel nothing but coldness.

Her face cracks and breaks, shifting and morphing into a face I'd never thought I'd see again- the face of my own father.

"You can't run from me, Riot. I made you. I know your every move."

The girls' body twists and bends in a sickening series of snaps. She looks at me, her mouth splitting across her face as it opens to reveal two large rows of pointed sharp teeth coated in a black oily substance.

It screams as it charges me and then dissipates into nothing, taking

what pieces of me I had left with it.
   I welcome the darkness as an old friend as it replaces the space I used to exist.

KAZ

    Wind blows through my thick coat as I chase the scent infiltrating my nostrils. It's strong and smells like Earth and brackish water. The Earth makes way for my massive paws as I drive them hard into it, propelling myself forward. Within moments, I break through the wood and into a clearing, coming face to face with wild wolves.

    They notice I'm much larger than they are and take off into the wooded area beyond the clearing, taking the brackish scent with them. I decide to stay and sniff around the area a bit, making sure that it was in fact the wolves that were in the brush.

    When Riot and I connected in that arena, something stayed behind long after the magic was severed. I couldn't quite place my finger on it but from the information Amira had given to me, once you perform connection magic with someone, it's a permanent change.

    In theory using the staff should have eliminated the permanence of the magic, but the effects were taking a long time to wear off- longer than I'd hoped. I hadn't expected us to actually be successful so soon, nor for it to be that strong. Riot's strength was first matched to mine, but quickly, he overtook me. The physical streams of power from the staff kept steady while it was over the lagoon. I used its waters to help keep the connection stable, but inside, I could feel him overpowering my shields.

    His essence broke through my mind, shattering any semblance of protection I had. He took root in me, leaving me weak and with a severed connection to my mate. I had to rely on scrying to communicate with her now. It was torture.

    He was torture.

When I was sure the smell was gone, I shifted back to my human self. The sun beat down through the trees, lighting my skin in golden hues. I missed her terribly. Before I could even think twice, I started a formation she'd made just for the two of us. The energy collected in front of me in a silver light. A triangle shape that created our mated star clusters in the center.

When the sigil was complete, I painted the trees with it, creating a door like portal. The trees within the affected area turned white in the bark, then black. The leaves went from pink to silver, and I kneeled, awaiting my queen.

The trees sighed as they parted for her, her face smiling. It took everything in me not to cry when I laid my eyes upon her. She appeared in her human form as she usually would away from the forest. I had no preference between the two so long as she was within my arms.

"My darling," she says, running into my arms.

The connection between us reminded me of two oceans meeting in the middle of a galaxy. Ever different, yet so cohesive. We ran our own paths, but we ebbed and flowed as one.

"There's been trouble, I sensed it immediately and tried to send word, but you were gone. I'd have thought you dead, but that I had time to consider it all told me you were still alive." She kissed me gingerly, then she broke away as if she remembered something.

"Riot, where is he?"

"Back at our camp. He's fine."

"He's secluded," she replied in an argumentative tone.

"He is."

Agreeing with her was easier than explaining what was going on, but usually she knew before I could tell her, however, with the connection weakened, I wasn't sure how much she saw now, if anything at all.

"The staffs, they worked then?" she said listening to the wind around her.

I nod in answer, not daring to speak lest I speak over them, and she misses something important.

"He's troubled, my love. There's so much-" Her voice catches and I take her hand, hoping to reassure her.

I press my will into her palm, hoping to soothe her with calm, stopping her thoughts in their tracks. This kind of serenity is never present when I'm shifted. Then, I'm her warrior. Now, I'm her protector.

LOCKE

My breath skips when I feel a block stopping me from taking her pain from her. She looks up at me, her eyes glistening with the threat of crystal tears. Centaurs were amazing and pure creatures that had captured my attention since I was a child. Their grace always a concept I resonated with.

"He's not been the same for a bit." I say, kissing her knuckles.

She frowns.

"How long exactly? Since the confusion magic?"

"Yes. Everything was going well. Once we made a connection though, everything changed. Even the green of his eyes have dissipated."

She looks up at me now and I can see the gears turning in her mind. I miss being there. I miss knowing exactly what it is she's thinking.

When she doesn't say anything, I ask, "How long will we be like this?"

"There's no telling. Just don't fall with him."

"Fall with him? I thought you liked him?"

"Oh, but I do! He's marvelous. He knows exactly what he's doing, my love. I advise you treat him better, however, think about the history of Meta. Think about all the Kings Meta thought would be their salvation who weren't."

I nod.

"The greed, corruption, hatred... it turns them all eventually."

She inhales.

"Riot is a huge risk we are taking. In fact, he's probably the worst candidate possible for changing Meta," she giggles.

"Indeed, he is, but he's also our only hope."

She nods.

"Indeed, he is, my love. He's destined for so much more. I just hope he can find his way."

Kaz left us in the clearing alone but shortly after he sprinted off, I too spotted a figure in the distance. I didn't want to leave him unattended, but since Kaz had already taken off in the other direction, I decided to go, wanting to avoid another ambush. I rushed into the brush. The figure, spotting me, took off leading me into a great chase.

After a few minutes, I lost the figure in a heavily wooded area. The trees were thick, and I can no longer see what direction I came from. There's a small wooden cabin that sat directly in the middle of the overgrown trees. Smoke pipes from the chimney and there are lights on inside. There's a small gravel pathway.

I decide it's worth knocking but before I can even make it to the door, a short, handsome man answers it. His dark eyes are kind and smudged with black, his smile, warm. He has three fingers on each hand and his torso turned goat at the midsection. He just stood there, smiling as I took him in.

"Welcome Traveler, to Quincy's Tavern!"

He stepped aside, gesturing me in. I noticed he wore a black leather cuff around one wrist and a tan one around the other. Around his neck he had a red scarf, goggles and an apron. I could tell he was wise beyond his years.

I crossed the threshold to find myself in a bar filled with many fantastical beasts and creatures I had never known existed. Not one paid attention to me entering the space. The man went behind the bar and accepted some wax seals from a large beast with tusks and slid him an amber jar filled with glowing yellow morsels.

"Good luck traveler!"

He turns to me now, patting the bar top in front of an empty seat and reluctantly, I take it.

"I'm Quincy." He smiles, taking an odd-looking device from under the bar and placing it between us.

He pours some brown beans into it and turns the handle; a crunching sound emits from it immediately.

"I've been waiting for you, Locke, Minotaur from Pantheon, " He says.
"You have?"

He lifts knowing eyes from his work and smiles as he turns to the back of the bar now and sorts through the slabs of tree bark set there. They are all shapes and sizes, but all are the same thickness.

He finds the one he's looking for and places it on the bar next to the contraption. A small fairy flutters over to us, dropping a loaf of steaming bread onto the tree plate and scoots away quick as lightning.

Quincy grabs a short blade and begins slicing the loaf.

"I have. For many moons. The stars told of your arrival many moons ago," he leads, still smiling as he worked.

"I'm sorry brother, I don't know what to say to that. I've never been told anyone was waiting for me in my life," I chuckle.

Normally, I'd probably be uncomfortable, but in here? I felt at peace. I felt welcome and safe. I felt *known*.

Quincy turned from me, offering a plate of food to another strange beast with three heads. While he traded goods with him, I took the time to look around at the bar. The back wall had a cheerful sign that hung right in the middle.

It read, "Welcome Traveler!"

The wall had vines of ivy crawling up them, but not so thick that you couldn't see the tan wood underneath. There were various shelves that floated in front of it, clearly illusioned by magic. They held leather bound books and various jars, contraptions and glass bottles. There were scrolls pinned up and even a silver skull with glowing eyes.

Quincy flung a black cloth over his shoulder as he approached me again.

"Sorry, friend. I have to tend the travelers who've found their way."

"It's alright," I answer almost too quickly.

He goes back to working on the black powder he emptied from one contraption, pouring it into another.

"Sorry but, found their way? What does that mean?"

"Well, you're lost, aren't you?" he asks

I watched him. Was I lost? He seems to gather what I'm thinking, and I suddenly feel like a fool for asking for clarification.

"Everyone who finds Quincy's is lost in some way or needs something. That's what I do, I help them find their way."

As his words are spoken, I feel like I'm looking for something, but I can't quite think of what.

"That happens quite often,"

A sparkle in his eye tells me he already knows what I don't.

"What happens?"

"The confusion, or, maybe it's realization."

"I'm sorry, I truly don't know what it is I'm here for."

"That's alright. I'm placed by the gods and I'm where I am when I'm needed. Seeing as you were the only one out there who saw me, you're in the right place."

"Okay, so, what do I do?"

"Do?" he chuckles.

He accepts various forms of payment from a few empty seats before placing another tree plate in front of me. This one has a bowl of bread with a milky soup inside.

"Eat, that's what you do." He laughs.

Deciding it can't be poisonous if everyone around me is leaving and finishing off their meals, I dig in. The warm liquid is aromatic and hearty. There are bits of carrots, potato and lamb. It's so good that I can't help myself as I shovel three spoonfuls into my mouth, savoring the taste.

As I ate, I noticed objects on the back wall coming into view that I hadn't seen before. A small shelf appeared at the very top of the wall, almost touching the roof. There was a small dark purple bottle with a golden cage over it. It had a crystal stopper, and I don't know if I'm dreaming, but I feel like I can smell it from here.

Next to it, sat a large, simple looking black collar. Leaning against the collar was a sheathed blade. Hanging below it, a small crossbow. All were equally interesting, and I could tell they had a story, but what caught my eye, even over the tantalizing heart bottle, was a rather plain looking wooden mallet and a very boring looking wooden stake.

I tore off a piece of bread as I looked at them, feeling their power and lure in full effect. I dipped it into the stew, hurrying to finish every last bite so I could talk to Quincy again, but just as I thought of him, he appeared.

"What are those trinkets up there," I say, mouth full of bread and stew. I point to the shelf, but Quincy doesn't even turn around.

For the first time since stepping into Quincy's Tavern, he looked worn.

"You can see them?" It's not really a question.

I nod.

He sighs deeply and crosses the bar, helping the last customer out of the pub. When he closes the door, he locks seven locks. I watch him glide about, locking and shutting all the windows. His hooves make a calming clacking on the wood as he goes.

When he's satisfied that the place is secure, he returns to the bar, cleans up my plate and then looks me straight in the face.

"What?"

"You can see them," he says, waiting.

For a moment, we just stare at one another.

"Well, those have a deep story. I can tell it to you; however, they are not for sale. In fact, I will tell you the tale, because I think it could be helpful, traveler."

"You can call me Locke, it's no problem brother."

He doesn't pay me any mind as he turns, using his air magic to lift the items from the shelf and places them on the bar in front of me.

"These," he says, gesturing to the artifacts.

"Are known as the Devil's Wares."

I swallow. No one ever talks about the gods anymore. To hear him speak so clearly of the one once known as the Devil was surprising, especially since he did it so effortlessly.

"Don't be frightened,"

"I'm not!" Again, my answer was much too quick for my liking.

He smiles.

"The gods are not dead, traveler. They are always watching. Always taking notes." He wags his finger at me.

"I have a feeling they are well impressed with you, Locke."

Warmth tickles my insides- a feeling I'm not used to as I possess Earth, and she's usually only made herself known by wrapping herself tight against my skeleton, like an internal armor built special for me.

"I've never thought about the gods that way. From what we hear in Pantheon, they've abandoned us completely."

"Ah, such a shame it is to be assumptive." He sighs.

"I'm not, it's just what I've heard."

"I think you shouldn't always listen to what you hear," he smiles.

"You're right. So, these items. Why are they so important?"

He looks down at the items thoughtfully. I can't help but watch his face as he scrutinizes each one.

"The story goes that these belonged to a very special kind of menace. One that got pure joy out of... sticking it to the living, let's say."

"Sticking what?"

"Anything, really. For instance," he explains, picking up the heart shaped bottle in his hand, showing it to me.

"The taste of lust," he puts it down, moving to the next one.

"The collar of greed."

He picked up the leather collar, looking at it as if he were considering its power.

"Okay what about the mallet and stake?"

They called to me most.

"Those? Oh, those are priceless... this mallet is doubt..." His voice was barely above a whisper now.

"And the stake?"

"Discouragement."

I looked at the plain objects, their features so unassuming and unlike the rest of the lot. Quincy must have sensed my doubt about them, because he continued on, louder now.

"They may look like nothing now, sitting here on this old bar top, however, together, they become hopelessness."

I looked from the objects to him now. He kept his eyes on them, not daring to look away as though if he did, they would be lost.

"These are tools that, when in the wrong hands, can do destruction beyond your wildest of dreams. When none of these other tools, "

He gestures with his hand to the other various wares between us, my eyes glued to the taste of lust once more and continued on.

"When they don't work? These plain tools get the job done every single time."

"How?"

"Ah, curious now, aren't you?" He chuckles but continues before I can answer.

"Obviously, Locke, there are many more things that one could do to someone worse than death,"

I nod.

"But do you know what's the worst thing someone could do to someone else's soul?"

I shake my head, unable to break eye contact with him now.

"Nothing paralyzes a soul more than discouragement," he picks up the stake.

"And doubt," he lifts the mallet now, one in each hand, looking me directly in the eye.

"These other items? They may cause a soul to act out such as in anger or lust, but Hopelessness? Discouragement? Doubt? They cause a soul to do…Nothing."

He smiles a knowing smile as chills run down my arms.

"Which is much more deadly. They respect no one, draining their victim of courage and bravery, causing their visions and dreams to be blurred and blocked out by anxiety and fears,"

I look back at the wares in his hands.

"When a soul has fully succumbed to hopelessness, they become an empty shell, allowing anything and anyone in. Even if the weapons of pride, greed, or lust, for instance, have no effect on you, beware the dull spike of discouragement and doubt."

"How though? How would one defend against something like that if it were out there?"

"It is out there, Locke. That's why you must help Riot. Help him hold onto what encourages and inspires his heart. You care about him, love is the greatest magic of all."

"That's not a real answer!" I almost shout.

"It's the one I have. You have to find other answers if you must seek them. This is the message I was given for you."

"Given? From whom?"

Quincy smiles, snapping his fingers and suddenly, I'm no longer on a barstool. I'm standing outside his cabin.

"Stay safe out there and if you ever need anything, just look for my tavern." And with that, I was thrown back into the thicket where Riot lay, alone, bleeding.

KAZ

Locke entered the wooded area from the opposite side of me just as I got there. We locked eyes for only a moment before rushing to Riot's side. I assessed the wounds as Locke got to work trying to wake him. There were no tracks that I could find and no scent from anyone other than Riot.

"Who could have attacked him?" Locke asked, becoming even more frantic when Riot didn't respond.

I shake my head.

"This is no attack. At least, not a physical one."

I can taste burnt champagne, the taste of dark magic, in the back of my throat and decide there's something more going on here. The rock ledge provides a better view of the ground, so I climb it as Locke tries waking Riot again.

"I...I think he's tranced, man."

He looks at me now, towering above him.

"What the hell are you doing?"

"Shhh!"

I pace back and forth on the stone pedestal, able to see clearly now the disturbed dirt, scraping of some kind. I could tell the footprints Locke and I had just made apart from the heavy markings that looked like a body had been thrown through the soil.

I signal for Locke to back away and he does, leaving Riot right where we found him. As a wolf, tracking skills are part of my natural instinct and looking at the ground from up here now, I can tell that this was absolutely no attack.

"There was no attack. I know a formation that can show us what happened here,"

"Are you talking about a replay formation? Those are highly advanced and illegal, Kaz. How do you know that the forest isn't under watcher magic? If they see you, we could all be killed. Not to mention, they'd find Riot!" Locke argues.

I jump down off the ledge and pat the spot next to me as I sit. Locke looks from Riot's tranced body, lifeless on the forest floor to me, shrugs and steps over him, joining me.

"These woods are clean, I checked. You really should know me by now."

I don't give him a chance to speak as I start the formation. My friend wasn't wrong in saying that replays were highly illegal, however, I'd been doing them since my mother first taught me as a child. Being careful was key and I never went anywhere I wasn't comfortable or sure of.

I place my hands in front of me, palms together, fingers towards the sky. At the same time, I move them away from my body, turning them at the wrists, until my palms are facing the wooded area. I make a box with them and then, bring them back to the starting position.

Once they are back in front of me, a series of complicated formations string out, Locke watching every move as I work. He was without a doubt, trying to learn what I was doing.

When the formation was complete, I held my hands cupped together in front of me.

"Are you ready?"

Locke nods.

"This may not be good," I say, trying to prepare him for the sinking feeling growing in my gut.

"Just do it."

I let the energy go and we watch as the magic replays what happened in the clearing. We see Locke run off, chasing something outside the parameters that I made.

We watch as Riot sighs what looks like relief and my heartrate picks up. We watch him go about cleaning up, everything seeming quite normal.

"Did you see that?" Locke says, pointing.

"No, what?"

"Watch him, he's craning his neck like he's trying to crack it or something," he whispers.

I'd been looking at the tree line, waiting to see who comes there, but Locke was right. Riot started acting strange as he sat, cleaning my tools. He stretched his neck more and more frequently as he worked until we could see him saying something, looking into the tree line.

Locke leaned forward, trying to see what it was Riot was looking at.

"This doesn't have sound?"

"Normally, it would but with magic being so scarce and this being so illegal, no. It doesn't."

"I can't see anything in the trees, who is he talking to?"

I scan, not wanting to miss a thing as Riot stands now, approaching the space just before the trees. He brings his arm up to something we can't see.

"He's... he's *glowing*..." Locke breathes.

Riot's head and shoulders were indeed glowing, but for what? No one was there. I'd never seen anyone do that without using magic.

"Perhaps he's doing magic?"

"Nah, he never glows when he does." Locke said, still sitting forward.

We watched Riot's back as he crumbled, falling to the floor as though he was trying to catch something heavy. He rolled and then looked back, and for the first time, we could see his face. His eyes were completely white.

"What the hell?"

"Shhh, just watch." I say, leaning forward now too.

Riot scrambled over to something we still couldn't see, picking it up in his arms and rocking it back and forth. It almost looked like he was begging and pleading the sky above. I recognized his jaw popping as he screamed something.

Then, he jumped back, digging his heels hard into the soft soil, pushing himself back against the rock ledge. His face was horrified as he watched something unfold that only he could see. Then, his eyes went fully black. He scratched at them, as if trying to pull them from his own face, yelled, and then passed out.

I looked at Locke as the magic dissipated. His face was sullen as he stared at his friend.

"He's tranced."

"He's being flared." I counter.

Locke walked over to his friend, concern drawing lines all over his face.

"I have to ask you this and I in no way am blaming you, but where did you go?" I ask.

I watch as Locke kneels, realization hitting him as he leans over his friend, face in hands.

"I thought I saw a figure on the other side of the woods. I wanted to avoid another ambush," He said, clearly upset.

I walked a few paces past the tree line, in the direction that Locke had taken off.

"This is open for miles. You would have seen someone plainly had there been anyone there."

"Are you calling me a liar?"

"Absolutely not. I'm thinking you and I were both tricked to leave him here. Then, someone flared his mind. Whether that flare already existed before we started traveling or it's new, it's a problem."

Locke looks at me with deep concern.

"What?"

"I think I need to tell you what happened once I left the area," he says, swallowing hard.

LOCKE

Kaz stared at me blankly as I recounted everything to him that happened once I'd found Quincy's Tavern. He didn't make a move as I explained to him every detail I could remember.

"Then, I spotted some wares on a shelf as I ate and apparently he was floored I could see them. He called them, 'The Devil's Wares."

He closes his eyes as his jaw feathers.

"They-"

"I know what they are," He says, holding a hand up in a stop motion.

"Well, I don't know why I could see them or why I was even in that place. I can take you there, if you want."

"No, you can't."

He turns now, rummaging for something in a bag he pulled from our supplies.

"Why not? He was super nice, and I felt safe. I felt at peace. It'd be good for you to eat something and maybe see the wares for yourself."

He slams the bag down as thunder rumbles overhead.

"Locke! Listen to me!" He yells.

"This isn't a game. This is *real* and I need you to step out of your Pantheon mindset for just a minute and *think*. Meta is huge. It's not the only island in the world. This whole thing with Riot's father, who, might I remind you is a *murderous* king, is bigger than any of us- *including* him!"

I'd never heard Kaz yell. I'd never heard him be anything other than confident and encouraging. His face was reddening with his words.

"I know it is, Kaz. That's why we are here. We are helping him. We have to do this."

"Why? Why do *we* have to? Why me? For fucks sake why *you*?"

I think about it for a second before answering him. I knew deep down he knew the answer already, but I wanted to give him one regardless.

"If not us, then who?"

That seemed to calm him as he furrowed his brows. There truly was no one else. Anyone who'd ever tried had made it worse. De-throning Arnoldous was only the beginning though, and I think Kaz knew that. There were centuries of work to undo and while I wasn't sure the entire job was for us, I was sure we were the spark to ignite the flame of change.

"You're right. But if I die, I *will* haunt you."

"Bring it in brother! No one is gonna die. Well, except Arnoldous Blair."

"One could only hope."

Kaz gives me a hug and we take turns trying to decide how to wake Riot. We try several attempts, to no avail, before Kaz offers another gut turning realization.

"We can't stay here much longer. We've been stagnant too long already."

I nod.

"He's tranced so I'll just float him on air formations between us as we go. We need to head north for a few more days' travel at this point."

"Let's do this then." I say, grabbing up the bags and starting off.

"Locke, north is this way." Kaz says pointing behind us.

I chuckle and follow him, Riot floating between us. When we came to a running stream, Kaz washed Riots wounds and dressed them with some gauze around his head as I drank and swam in the river.

"It's kind of nice not having to watch him so much," Kaz chuckles when he's done.

"Come on, he's not *that* bad."

"He's awful," Kaz chuckles.

"And I'm starting to like him."

I light up inside hearing him say those words.

"The things I saw in the arena when Riot came storming in through my mental shields, they were awful."

"I've been meaning to ask what you saw, but I thought you'd not want to tell me," I say, getting out now and drying off.

"I don't. I will though, in time."

"What happened to you when you left the clearing, then? Come on Kaz, you have to tell me *something*."

He thinks about that and gathers some water for me in a canister he brought along.

"I saw Amira. It was nothing special, I called her to me and she already knew our troubles." He said, closing his eyes and tilting his head towards the sun, his pale skin needing it.

His magic was being tried having to support Riot on borrowed air magic. He couldn't use his water during a long-standing formation, and I knew he was getting tired.

"If my calculations are correct, we are just south of the Brine Scallop River. Once we pass that, we should be at the tip of Meta."

"When do we hit lands not controlled by the king?"

Kaz shot me a grim look.

"We don't. I told you, there are islands outside of Meta and he controls pretty much every single one of them."

"Well, fuck."

"Exactly. He will have forces in all of them. That's why Nobility is our best shot. If that doesn't work, I don't know what will."

I sigh, mostly because he's right. If Nobility doesn't work for us, there's no place where Riot's father doesn't have control. I'd never been this far out of Pantheon before. I've never even left Meta. In fact, Meta was so large, we hardly ever spoke of the other islands or lands.

When the sun rolled behind more clouds, we walked on in silence. Kaz was concentrating on keeping his formations up, but they weakened the more Kaz became exhausted.

"Maybe we should stop?" I offer, finding a nice ring of trees with low, wide branches we could climb up to the top and rest in.

Kaz looked around thoughtfully.

"We still need to wake him," he says, gesturing to Riot who was now only inches from the rock and leaves.

"We can figure it out tomorrow, you're exhausted." I offer, hoping to encourage him.

"Not really. We are about an hour's walk from the edge."

"We are? Hey, something I didn't think about before, how are we going to cross water?"

"You have Earth right?"

I nod, not really getting where he's going with this.

"That's how."

"Oh no. No, no, no. I'm not angering Mother Earth by destroying her sculpt of the land."

"You're not destroying it if I teach you illusion magic and we just replicate it." Kaz says, whipping out the blade he'd made and starts creating a tap in the tree.

"Yes! Look at this!"

Kaz holds up his blade with a silvery shimmering slime hanging off the end of it.

"Ew, gross!" I sputter as I watch him put the stuff into his mouth.

He closes his eyes, moaning as if it's actually any good. I watch as Kaz empties the water canister and gets to work on the tree, making the hole bigger for the canisters opening to fit into.

"Hey man, that's my water! I need it unlike you."

"Silver Sap is better than water, Locke. With this stuff, you'll get everything you need."

"I mean no disrespect, but how do you know all of this? You've always got some kind of know-how."

Kaz chuckled as he worked the canisters into the hole now.

"I told you; my parents have spent their lives traveling and learning and training other packs. They don't pay my parents with money; they pay them in an exchange of knowledge which then gets passed on to me.

"I've never seen you once call anyone. How do you get the knowledge? Where are your parents? Hold on, all of a sudden, you're super mysterious, brother."

"Wolves can communicate down our own consciousness. When they learn something, I learn it too. At the same time."

"Ew, so do you experience their thoughts all the time? And like… when they do it?"

He punches me in the arm.

"No, you freak, and even if I wanted to, we all have shields. Think of it like a singular pod where anyone can go and exist and then, branching off that pod are hallways with smaller pods. The smaller pods are each wolf in a pack and the hallways are where the shields are. We choose what comes down our hallway."

He pulls the bottle from the tree now. I can see it's filled to the brim.

"Here, take some off the top. You don't need a lot. Too much will have you feeling like you're on Faerie Shrooms or something."

I take the canister from him and reluctantly slurp some off the top. The texture is awful. Thankfully its warm so that helps a bit as I gulp it, not wanting it to sit on my tongue for too long.

I pull my face into a look of disgust as Kaz laughs, but then, I feel it. The slime dissipates and is replaced by a feeling of energy. It smothers all my tired, all my worry, working its way over my muscles. I even felt earth loosen its grip on my skeleton.

"Woah, what is that feeling?"

"That's natural energy. It's saved many lives of wolves throughout the centuries. Especially when food was scarce so long ago during the height of the Cardinal war."

"Food was scarce?"

"For wolves, yes. I imagine for many other factions not royal outside of Pantheon also experienced hardships of many kinds."

I'd never really thought about the other factions who lived in Metos, and I guess outside of it too. I assumed all my life that all factions existed within city confines and that they all fought to be a part of Pantheon.

My family fought for generations to be considered for a life in Pantheon. I knew my grandfathers even tried necromancy to bring Baphomet back to help them get there, but that stuff never worked on a god.

I watched as Kaz, now energized by the Silver Sap, hoisted Riot onto one of the higher branches. The sun was setting, and we were on the verge of being plummeted into darkness. These are the most dangerous hours for us. Tonight though, both of us would be able to get some rest with Riot still tranced.

I climbed the massive branches until I was one above where Riot now lay, still tranced, dead to the world around him. The branches were staggered perfectly so that on my left, I could look down and see him and, on my right, I could see Kaz who was one branch below Riot.

The thick, flat branches gave enough room that even I, as massive as I was, could stretch out comfortably.

"Dream well, Friend. Tomorrow, we leave Meta."

Kaz bid me rest for the evening, and took his place, using a duffel for a pillow. From here, I could see the stars through the canopy of trees. Kaz's words floated through my mind as I watched them, twinkling down on me. Everything he's said has been true.

I watch the stars and decide to do something I've not done since I was a child. Not out loud, but in my mind, I decide to talk to them.

Locke here.

Sorry it's been so long. I just wanted to say thanks... for keeping us safe as we run. Please watch over my family. Especially my mom as she deals with those miscreants she calls my brothers.

I chuckle to myself.

Look, I don't know why you sent Quincy to me. I don't even know if that was fully real but thank you. Thank you for reminding me I'm a good Minotaur. A good man. I'm trying. And if you really are impressed with me, if you really are proud, send me the support of the gods. I'm doing the work in your name, the least you could do is back me up.

A cluster of stars right over head of me brighten and twinkle in a fast pace. I've never seen them do that, but before I could question it, I was out, images of the cosmos greeting me as I swam through their unending abyss.

———

The sound of bark cracking and breaking somewhere below me wakes me up. Slowly at first, and then all at once as I hear grunts of struggle below. I peer over the edge of my branch before jumping down in case there's an attacker, but all I see are broad shoulders.

It takes a moment for my eyes to adjust to the darkness around me as Riot's branch comes into view. I'm shocked to see it's empty, and that the broad shoulders below belong to him.

"Hey! Hey!" I shout, hoping to distract him, jumping down.

I catch myself as I drop to Riot's abandoned space, cutting my forearm in the process, but I don't have time to stop and look at it. The space from Riot's to Kaz's branches is almost double. I look around for something I can throw, but there's nothing.

Saying a silent apology to him, I thrust vines out of my palms, frantically, aiming for his neck. They grapple him with little to no effort and once in place, I grab the ends and tug as hard as I can. Riot flies off Kaz and hits the ground below.

When I don't hear any scuffling about, I drop down to Kaz. I can see he's half shifted, claws out, fangs protruding. He just lays there staring up.

"Kaz? You alright?"

His chest heaves. I can already see the bruises around his neck, even in the darkness.

"I'm fine," he rasps.

I help him to a sitting position and look around for where Riot ended up. He's a few feet away, curled into a ball, his back to us now.

"If I've ever been sure of anything in my life, it's that his mind is flared, and his father is the culprit." Kaz says through gritted teeth.

His voice is broken from being choked. I hand him the canister of Silver Sap, hoping it would help and am relieved when he drinks. In awe, I watch as the bruises on his neck start to fade, leaving behind only small traces as his healing energy comes back.

"What happened?" I asked him, hoping now he will sound better.

"I'm not entirely sure. I was asleep, but very quickly I became aware of my dream state. I had a vision of Riot being twisted and torn over and over and-"

He stops abruptly, as if the memory of what he saw breaks him a little.

"And what?"

"And he asked for me to help him. He asked for me to kill him so that the pain would stop."

Kaz has never been afraid to kill. Never once questioned a soul begging for mercy. I've known him most of my life having met him when I was ten. He was twelve and he has always been poised, but ruthless. I've watched him rip out the throats of many who've wronged him.

But now, sitting here, looking at him, I could tell that the thought of it made him sick. I took a seat in the space next to him, folding my hands in my lap.

"Did you?"

"No, of course not. In my dream, when I told him no, he started freaking out. He cried, then screamed and then laughed manically, telling me it was my fault, all that would come from this. From letting him live."

I watched his face as he kept his eyes plastered on Riot's back. It was like he expected him to attack again at any moment.

"Did you attack him in your sleep?"

"No, not at all. When he said that, I felt the air leaving my lungs, my chest was burning, screaming for air. I jumped awake but was met with burning green eyes. He was there just choking me."

"Why would Riot do this?" I mumble more to myself than to him.

"That's the thing though, Locke. It wasn't Riot's eyes that were staring back at me. It was his father's."

KAZ

    We sat, staring at Riot's back until the darkness turned blue with the rising sun. Now we knew for sure that Riot's father was watching us through his eyes, and he wanted both myself and Locke dead. Luckily, we didn't have too much travel left.

    "I'm gonna go take a leak and I'll help you with Riot. Just... Don't approach him," Locke says, standing and stretching.

    After I'd told him about my dream, we'd sat in silence the rest of the night. I could feel the Silver Sap working on my energy and the wounds inflicted to my trachea from within. My parents had always said if you could find Silver Sap, you could survive nearly anything.

    I finished off the canister and decided to refill it while Locke finished his business. Not wanting to turn my back on Riot, I made a new tap in the underside of my branch. I should have done this the first time, because gravity helped it flow much more nicely.

    When Locke finally returned, he knelt next to Riot and tried waking him.

    "Riot, come on. Are you hurt?"

    Surprisingly, he sat up. I watched while I shoved the canisters' oopening into the hole and licked the sap off the tip of my knife.

    "Where the fuck are we now?" he huffed, looking around.

    "Almost to our destination," Locke answered him carefully.

    I assumed he didn't want to give away too much detail, now that he saw I was right, and Riot's mind had become his father's personal fountain of intel.

    Riot touched the scabbing over his eyes lightly.

    "Why does it hurt? And itch?"

Locke looks at me and I try my best to give him a cautionary glance as Riot follows his line of sight to me. I make myself overly busy with the canister and sap.

We need to find out how much Riot remembers. How much he knows. Flaring the mind of anyone is an evil act. It's illegal under the Loyalists law, but the King gets away with everything.

"You had an episode," Locke treads carefully.

"Oh. I did this?" his voice breaks a bit.

I can see how tired he is. This is him now, no king in sight.

"Riot, how much do you remember from the past few days?" I try.

He looks around at the space, the silver sap leaking from the branch to the ground now, and then between Locke and I.

"We were in the woods and I was sorting the duffels. Now, we are here."

Locke shoots me a look.

"That's it?"

"Yeah. Why?"

Locke sighs deeply, pulling Riot to his feet.

"A lot has happened, although you were asleep for most of it,"

"I wasn't asleep, I was in literal hell."

LOCKE

Riot's admission to having been aware of where he was while we thought he was in a tranced state was nothing short of shocking and unexpected. He helped us clean up without saying much after apologizing for attacking us both. Apparently, he didn't remember attacking me either during our travels.

When we were finally on the move again, Kaz was the first to speak.

"Do you remember anything... from Hell I mean?"

Riot shook his head.

"No. I just know and *knew* that I was there."

In my gut I felt that he wasn't giving the whole truth. It sort of felt the way he did before all of this began. His being distant with Kaz. I could suspect that I wouldn't know if he was his normal self again until I could get him alone, just the two of us for a moment.

After about two hours we came to another running stream and Kaz offered to find some aloe while we drank and bathed. I missed having a shower and bathroom and privacy. I missed comfy beds and real food. We'd been eating fruit we found along with the Silver Sap, but the further out of Meta we traveled, the less frequent we were finding the sap trees.

"Riot, please talk to me," I beg him, worried that I'll miss my chance if I wait too long after Kaz disappears into some bushes.

"About?"

"Hell. You. Anything!" I snap a little too harshly.

He laughs a shallow laugh, shaking his head as he draws in the sand with a stick.

"What's funny?"

"That you want me to talk to you, tell you everything, yet you don't even care about me. I was second on your list. You just want information from me."

"Well, yes, but I do care about you, Riot. Haven't you learned that by now? You're like a brother to me." I plead.

Riot doesn't look at me as he keeps his attention on his art. I keep my attention on him, searching his face for any sign of the guy who'd become my friend.

"No one is my friend. No one cares. I'm just a pawn in all this, just like you. Only difference is, you have a choice. I do not."

Kaz reappears holding a large, spiky aloe and sits beside Riot. He uses his knife again to cut it open and remove the outer parts before offering some chunks to Riot for his face.

I watch Riot as he eyes the knife and make a mental note to let Kaz know later on.

"Put this on. I'll give you the rest throughout our travels. It should soothe the itching and help it heal, although there's one I'm not so sure will be going anywhere." Kaz says, shoving the rest into a banana leaf and putting that into his own duffle.

Riot takes the chunk and rubs it on his face. I offer him some more strips I made from the only other shirt I had.

"Oh what, so I can't see, and you can kill me?" Riot spat.

"No, of course not. It's for many reasons, but the main one is to protect your wounds, so your face isn't ruined." I say.

He looks to Kaz and asks, "Is it to help my face or is he gonna kill me?"

A sharp pang of hurt echoes through my chest. I can't believe that Riot would ever think I would hurt him, let alone kill him. I looked at Kaz over Riot's shoulder and I think he could sense what I wasn't saying.

"It's to help your face." Kaz replied in a soothing tone.

It sounded as though he too felt hurt by the assumption. Riot nodded and took the cloth from me without further word. He handed it to Kaz, staring me down as he turned his back to him. He didn't break eye contact with me until the cloth was over his eyes.

Kaz led Riot, one hand on his shoulder, as I trailed behind. I tried reminding myself that it wasn't personal. That this wasn't him. We walked in total silence, Riot's breathing catching every so often in his throat.

Before long, we broke through the mountainous terrain that had taken over from the forest a few miles ago, to a cliff that towered stories above the glistening water below.

"Alright Locke, now, I teach you illusion magic."

"You're going to teach a *Minotaur*? Illusion magic?" Riot sneered.

Kaz pulled him to a flat rock and sat him on it.

"We're on a cliff, Riot. Don't walk or you'll fall."

"You got it. It pays, being honest." Riot said, clearly meaning it to be a jab at me.

"I am honest," I start but Kaz shoots me eyes to stop.

Riot scoffs.

"Locke, focus on me," Kaz says, taking a stance with his back to Riot.

I was thankful for his chosen position as I didn't feel safe having my back to Riot right now, even if he couldn't see. The wind blew and it carried with it the smell of the ocean below us.

I had to put all of this to rest and focus. I still had a job to do and parents, a family who loved me to get back to.

"Locke will try to focus, but he's still wishing he had more to live for than his sad, sorry broken family."

"Locke, don't listen to him," Kaz says, low so that Riot won't hear him.

"Don't soothe him Kaz, he's a *Minotaur*. They don't have feelings they just live to eat and be a disappointment."

This wasn't real.

He didn't mean it.

"Locke, what you're feeling right now can be used for illusion magic. Take it and imagine the earth. What are your favorite parts?"

I ignore Riot and focus on Kaz the best that I can.

"Uhm, everything,"

"That's not good enough, give me details."

"Uh- the soil." I say, trying not to look at Riot.

"Okay, what about it?"

Riot crosses his arms where he sits, tilting his head as if trying to listen to my answer, a sick smirk crossing his lips.

"Oh, this is gonna be rich,"

I ignore him.

"The way it smells. It's crisp and clean and earthy. It's life, it's death. It's the essence of who we are," I say, proud of my answer.

Kaz nods.

"Great now imagine a circle of it floating just here, between us."

I focus trying to imagine what soil made by me would look like, but I'm distracted by Riot's ever growing smile as he listens for my success but hears only my failed attempts.

"It's okay Locke, don't be ashamed of yourself. After all, that's your parents' job."

I charge at him, but Kaz catches me.

"Shut your fucking mouth Riot Blair!"

Riot laughs out, clapping his hands clearly amused at my anger. Kaz throws a hand towards him just in time to deflect him from ripping the bandages off from around his eyes and pins them together in a ring of red light in his lap.

Despite being bound, Riot continued to laugh maniacally.

"We have to get out of Meta, Locke. I need you to focus. That's not Riot anymore. He's not himself. Focus on the soil. What else?"

"The flowers. There's as many of them as there are souls that have passed on," I say, listening to the wind now as Riot shouts another insult.

Insult after insult comes but I don't hear it as it falls onto the strengthening winds, and I push everything I love about my element out of my mind. As it starts to work, I squeeze my eyes shut, feeling the ground beneath me lift. Kaz runs, grabbing Riot and pulling him onto the land I'd made.

"Okay Locke, now that you've made it, I can stabilize it!" Kaz shouts over the wind.

He makes a formation and just like that, we are floating off the cliff edge and over the water.

KAZ

I'm impressed that Locke made his first illusion magic, but I don't say anything just yet. Riot was on a rampage, and I needed Locke to keep blocking him out. If he faltered for even a moment, we could end up in the blue waters below.

"We did it," Locke breathes.

I know he's broken and tattered from all that's been going on, so I smile. I smile for *him*.

"We did. We made progress. I hate to tell you that this was the easy part. Now, the real test begins."

"I know," he sighs.

"Luck is what got you oafs this far."

"Riot, I'm warning you brother," Locke says through gritted teeth.

"I don't know what it is that makes you so stupid, but it really works for you." Riot sneers at him.

I can feel Locke tense beside me and say a silent prayer to Hades that Nobility isn't as far as it looks.

The day wears on and I start regretting not having Locke make the slice of land larger. We had just enough room to sit or stand. Riot had made numerous threats to jump so I propelled us faster over the ever unfolding expanse of water before us.

"Imagine we saw real Kraken," Locke says excitedly as the sun starts disappearing over the horizon.

"Let's hope not. Although, there are far worse than the Krakens out here."

"Like what?"

I looked Locke in the eye.

"Sirens. Wild ones. Ones that don't have class or morals."

I watch as Locke considers what I've said. He sighs deeply and I catch him looking down at the passing waters below. The sun sunk below the horizon finally, handing the night its stars as we raced over the darkening sea.

My parents had always taught me to have back up plans, however, if Nobility didn't work for us to hide in while sorting all of this out, I had no idea what we would do next. I tried reaching out to Amira via our bond, but nothing went out.

I was heartbroken having to leave her back in Meta, but I knew she understood what I was doing and why. Her trust in Riot's character was the only thing fueling me to continue on with this insane task. I tried reaching out to my parents. I was again met with nothing.

They have had me blocked since the fight with my father. He was always so quiet, never really voicing his opinions, but he stood for everything a wolf should. He was fierce and loyal. He was fiercely loyal. His every interest was formulated in the favor of those he held alliances with. He was working under the Outliers, in all the uncharted lands, trying to create his own army of those willing to work with wolves to one day stand against the Blair King.

I'd grown up watching and learning his tactics, his alliances, and everything he knew, but when he'd given me my own pack, I'd been young. I wasn't confident in leading others; not like I was in leading myself. I had never shied away from anything, and not to mention, I loved a good kill. I lived for it. Having my own pack put a damper on my recklessness. I'd thought I'd known better than him and added more to my pack, but not wolves. I added in beasts of all kinds.

My actions angered my father, but he'd allowed me to carry on, giving me the freedom my mother said I'd deserved. I traveled all over, looking for more, building an army of my own. I wanted to stand next to my father the day we finally would end the rule of the Blairs.

My soul yearned for that day.

But then, he'd found out about Amira, and he was livid. He still is. He believes I should marry a wolf. Therefore, we fought. When he won because I couldn't bring myself to do the unthinkable, he threw me out for standing my ground. Luckily, he didn't sever the connection completely. It was the only sense I had left of being at home. That and the fact they said I was still their son, but I'd never be respected by the wolves again.

I pursue my life with Amira now because she's all I need and as I look to Locke, standing there, eyes closed, nose in the salty sea air, and Riot, completely broken, flared by his own flesh and blood, by his father, I couldn't help feeling like I'd found my home- as much as none of us were willing to admit it, I could admit it to myself.

———

Within a few hours, I could see Nobility in front of us. My gut clenched.

This was it.

"Holy shit," Locke breathed.

I looked at him and watched his face as he took in the sheer mass of Nobility. It sat on a crescent moon shape. The entrance to the city was through a tall white glistening castle that shot into the sky, towering above the clouds. His eyes followed it up.

"What now?" Riot groaned.

I looked at Locke who looked at me, sullen and worried. I could tell that we shared the same inclination about Riot. From my days of traveling and trying to build my own pack, I had friends in many places- including Nobility.

Suddenly, I remembered a very special someone who may be able to help us here, but first, I needed to see if Riot could enter. I anchored our path to the island's edge. The docking station is made of pure clear crystal that is filled with rainbows that glisten off the full moon above.

Nobility was filled with a special kind of people. It was a melting pot and a safe haven to many, but its natives were a special breed not found anywhere else. They could hear for miles. The normal faeries all had shorter, variously shaped ears with more rounded points while Nobelists were much sharper.

In fact, most of the natives from Nobility, called Nobelists, sported sharp features. They had sharp noses, monolid eyes, and sharp mouths. They were all uniform in appearance, but each one had a unique look. Most of them had pale white hair that was tied in a series of knots and braids on top of their heads. A bar of color that spanned temple to temple across their eyes signified their earned positions.

My friend, who I'd met so long ago, had taken the time to educate me on his people's classes and statuses. They were all equal, but each had a job and a position. Everyone born here was taught to exist as a leader in their society, others-centered, generous and open-hearted.

They dressed in all white, with bandoliers filled with otherworldly weapons. My favorite of which being what he called, Fruit of the Spirit. It was a dagger with the blade no longer than the palm of the Nobelist who'd earned it. The blade was crystal clear with rainbows throughout. The hilt, a bright silver, inlaid with rainbow moonstones.

As we approached the island, I could feel the natural peace of its energy soothing my insides. The clouds that surrounded it, moving away, making room for our arrival. When our illusion finally met with the edge of Nobility, I tethered Riot to its base, making sure he would not cross without permission.

"We're here," I say once we have fully docked.

I spot a guard I know too well. Mordechai tilted his head in a nod, and made his way over to us, eyeing my comrades on either side of me. The Nobelists moved with purpose, shoulders squared, backs straight and heads held high. It was just how they were made.

"Kaz Arnsen! My Noble brother. How are thee?" he said, his voice booming. Even though I'm used to the weird ways in which the Nobelists speak, it's always funny hearing the variations of a language lost.

Despite the lack of emotion on his face, his voice was cheerful and inviting. He sported a golden bar that glistened, the highest honor to wear as a warrior of the warriors. He's highly decorated and the people considered him kind and caring.

"Mordechai, my friend!" I step off the illusion and onto Nobility, hugging him. I was happy to see he was well and whole, as always.

"I'm glad to see you here, although I hope you bring with you no trouble?" He says eyeing Locke and Riot still standing behind me.

"No, no. They won't be. The blindfolded one is Riot Blair."

He tenses.

"You've done it? You've gotten him out of Meta?"

I nod as he eyes Riot cautiously.

"Then you are successful, as we always knew you would be."

I chuckle.

"Not yet. We are working towards it. I'm afraid I do bear sad news though," I start.

He looks to me now.

"Riot. He's flared."

Mordechai gasps rather dramatically and looks back to Riot. Locke smiles halfheartedly as if to offer some kind of reassurance that I was telling the truth.

"Flared, you say? Interesting. Then he is completely broken, possibly even shattered. He may even be dead." He breathes.

"Flared by his own father." I add.

Mordechai lays a hand on my shoulder now, the other flies to his mouth. His long, thin fingers covering his lips as he surveys my friends again.

"We shall offer you safety and the tools necessary to heal, if he shall pass the test. Thou have explained the way Nobility works to your brethren, correct?"

I nod, looking to Locke now.

"Locke can see you. He's the Minotaur."

"Fascinating."

Mordechai walked now, guiding me along with him to our docked slice of Earth.

"Brave Minotaur. What is your family name, son?"

"Montoya, sir." Locke says, puffing up his chest.

Mordechai lifts his brows, clearly impressed. Although, I would bet that he and the other Nobelists could find anything impressive about anyone, given the chance and of course, asked for their opinion.

"Montoya. Your father fought hard for a place in Pantheon." He muses, tasting the facts on his tongue.

Locke stands proudly.

"Welcome, to Nobility, Locke Montoya."

Mordechai offers him a hand. This was the real test. Locke takes it and steps off the illusion bravely.

"Wow, this place is amazing!" He yells, finally seeing all of Nobility and what it has to offer.

"Riot, you're gonna love this, brother, if you're in there."

Riot stands motionless.

"I have to be honest, Locke. I don't think he can hear you. I don't think he will be able to come to Nobility. The mind flare was the worst thing that could happen to him."

"We failed. We failed to get him here before the flare." Locke admits, sounding utterly defeated.

"A pure heart as well. A rare find, especially in Minotaurs who are notoriously ferocious. Tell me, kind warrior, what has softened you so?" Mordechai takes his hand, caressing it as if to press the secrets of Locke's mind out through his fingertips.

"I just... It's just who I am,"

"A pure mind as well. Fascinating."

Locke chuckles a bit and I know he's thinking he's anything but pure of mind. It was true Minotaurs had a bit of a sex drive but when it came to Locke? The right girl, or, really any girl, could be his wife. I had to chuckle too at the thought.

"Alright, let's see how your friend does. If he is unable to see Nobility, he will be unable to see or hear you while you're here. Dost thou have a plan if that happens?"

"Yes, I do."

Locke shoots me a questioning look.

"Very well."

Mordechai flicks his wrist, lifting the blindfold from Riots face. It lifts, slowly. I'm pleased to see Riot's eyes are closed, but around his eyes are black veins, leading to them. His lips are gray and colorless. In fact, if he hadn't been standing there, I would have thought him to be dead.

When the blindfold has reached his forehead, pushing back his curly black hair like a headband, he opens his eyes. The emerald green they usually are, is gone, replaced by black.

He just stares.

"Why don't you try calling to him, Locke. I must warn you though, the eyes I am seeing I have seen many times before, and your friend is no longer inside of that body which has become a vessel."

Locke swallows hard as I reinforce Riot's magical bindings. I look at Mordechai and decide I should probably also tether him to the ground with another lead, so I do. A red chain forms from his wrists and tethers with force to the floor. A sickening smile crosses his face as he stares into the distance, past us, past Nobility.

"I know you're there. Just because I can't see you doesn't mean I can't sense you." He sneers.

"Riot, can you hear me?" Locke calls out.

Riot just stands there.

"It seems that it is as we feared. Whatever your plan is, Kaz Arnsen, I would do it now."

I look to Locke, nodding my head.

"You stay here with him; I will go and see Sterling."

"Sterling! Oh, he will be most overjoyed at your presence here in Nobility. I wonder though, will it be safe to leave your friend with the shell of none other than Riot Blair?"

"You've not seen Locke in action," I say.

"He would be able to handle anything thrown his way with both grace and tactful success."

With that, Locke steps back onto the platform as Mordechai turns to guide me through the silver gates of Nobility just as he had many times before. I knew these gates, walls and people well.

I didn't dare look back at them standing there as I followed Mordechai.

Once we were through the gates and inside the castle, Mordechai led me to an unassuming wooden door that led to a long narrow hallway made of stone. It was drab and dark, barely lit by yellow faelights. I followed closely behind as we walked in silence. We came to a small sitting room with pictures covering the walls of the warriors that served Nobility over the centuries. A few benches sat around the room, and in the center was a piano, made of clear crystal.

"Sterling is upstairs working on his latest project. You know where to find him. I'm going to go back and keep watch over your guests, so I will see you then." He nodded, leaving me in the small sitting room.

I watched him go, hoping he could help Locke some in my absence. Then, turning on my heel, went through the door. There was a small spiral staircase that led upwards to a large room with a dome for a ceiling that opened on one side in a crescent shape much like the one the entirety of Nobility sat on.

There were charts and telescopes and crystals of all kinds scattered throughout the room as decoration and I assumed for research. There were rugs all over the floor in mismatched patterns and directions, erratically placed. The sky above the open dome was illusioned to be magnified like that of a telescope and in it, was a cluster of stars that jumbled my mind.

The twinkling mass was sort of shaped like a crystal, the stars that were being studied shone brighter than the ones that surrounded it. I tried and failed again to make sense of it. Looking around the room, I spotted a long desk piled high with paperwork all scattered along its surface, stacks of books in its corners. Then, there, in the center of all the static madness, was Sterling.

His long hair flowed in front of his pointed ears, his silver eyes, flecked with yellow, inches from a line he was connecting to another. His silver crown of leaves glinted in the light that bounced and bobbed over him. A faelight of his own creation.

"Working hard or are you hardly working?" I greeted him.

He peered up at me over his pencil, a smile that said everything tugged at the corners of his mouth, exposing his perfectly white teeth.

"Kaz, you son of a gun!"

He dropped his pencil, rising to his feet and, rushing down the stairs faster than I knew to be humanly possible, pulled me into a brotherly hug.

"What are you doing back here you wolf? Last I'd heard from the Third Sister, you were marrying Amira finally! I figured you'd be long out of Meta by now, but never expected a honeymoon in Nobility!"

"We did! It was marvelous. I'm sorry you couldn't attend,"

"Ach! Nonsense. I'll have none of that. We will celebrate when the gods allow it, my friend." He clapped his hand onto my shoulder.

I smile at him. He was the closest thing to a family member I'd had since the incident with my own father, and even though he wasn't much older than me, he felt like a fatherly figure at times.

I sighed deeply though as the thought of what I had to tell him crashed into me, effectively taking every calming feeling I'd since gained with it.

"I'm afraid this visit isn't a leisure one," I say, and my face must've given way to how serious this was since he led me to a seat near his messy desk.

"I'm all ears, my friend."

LOCKE

I watched Kaz walk with Mordechai into the huge castle. When the gates finally locked behind them, a sinking feeling weighed me down right to my core. Riot stood there stoically so I pulled his blindfold back down over his eyes. He didn't flinch. He didn't try to stop me. Instead, he kept his sick signature grin plastered on his face.

"You will never be able to suppress me or my power, Locke."

"I know that's not you, Riot." I mumble.

"You don't know me or what I'm capable of. You don't know me or my desires. You're daft and blinded by your heart. A foolish man."

"My heart makes me who I am. It makes me care about an insufferable asshole, like yourself."

He chuckles.

"What for? You should only care about yourself. It leaves less room for disappointment."

I roll my eyes and look away. Trying not to let it bother me is hard, but I know this is the flare. His soul had been pulled from his body and I could only hope that it wasn't lost somewhere we couldn't find him.

Before long, Riot got bored and stopped flinging insults. The gates opened and through it came Mordechai again. He walked over to us, smiling and gesturing for me to cross the threshold. I took one look at Riot and stepped off, relieved for the distraction Mordechai's presence would provide.

"Thou face tells of worries beyond your control," He sighs, searching me.

"Yeah, well. He's like a brother to me. I see a lot in him," I say, looking back at Riot.

"I see a lot in *you*," he answers.

"Nah, like he said, I'm no one." I chuckled.

"Such a shame it is to be blinded by a pure heart."

I snap my attention back to him as he looks down at me with those sharp features. I could see how he could be easily horrifying if he had to become the warrior I knew he was.

"What do you mean?"

"A pure heart puts others before themselves, always. No matter the detriment to themselves or their own wellbeing. A pure heart is both a gift and a curse."

I don't say anything, as he smiles. I'd never thought about it that way, but he was right. Where my brothers and my father were ferocious and notorious, I was always worried about them and their well-being. I picked up where they lacked it. I followed them around, making sure they were safe, and their needs met.

No one asked me to do it, I just did.

"You're welcome here anytime, Locke."

I smiled at him.

KAZ

After I'd told Sterling everything that had happened since meeting Riot, and even before then, too, he stared at me. I'd told him everything about my father, my pack, my friends and Amira. I told him about Riot and Locke begging me to help them. About Riley and the things I saw her do. The conclusions I'd made about her existing between humanity and immortality and that I'd told those thoughts to Riot. He sat; chin perched on his fist as I spoke. He nodded where appropriate, listening intently.

"So, I'm here now, with Riot out there, unable to see Nobility. His father has forces all over. We've escaped Meta, but with a flared mind, he's still got a hold on Riot. Amira said that Riley is more powerful than any of us could have imagined. I'll be honest, I have no idea what to do. I'm lost."

Sterling takes me in, studying my face and processing everything I'd just told him. Without saying anything, he stands, moving over to a wall piled high with all kinds of trinkets. He starts moving things around, looking for something.

"What are you doing?"

"Packing."

I stand now too, moving closer to him as he removes his crown of silver leaves, placing them on a shelf.

"Packing? You can't possibly mean you're leaving Nobility?"

"I'm coming with you. I know the lands outside of Meta better than most and I think I can help you. If you think you've found the one who exists between humanity and immortality, then I think I believe you. I think you've found the next host of Ophiuchus."

"Ophiuchus?"

He nods and pulls a satchel out from under a pile of other fabrics. He points to the magnified sky behind me and starts shoving various objects into a bag.

"You have a problem with a snake. Ophiuchus is known to be a snake charmer, tamer, whatever you want to call it. She could fix your problem. She could fix Meta."

I look at the cluster of stars again and I'm just as lost as I was the first time I looked at them when entering the crescent office.

"What is it?"

"That? That's a constellation," he says through gritted teeth as he pulls something heavy from the shelf.

"Specifically, it's the constellation Ophiuchus. The stars have been telling of its coming again."

"Again?"

He sighs, flinging his bag over his shoulder as I turn to him now.

"Yes, again. Ophiuchus is a constellation of its own entity. It's not really understood among the many astrologers who've tried to study it, but it seems to choose a host at random."

"So it's an entity? Like a spirit?"

"If only it were that simple. I've been studying it now for quite some time and it seems as though it were created by the universe itself."

"So... like another god?" I can't believe what I'm hearing. Of all the unthinkable things I thought I knew; this was by far the most impossible.

"Sure, but more than that. It is the nexus of all energy from the past, present and the future of every reality on any timeline."

"How is that possible?"

He closes the crescent ceiling, forming a full dome yet again. We make our way down the staircase and into the sitting room before he speaks again.

"It's not. It's happened before, but by the time the powers were able to fully emerge, the host died."

I didn't say more as we walked back towards Riot and Locke. If what Sterling was saying is true, then what we were doing wasn't just about the king, Meta, or Riot. It was about so much more. And if Riley really was the next Ophiuchus, she may be in danger.

We had to find Riley.

We emerged through the front gates again to find Riot still standing where we left him. Locke was sitting on the edge of the island, talking and laughing with Mordechai.

It was nice seeing him back to his normal happy self, even if it were just for a moment. Mordechai was the first to spot us and smiled.

"Mordechai, it's lovely to see you again today."

Mordechai nods his head as Locke jumped up, wiping his hands off on his shorts.

"Locke," he says, offering his hand to Sterling who just looks at it.

"Nice to meet you, Locke. I can see from Mordechai's demeanor; you've made quite the impression."

"Indeed, he has!" Mordechai booms, clapping Locke on the back with a massive hand.

"We have a lot to share," I offer.

Locke's face dropped, reality hitting him once again of why we came to Nobility.

"Since Riot is the affected one, and here he can not hear us, I think it best we fill you in on my suspicions before we travel. Mordechai, you'll stay here to hear what we are thinking. You'll need the information as you're to stay here and take on my job, while I assist Kaz."

Locke looked from Sterling to me, confusion written all over his face.

"I guess you know everything then?"

Sterling smiles.

"I told him everything, yes. Sterling has quite the information Locke. Remember that day in the park? When we saw Riley freeze time?"

Locke nods, wide eyed and hanging on every word I said.

"Riley is quite possibly the next incarnation of Ophiuchus, or, from what Kaz here has told me, a very powerful being." Sterling begins.

He tells them everything he told me, and by the look on their faces, they too think it's entirely possible and entirely crazy.

"But if she *is*, this... this Ophie thing, then what does that mean?"

Sterling looks at Locke and shrugs.

"To be honest, I don't know. I've been studying it for some time, but outside of my own findings, I don't know much. There's not a whole lot on it and most astrologers don't even acknowledge its existence."

"So, Sterling has offered to come with us and help us."

"Look, I've not said this before, but Riot has always had something for Riley. I'm not sure what it is but under all his outward acts, there's been something else. He acts like it was for his own plan against his father. However, it's always been more."

Locke spills this information that would have been helpful so many months ago. I look at him, completely stunned that he never thought it important to mention until now.

"Why haven't you said this?"

Locke shrugs.

"I didn't think it was important."

"We've been trying to get a leg up on the king for how long? His father has thought all this time that Riley had an idea of how to open the tap or that perhaps she was a backdoor to one, and only now you're telling me that they've had a connection?" My voice becomes higher and higher so that I'm almost yelling.

"I don't know that they've had a connection, I just know that Riot never seemed fully against her."

"Fucking Minotaurs," I say, despite sounding like Riot.

"Thank you, Locke. This information, no matter the timing of it, has been utterly helpful."

"How so? We should have known this months ago!" I shout at Sterling, frustrated now.

It all made sense now, his father tracking him to see where he was. It's not just Riot that he's after, it's her. I wondered how much more Locke knew that he hadn't told us. How much more did Riot know that he hadn't said before?

Using confusion magic on him was the wrong move. I knew now that it had opened his mind, scrambled it even, and that had been how his father had found a way in. The flare possibly existed before the confusion magic, but there was no way to tell now.

"Because we know now that your friend's father was looking for Riley and Riot possibly felt connection to her. If we are looking for Ophiuchus, then we are quite possibly looking for her, and he may have a link to her," Sterling says, nodding to Riot who still stood statue still on the illusioned piece of land.

"He could. What if he doesn't?" I ask, aware that this could be the wrong path entirely, but getting a leg up on the Blair king was worth it, no matter the leg or what it happened to be attached to.

"We will cross that bridge when we come to it, however, if Riley is the one he sought originally, then I can bet it's the right move. There are no taps. The gods don't make mistakes."

"Right, and we witnessed Riley using all four of the elements," Locke adds.

Shock struck Sterling's beautifully dark features, but quickly dissipated as he became his stoic self once more, questioning me instead.

"Did Vertez know this? That she could access all four elements?" I ask.

Locke shakes his head.

"No, Riot was already onto him. After Vertez tried to drown Riley at the Glistening Cove party. We went solo. Simmer was to keep him at bay and had been until we disappeared. That's when we came to you."

I nod thoughtfully.

"There's another island that we could hide out on. It's a poor one so most of the people there wouldn't be in favor of the king. They may not even recognize Riot right away either," Sterling rummages in his bag, and pulls out a large, rolled paper.

"I'm in no matter what. We just need to at least pull Riot back from wherever he is, then find Riley."

"We will do our best Locke, I promise. It may come down to finding Riley first, but we will do our best."

I watch Sterling make promises to Locke and for the first time, I feel like there's hope in all this. Nobelists didn't make promises for no reason. Sterling truly believed that he could solve this.

"What is it called? The island, I mean." I ask, never having heard of a place like that.

Sterling looks between us all and then at Riot as he says,

"Twin Seouls"

LOCKE

    Kaz had never heard of the island his friend suggested to us, and neither had I. Sterling helped us move to Twin Seouls by culling him himself and Riot. Kaz took me and our things. We arrived there within moments, leaving the beauty and serenity of Nobility behind. I promised though, that I'll go back and see Mordechai again. Before leaving, he'd pushed something into my hand, whispering for me to not look until I was alone in my own quarters.

    I clasped it tightly in my hand, not daring to let go while culling, but once we landed, I hastily shoved it into my pocket before anyone could see.

    "We're here. These lands don't have leaders either. The people here are poor and therefore tread the line of morality. Keep what's important to you close."

    Sterling heaved one of our duffels onto his armored shoulders and led the way. Surprisingly, the island wasn't gated, and everyone wandered all of it. There were no divides or sections, and everyone existed out in the open.

    As we walked, Kaz leading Riot, still blindfolded, the people looked our way. Some stopped in their tracks completely. Some merely glanced.

    "I thought Sterling said the people here wouldn't know Riot," I whisper in Kaz's ear.

    "They don't. It's Sterling they are looking at. A Nobelists' presence holds great weight."

    Just then, a woman with short hair and many necklaces steps into our path, bowing deeply.

"Nobelist warrior. What brings you to Twin Seouls?"

"We seek shelter for a long stay." Sterling answers her, nodding his head.

"I see. There's a small group of outsiders who have convened on the west side of the island. They aren't from here but have made their own community. They have lots of room there." She says, looking up at Sterling now.

"Is there no room here? In the mainlands?"

"I'm afraid not, sire. We have opened our homes to the refugees."

Sterling looks over his shoulder at us, questioning what we knew of what the woman was saying. I stare blankly and Kaz shakes his head. He looks at Riot, then the floor before turning around again.

"Refugees?"

"Haven't you heard? The king has put a bounty on the heads of anyone who's a known Separatist. Anyone not aligned with the King have fled or have otherwise gone into hiding."

If the news shocked anyone else, they didn't make it evident on their faces.

"The west side of the island, you say?"

She nods.

"Thank you. Your kindness will not be forgotten."

She saunters off back to her family who I now noticed waited in the doorway of a cobblestone hut. I watched them and felt a pang of guilt that they'd been here their whole lives, never having a chance at Metos or even Pantheon. Did they even know it existed?

"I'll find out how far the travel is from here to the west, stay put." Sterling orders, dropping our bags and walking off towards a pub.

"There's not much for us to do but just wait," Kaz begins, leading Riot over to a bench.

I follow as he sits him down. The town looks more like an open park as the people hustle about, working on various tasks. It almost looked fake or scripted. I narrow my eyes as I watch them.

There were women on looms, men that were farming. Some kids skipped rocks nearby, while a teenage boy led some goats to an open pasture.

"Do the people here know about Pantheon?" I ask Kaz.

"I've never been here, but I would assume so. If they know of the King, they must know of its existence." He says.

I nod, watching the people as they work.

"Are they human?"

"I'm not sure," he shrugs.

No one around us used magic, they all worked by hand. The people looked normal. They had to be shifters or witches. Especially if they'd offered refuge to those running from the king.

A skinny man dressed mostly in rags stared our way while hoeing his garden. I decided to approach him while he worked to ask. It couldn't hurt to know.

"Hey,"

He looked up at me and signaled for his children to run inside.

"I don't want to hurt anyone,"

"I wouldn't think you did, but the conversation you're wanting to have isn't one I want my children a part of, if that's alright." He turned his attention back to his garden.

"Oh. Uh, right. I just wanted to ask what faction you belong to." I say.

Regret washed over me the moment the words left my lips, but I couldn't take them back now. The man looked up at me from the place he knelt now, a scowl on his face.

"Why so you can order me around? Take everything from me?"

"No? Why would I?"

A woman's voice comes now from somewhere behind me.

"You already have, all these years."

I turn to face the voice. It belongs to a woman who bears resemblance to the kneeling man.

"Anyone who's ever pledged allegiance to the king has sentenced us to this place."

"That's not a fair assessment." I argue.

She steps forward now, approaching me until she's a breadths pace away. Up close I can see the red flecks in her irises.

"It is."

"Locke!" Sterling yells, running over to myself and the townspeople.

"What an interesting name, one that won't be forgotten easily. If you bring harm to Twin Seouls, Locke, I'll see to it that we seek you out specifically." The woman threatens me.

"He won't. You have my word." Sterling answers her when he gets to us.

"And who are you?"

KAZ

"A Nobelist."

She narrows her eyes at him. I notice now the lines in her skin are like the lines in a tree trunk.

"Good luck to you both. Because you're going to need it." She says, turning and walking away from us. I look back at the farmer and see he's gone.

"Locke, I've found a shortcut through the mountains. On the other side are the outsiders."

"Any word on who they are?"

"No, no one seems to know. They culled in and promised no harm. The city pushed them out there so that they had their own space. They had a ton of injured people."

"Injured? From what?"

He shrugs.

"No one has any information on from what or from where. They just showed up here and as they grew, they moved out there."

"Could we cull over?"

"We could cull closer, but into the town is a no go. It's most likely spelled, but we also don't know what's there. There's no reason for us to risk our lives."

I could appreciate how tactful he was. I would have just culled in, biceps blazing. I followed him over to Kaz and waited while he filled him in, watching Riot the whole while.

He remained motionless and without any indication on his face of thought or that he was even listening to us.

"Well, we better get moving. The closest we could cull in is between the peaks and then it's about an hour's travel to the town." Sterling says, grabbing a bag and offering his hand to whomever was to travel with him.

"Take Riot again. I need to speak with Locke before we go. "

"We shall await you on the other side." Sterling bows his head and takes hold of Riot. They are gone in an instant in silvery wisps of smoke.

Locke sat with me watching the town of Twin Seouls. Riot and Sterling had culled away already, but we sat.

"I'm sorry," I say.

I'm not sure what else *to* say. Locke had been on the receiving end of Riot's bullshit for some time now. I knew what the stories in the media said when the three of them had started at Pleaides, and what the king wanted people to believe, but I'd known Locke almost all my life and I knew his family were once just as poor as these people, fighting for their chance at a place in Pantheon.

We sat watching them as they worked. The dirt streets were uneven, and the houses were modest, gray and had thatched roofs. The people all wore the same kind of gray clothing, and chickens ran in the street freely. It was a long way from the home I was used to. It was a long way from Pantheon.

"I never thought I'd become so conceited, so... utterly blinded by Pantheon that I'd forgotten where I'd come from," he says, watching the farmer who was back in his garden.

He paid us no mind, but his sister stood in the doorway of his cabin, watching Locke. Watching me.

"You're anything but conceited, Locke. You've just moved on from a life like this. Everyone dreams of getting into Pantheon, into a better life. You just actually did it."

"My father did it."

"Nonetheless. You have no reason to feel guilt." I say.

He bows his head.

"I asked you to stay behind because I wanted to prepare you. This thing with Riot, he could already be dead. Not to mention, people are hunting him now. We have to now assume that anyone is an enemy," I say, hating myself for having to vocalize it.

He nods, head still bowed.

"Locke, this could all end very badly and I guess what I'm saying is, now is your moment. Now is where you could go back to Pantheon, grab your family and run."

"Run to where? His father hand picked me, Kaz. He picked me and Vertez. Vertez has very clearly chosen his side. I have chosen mine."

"What if your father, mother and brothers stand on a different side than you?" I ask, looking at him now.

"Then that's the way the gods intended it."

I clap a hand to his shoulder and nod. He was beyond brave. I wish I'd been that brave to walk away from my family when they'd proven to be against me, but I hadn't. In their own way, they still controlled me.

"Then so be it."

I stand, offering him a hand, pulling him up with me.

"Let's do this." He says, keeping my hand in his grip.

With that, I cull us away.

We culled in on Sterling and Riot who were waiting for us between the peaks under a massive apple tree.

"Sorry, didn't mean to take so long,"

"No troubles at all. It seems he's completely mute now." Sterling says, looking to Riot.

Locke walks over to him. Guilt floods my core.

"We better start moving. There's a whole town of people about an hours walk away waiting to meet us."

"They know we are coming?" I ask.

Sterling looks to me now, eyes glistening.

"No, but I did send whispers on the wind hoping that they would get the message before our arrival. Let's make pace, comrades."

We picked up and followed Sterling, unsure and unaware just how close we were to the answers we sought.

STERLING

We made fast pace through the peaks, if not for my pushing the others to keep on going, then for their curiosity at what lay on the other side of the hills that sprawled before us. I knew Kaz was good for making time, I'd seen him in action a few times over the years as he assisted the men of Nobility.

Although he refused the title, he was seen as a warrior there, though I doubt he displayed or bragged about that title to anyone. Even his mate held titles there for her mind and her caring nature. Amira had even lent us some resources when we'd needed them the most. I'd do anything for a man who could put his faction aside and link arms with another people purely because they stood on the same side of an opinion.

That was just what Kaz did. Without asking. Without question. He assisted Nobility when we needed him the most. He'd brought wolves and factions of all kinds to make sure we had everything we needed when Lurgans had broken into our lands. Assisting him now was both an honor and a repayment, although I could never repay him fully.

I could hear sounds of the town as we approached the bottom of the last hill and sent whispers on the wind one last time in an attempt to avoid any possible repercussions.

"Alright. This is the last hill standing between us and them," I announce.

"Does it sound dangerous?" Kaz asks, holding Riot in place.

"No, not that I can tell. They sound as though they are underwater. It could be a barrier; it could be that they are truly underwater." I explain.

"Please, don't be sirens." Locke begs the sky above.

I smile.

"Even if it were, I'd protect you all."

"He has an impressive wingspan," Kaz laughs.

"Nobelists shift?"

"No, Locke. Not shift. Has anyone told you what Nobelists are?"

He shakes his head at me, and I contemplate if I should do this now or later, but Kaz speaks before I can.

"Let's just say they are sent by the gods to us."

"Not all of us, but some of us, anyways." I add.

I watch Locke's face which doesn't really seem to be registering what he's hearing. He shrugs, and gestures towards the hill.

"Let's do it,"

We start up its steep path, the only sound filling our ears is the gravel below our feet. The walk is short and easy for us, our true forms kicking in from deep below our core as a defense mechanism. I can feel everyone's power, even Riot's, coursing through our veins.

My instincts kick in and I decided I should ask the others to wait, just in case. Unsurprisingly, I'm met with push back.

"No way. We go together or not at all," Locke huffs.

I accept it for what it is, saying nothing as Kaz and Locke eye each other and then Riot. Kaz looks past me to the top of the hill, the wind blowing his hair around him. I turn and lead them over the hill, ready for a fight.

But as we make our way over the hilltop, I'm surprised at the sight before us. It stops us dead in our tracks. I don't think the others can see it, but there's a huge, beautiful dome made of white light that shimmered like its own set of stars. I looked back at the others, their eyes on the land.

The hill flattens into a stretch of land that rounds on itself like a cul-de-sac, surrounded by snowcapped mountains. There are all kinds of makeshift tents set up around the ring of land. In the center sat a huge fire, roaring life into the space all on its own.

A tall man approaches us, smiling a bright smile.

"Welcome," he says carefully, but cheerfully all the same.

"Hello, sir. We were sent by the people of Twin Seouls. We are seeking long term shelter. One of our own is injured and we're looking for a safe place to heal him."

"Why wouldn't they allow you to stay in the town?"

"They said they were full from the refugee intake."

He eyes us, his stare landing on Riot. Luckily, he was paler now, and thinner already than when I'd last seen him in the papers. These people shouldn't be able to tell who he is with the blindfold on. I watch, maintaining a calm demeanor while the man looks him over.

"I see. Are you Loyalists? You look very regal for mere Outlier travelers."

"A Nobelist, sir. As for my friends, they hail from many factions, but none are aligned to the crown." I assure him.

He tears his gaze from Riot and back to me.

"We are short on space, but I can squeeze some quarters in for you. Our priestess will be back tomorrow, she can decide your fate then, but you'll be safe for the night."

I bow low to him.

"Thank you for your kindness, sir. Even for the night, it means a lot. Your kindness will not be forgotten."

He nods his head tightly and leads us into the town center. The people are busy attending to the wounds of their own people to have even noticed us entering. Riot was still cuffed, being led along by Kaz, but when we got near the fire, he moaned out loud.

"Your friend can feel the power of our lifeforce," the man commented.

I look over my shoulder at Kaz who widens his eyes, shrugging. I'd hoped it hadn't been heard, but in the spirit of keeping him at bay, I confidently spewed the best answer I could manage.

"Yes. Would you mind if we create our own fire for him near our quarters?"

The man looks at me like he's trying to figure me out. Figure us all out. I can sense that he's confused still by the town sending us up here so I force my face to be as grateful as I can manage.

"I suppose that would be fine. It's your responsibility to keep it under control. You'll be held responsible for any accidents."

"I wouldn't want it any other way," I assure him, bowing slightly at the waist once more. He nods again and gestures towards a tent that appeared in front of us seemingly at his command.

"Everything you need should be inside."

I motion the others in as I step aside. They walk between the man and I into the opening as we watch each other, clearly wanting a moment alone. Kaz leads Riot in, Locke following him closely. I hear him gasp in awe as the tent fabric closes. I spare no time in jumping in first, hoping to evade whatever other questions he had for me about our party, but he beats me to it, holding up a finger to silence my opening mouth.

"I mean no malice, sir, but we are dealing with casualties of our own, our resources are very scarce."

I nod in understanding. Taking him by the elbow, leading him a few feet away from the tent through some women who were rushing across the path with plates of hot food.

"We aren't here to take anything from you, I can assure you that. I am from Nobility."

"Ah, so you are more than trustworthy," he smiles.

"I am. I can see your people are hurting and if there is anything I can do to repay your kindness during our stay, please ask. I will oblige to the best of my abilities."

"Our priestess will be back tomorrow, as I said. I will pass the sentiment along." He promises.

"If you don't mind my asking, what happened here?"

"Not here, a place we used to call home. We were attacked suddenly. We are still trying to make sense of it all, but I've said too much already without permission." He says, looking around nervously.

"I understand. You said Priestess? You're witches?"

He nods. I had known but to see him admit it openly since they were convening here meant that things were indeed as bad as I'd feared.

"Are you from Metos?"

"I'm sorry, sir. Until my Priestess returns, I don't think we should converse any further. I'll be back the moment she arrives. Until then, I advise you not to leave your tent."

I nod and he takes off. I survey the area, marking our ways out if anything were to go too far left. I try to pull the dimensional planes to me, feeling for a portal to cull and I'm not surprised when I'm met with nothing but a wall of resistance. It was armor of a wounded people.

The place was protected heavily by not just magic, but dark magic. I looked around at the people dressed in their bright clothing and brightly colored tents, a stark contrast to the darkness of their shields.

Most of them looked back now as their interim leader stalked away from me, his eyes pasted to the floor. I bowed my head at all of them, feeling my wings perk up from under my skin, but I willed them back down.

Backing up slowly, they eyed me. I turned on my heel and disappeared into the tent, securing it tightly behind me. When I turned around, I saw that Locke's reaction had been more than precedented.

The tent sprawled into a beautiful four room floor plan with a sitting room, kitchen and fire pit. The kind stranger did indeed provide everything we would need. Even if this was just for one night, I could comfortably remove Riot's bandages and try to treat him.

"Kaz. I would like some time with Riot, but first, perhaps we should all freshen up. You could work with Locke on some formations and hand to hand combat while I work with Riot."

"What are you going to do to him?" Locke asked from his spot around the small fire.

"He had moaned near that fire. Have you guys tried anchoring his soul?"

They looked at one another. I assumed not, but there were only so many things we could try to do without directly severing the ties to his father. That kind of cut to a connection would require the death of one of them and since Pantheon wasn't safe now, there was no telling when we could get to Arnoldous.

There stood many guards, Royalists, Loyalists and now, sons of nearly every mother in Meta looking for Riot between us and him. We needed him here as soon as possible. However, every day that we had him, his father was one step closer to losing, even if his mind *was* flared.

"No, never. I didn't know we could." Locke answers.

"He's a Sagittarius and a Basilisk, right?"

They nod in tandem.

"Interesting."

The clash of cold and warm. The clash of differences. It all made sense now. He was destined to always be pulled in two directions, but I know deep down that a star could not shine without darkness. I just now have to find out how to try and help Riot Blair see that.

"His darkness has indeed taken over. It's going to be very hard, pulling him back here, but I will find a way to do it. No matter what that means." I promise them.

Kaz looks at me, and I swear I can see his eyes glisten. Locke looks over at Riot.

"What if I feel like I don't want him back?" he whispers.

"Locke?"

"Kaz, just... he's been trouble and you used to always say he was the biggest risk we were taking. What if that's all he is? What if I'm wrong about him being my friend? About saving him?"

Kaz smiles, but it's not one of joy. It's one of regret.

"I never should have doubted you, Locke. You see something in him for a reason. There's no reason to change your mind now."

"Yeah well now, we've dragged Sterling, Mordechai and all of Nobility into this and where are we currently standing? In the middle of a town filled with people who have no idea that we just carted the most hunted man in all of Meta into their already broken society, literally adding fuel to a fire that's already burning!"

He yells, standing now.

"They have no idea! We just did this against their will, and they gave us their *already* slim resources! Are we the bad guys or the good guys here?"

He looks at me now.

"Is there really a side, Locke? That's the whole problem and how we got here, isn't it? Because of sides? Lines drawn in the sand where there should be none?"

"Locke, I think you just need good sleep. A shower. Food. These people didn't have to give us shelter and it could quite possibly be only for one night." Kaz assures him.

Locke wanted to fight him, but counting that he would be outnumbered, nods and allows Kaz to lead him away to the closest room.

I take a seat next to Riot, feeling the heat of the fire as I sat much closer than I'd normally find comfortable. For Nobelists, we didn't control the elements. We were more ethereal, and our gifts compared to those of the gods, so too much of the elements affected us in their own ways.

When Kaz finally returned to the living area, he took a seat across from us.

"I'm sorry about that," he said quietly.

I shake my head. There was no need for him to ever apologize for the thoughts of a mind that's been betrayed. Locke struggled with many things but right now, he blamed himself for his friend's condition, as silly as that may seem to him.

"Don't be. This is no one's fault other than the man who did it to him. The king. We will get Riot back, then we will move forward with what to do next. The covens leader will be back tomorrow, until then, we stay inside."

"So what now?"

"Riot Blair needs warmth. The Fire is a good place to start."

I stand, leaving Kaz alone with Riot.

This was for them to figure out.

KAZ

Riot sat across from me. I stared at the shadows that danced across his face. His cheeks had sunken in, his lips grey. He looked half dead and was getting worse each day. The fire didn't look like it was working. I crossed the room to take the seat Sterling had been sitting in, surprised at the cold air between us, emitting from his body.

"Riot, if you're in there, you need to come back to us," I whisper.
Nothing.

Sterling was an ethereal being. He knew what he was talking about. In all my time of knowing him, he had never been wrong. Had never steered me wrong. The fire wasn't big enough, but he'd said not to leave the tent. There had to be more I could do.

Locke joined us now, sitting opposite me.
"Is it working?"
I shake my head no.
"You're connected to him, do you feel anything?" he asks.

The truth was I hadn't felt anything *but* Riot since the arena weeks ago. I'd spent most of my time so focused since then on trying to feel Amira again, that I hadn't noticed Riot's energy was completely chaotic on the other end of our connection.

I tapped into it now, reaching out to him but was met with a tornado of emotion, violence, and loud screams.

"Locke, I can feel him," I breathe.

He jumps up, rushing over to Riot. He yanks the blindfold off to reveal Riot's eyes are wide open, fully black and lifeless.

"Riot, it's Locke, brother. Are you there?"
Nothing.

"I can feel him, but he's pushing me out."

Locke sits back.

"This is hopeless."

"It's not. If Kaz can feel him then he's not dead." Sterling says, from his doorway now.

He was topless, with nothing but a towel tied around his waist. His skin glinted off the firelight and as he turned to the kitchen, two massive, silvery black wings were tucked tight against his back. They were a sight to see.

"Woah dude!" Locke exclaims running over to him.

Sterling whips around in an effort to hide them, back to the wall as he flung out one massive muscular arm to keep Locke at a distance. He's a warrior that's been through more wars over the sands of time than I could count. He'd never told me about them, but if you truly looked at him, you could see them, their fires danced in his eyes. They lived in the gold bar that crossed his perfectly symmetrical face, in the silver flakes of his yellow eyes. They lived in the scars along his arms.

"Can you open them?" Locke asks excitedly.

Sterling shoots me a look like he's asking me to get my dog off of him. I couldn't help the laugh that escaped my throat as I watched the two of them, both abnormally large, dancing around the kitchen.

"No." he hisses.

"Sheesh. Why not?" Locke says, backing down.

"Because if I have to open these, you'll be very upset," he said and I swore I could see him tuck them closer to his body.

"If he had to open those, there would be total destruction," I say, knowing fully well what those powerful wings would do.

"No fun," Locke scowls, coming back to the fire and back to reality.

I had to admit the small glimpse into the way we could be was fun for the moment it lasted, but just as I started to mourn a normal life with normal friends, it was quickly washed away by another realization; if this had been a normal life, would I even know them?

"What weighs heavy on your mind, friend?" Sterling says, having found a shirt and some pants. It was remarkable how you couldn't see his wings through clothes, even with how massive they are.

"Just what to do next, I suppose."

It was already late, and I'd elected to have Silver Sap over looking for food from the already scarce portions the villagers had to offer. I didn't want to make their lives any harder as they tried to rebuild what was left of them.

After what Locke had yelled about, I could understand his thought process in dooming these people to the presence of a Blair without their knowledge. I didn't want them to have anything else to blame me for if they found out the identity of our injured friend.

"I think I'll be turning in for the night. Who will watch over Riot, though?" I ask, feeling what was left of the damage to my throat Riot had caused the last time I'd tried to sleep.

"You need rest, I'll watch him." Sterling said.

Locke opened his mouth to object, but Sterling cut him off.

"I don't need sleep anywhere near as often as you do. I had a long sleep before your arrival. I can go for about a week now. And anyway, I'd like to meet the Priestess of these people bright and early." He said, sipping from his mug.

He narrowed his eyes at Riot, who still stared blankly past us all.

"Besides, Riot won't be going anywhere, isn't that right? And if his father chooses to look, all he is going to see is the hell I project back to him."

"Hell you project back?"

"Yellow eyes are no mistake, Locke. I am a Nobelist. We are physically incapable of lies, manipulation, torture, and the like *except* where it is necessary to protect the cause. And there is where we become a fatal warrior." Sterling says, staring directly into the eyes of Riot Blair.

I'd always thought Nobelists looked like elven angels, but I knew all too well the true faces of these warriors. There was so much more to them and I knew if anyone ever had to see his true face, it would be actual hell.

"As interesting as this is, I'm beat. I'm sorry, I just need some rest." Locke says, standing now, and bidding us all goodnight.

"Are you sure you'll be alright out here with him?" I ask once Locke has gone to his room.

Sterling nods.

"I've dealt with far many more monsters in my life. A single flared one is nothing."

"I trust your word."

Sterling sneaks a glance at me and I can see the concern on his face for just a moment.

"Then why are you still sitting here?" he asks.

"When you were out of the room, I reached down my bond with Riot. I have been so frantic to get my bond to Amira back, that I didn't even notice the chaos and scrambled mind weren't me. All this time, it's been him. All this time, he's been right there. Back in the forest, when we were leaving Meta, I'd had a nightmare. Or, at least, I thought it was my nightmare, but I woke up to being choked by Riot." I say.

"You told me," he sips from his mug again.

I nod.

"What was the nightmare?" he asks.

I inhale deeply.

"I dreamt of horrors like I've never seen before, Sterling. I think I was Riot, maybe at some points, I was me, but I think I was mostly him. Anyway, I dreamt of this very specific smell. It was bourbon, something sweet and vanilla. Then, I saw snow and a cabin. When I felt myself falling into them, I saw green eyes much like Riots, but more yellow and the pupils were slits."

Sterling set his mug on the floor next to his foot, and leaned forward, elbows on his knees, listening intently, eyes on me. I swallow, pain searing through the parts of my raw throat still healing from Riot's powerful grip.

"Go on,"

"When I started to settle into the feeling I had... I began to feel like I was exposed. Sprawled out under a microscope and then severe pain took over every inch of me. It happened over and over and all I could hear were screams."

"Did you hear anyone?"

I shake my head no.

"There's more but... I can't."

"That's alright, Kaz. You don't have to. This is more than enough."

"I will say this though. Just before I woke up, I saw something. A black crown with glowing green stones. Then I felt the crushing in my throat and woke up to Riot on top of me. I'd tried to shift. I didn't want to hurt him or anything, I just wanted to get him off me, but he seeped into my mind, holding my power in his hands and completely stopped me. It was something I've never felt before. I didn't even know anyone could *do* that. It felt like he was touching a bit of my soul. It felt like he had my very essence in his hands. Like he was molding it, squeezing it to death.

It was sensitive and it haunts me, even now."

Sterling stares at me, his face blank. I can tell he's taking it all in and trying to make sense of everything I've said and that he's seen.
"Thank you for sharing, really. I'll have to think about it, to be honest. Do you mind if I relay your story and what you've told me if I think it could help? I have some contacts back in Nobility that may be able to help or offer some guidance."

I shake my head no.

"I trust you, Sterling. I know you'll do what is needed and what is right, otherwise I wouldn't have sought your help."

I stand now, ready to leave him alone with Riot and he nods, bidding goodnight. Before I can enter my room though, I have to tell him one more thing.

"Thank you, Sterling. For everything."

And with that, I shut the door behind me, alone for the first time in months.

STERLING

Kaz thanking me gave me an uncomfortable feeling inside. I never in all my years of serving this realm had been thanked for anything. I was thrown from my pedestal in my realm for a misunderstanding and I was given this role as a punishment. No one owed me thanks. This was my punishment to bear, and I was happy to do it.

I stared at Riot Blair. He sat, eyes unmoving. He was a lot more like me than I'd cared to admit out loud. I've watched him, even his family through the media and other means over the years. I've watched many people of this realm through my sentence here, but none have ever been as interesting as the Blair family. Before them, were the Mantrovere family, but the family of Blair's quickly took over.

I glanced at the time. It's just past eleven at night. When I'm sure the others are asleep, I throw a shield over Riot, the fire and myself. I sit back, finding Riot's eyes. I have eight hours to get the reaction I want. Eight hours to go in and find his father. Eight hours to find Riot Blair.

"Let's start with your father, Arnoldous Blair."

No reaction.

I chuckled.

"Unfit king. Pathetic man." I search his eyes.

Still nothing.

I decide to bet on the love a son has for his mother and try again.

"No? Okay. How about Cordelia Blair then."

His eyes focus, snapping into mine. The reaction is minimal but it's enough. It's exactly what I need.

"Hello, *Riot*." I say, a hair above a whisper.

He doesn't move a muscle, but I'm in just as mental shields close behind me.

"You have to be faster than that."

"*Who are you?*" a voice echoes through the darkness. It's neither masculine nor feminine.

I scoff.

"Wouldn't you like to know?"

"*Leave.*"

I laugh.

"Who are *you*?" I ask as a distraction as I press on into the darkness lain out before me.

All minds of a soul that was flesh and blood had the same layers. The more they found hopelessness, the darker the layers became, but they had the same foundations. I've lived long enough, have been through many minds, and knew my way around them.

"*Leave*," the voice comes again.

I press on.

Before long, I came to a black castle, broken and sharp. There were windows for rooms that didn't exist beyond their glassless panes. The ground was cracked stone, the castle made from the same stuff.

"*What are you doing here?*" The voice came as I pressed on towards the castle.

A small child with no face appeared in front of me.

"*Hello*," the voice was small and bright.

I looked down at it momentarily, but quickly went back to the castle. I was used to all the tricks in the book. I *made* the book.

I placed one foot after another on the steps, pressing on past the child.

"*Stop!*" it yelled.

I moved with purpose, ignoring the lull and draw the voice had on me and pulled open the large broken wooden door in front of me. Once I stepped over the threshold, strong winds started blowing in a circular torrent.

"You'll have to try harder than a child and some choice weather!" I shout over the howling wind, pressing on even still.

Immediately, the wind stopped.

The room just beyond the door transforms before my eyes. The broken castle became whole again.

That's right, show me.

The walls and floor became black marble. A staircase sprawls in front of me and I suddenly know this castle. It's Stone Castle. A cursed castle that once went by another name, but I dare not think of it while in here.

I press on, not daring to stay still for too long. The walls crumble behind me as I move, back to the way they were when I entered it. The ones in front of me forming again. I backed up, and the ones in front of me crumbled. The memory was moving with me.

Clever.

I ascended the stairs and when I reached the top, no landing greeted me. I cautiously put one leg forward where it should have been and thankfully, the floor materialized beneath me. I pressed on.

"Where are you going?"

"Why don't you tell me who you are and why you've taken host in the mind of Riot Blair."

Ear shattering screams filled the air around me. I flinched, covering my sensitive ears as quickly as possible as the illusion of whatever memory I was about to see broke around me, the illusioned ground no longer catching me. The familiar feeling of falling flips my stomach and I throw my wings out to catch myself.

They burst open, sending a shockwave of power out, crumbling what's left of the castle. I propel myself up and over it, looking around for anything else in the blackness as the screaming becomes louder.

"You will have to do better, even still!" I call out.

I lower myself to the ground as the screams turn to maniacal laughter.

"What do you want, demon?"

"Demon? Aren't we a little old for such names?" I sneer.

Tucking my wings in close again, I walk on, past where the castle once sat in front of me.

"What you seek is not here."

"I seek the soul of Riot Blair."

I spot a small pink shape in the distance and walk towards it.

"You won't find that here,"

"Oh, I think I will. I have never failed,"

The pink form was taking shape now, and I could tell from here it was a little girl. The ground I was walking on turned to cold icy water.

"Children? What is it with children?"

"You've never failed? Is failure not how you ended up here in this realm?"

I chuckle.

"Very good! You can read the memory of a thought. Although, that doesn't impress me."

"*No? What would?*"

"*Very Interesting,*" I muse.

"*What is?*" The little girl asks now.

I kneel now so that I am on her level and smile.

"What's interesting is that you're not brave enough to face me, yet you call me by old vernaculars. What's even more interesting, is that by not answering me, you've given me every answer I need."

She scrunches up her nose and I can see the rage taking form as her teeth slowly grow to points as she speaks, two rows of fangs forming where her canines used to be.

"*How so? What is it you think you know?*" she frowns.

"You're not ethereal. You're of this realm. You know Riot personally, and you know my kind. And you know what else? You're going to lose."

She looks at me blankly, and then, she begins to laugh. Her mouth widens, splitting her face, her jaw dislodging, the cracking of bones fills the air as she opens it to attack me. I stand now, looking quickly for what it is I need. She bursts forward into a large Basilisk with three heads and right there, in her eyes, I see him. He's got his back turned to me, small and childlike.

I beat my powerful wings towards her, and he snaps his head around at the burst of sound, seeing me just in time as she throws me out, back into myself.

Riot sat there, across from me, right where I left him, but there was a semblance of a smile across his lips. The fire was dying out, but I could see a single dried tear on his cheek.

"I'll find you!" I shout to him as I watch his face disappear into the blackness again, the smile gone now, his light gone from his eyes. The green fades to black.

I don't wait for the others to wake up. The moment Riot is gone again, I blindfold him and run from the tent out into the foggy morning air. There had been a tent I mentally noted when we arrived yesterday that was clearly for the Priestess.

I made a direct path for it. Luckily the rest of the village was still sleeping. When I got to the tent, I announced myself.

"Priestess! My name is Sterling, I seek to speak with you."

No answer.

"I need to speak with you immediately."

The tent fabric flings aside, the man who greeted us yesterday standing before me now, livid.

"Are you mad? I told you I would find you when she arrived."

"Are you telling me the feminine energy coming from behind you is yours?"

"It's alright, Tambo, you can let him in," a voice greets me.

He huffs, stepping aside and letting me into the tent, snapping it shut securely behind me.

"Priestess, my sincere apologies." I say, coming into the space.

It's quite plain in comparison to my own tent. It houses a seating area and a small room off to one side, of which the Priestess enters through now.

"It's alright. I'm sorry I was away when you arrived. I hope you've found what Tambo was able to provide you accommodating?"

I nod, trying not to stare. She was breathtaking and her aura was tantalizing.

"It is more than enough and has served its purpose, even if it shall be only for one night."

She lets out an airy laugh and calls my bluff.

"I'm not one for small talk, so what is it you came here for? Then I'll decide how long you stay." She says, lifting a chin to me, challenging me.

"I'm a Nobelist and I would be more than happy-"

"To assist where you can, yes, Tambo here has passed your sentiments on to me. That doesn't answer the question though." She says, cutting me off.

"Very well. We were seeking refuge from the king and his supporters. We fled from Meta. One of my men are injured and his mind is not as it should be. I am working to bring him back, but it's proven difficult," I lead, not wanting to give away too much.

She eyes me thoughtfully.

"I see. And why wouldn't the villagers let you stay there if all you sought was refuge?"

I knew the reason was because we were from Pantheon, and anyone could smell it from a mile away. They didn't trust us, and rightfully so, but I tread carefully now when I open my mouth to answer her.

"They said they were full of other refugees and led us here."

"Tambo, please leave the tent and see to helping where hands are needed. I need to speak to him alone."

Tambo nodded without further word and left us in the company of one another. She turned now, walking over to a long chaise and taking a seat. She looked at me expectantly, like she was asking me to sit down. I obliged, taking a seat opposite her, regardless of every bone in my body urging me to blurt out anything and everything I could to get her to help me.

"Now that we are alone, just tell me the truth." She says, leaning back.

"I never lie," I say.

"Alright. Why don't I meet your friend and see if there's anything I can do?"

I shake my head.

"I'm sorry to be so bold, but I need your word."

"You have it. I'll meet him and do whatever I can."

I nod, knowing she won't make a promise without knowing what it is she's going into, and I can respect that. I stand, hoping she will follow my lead, but she doesn't.

"Will you accompany me to our borrowed quarters?"

Just then, the man bursts through the tent, eyes wide with horror.

"Priestess, come quick!" He shouts, running back out the way he came.

With one hand on the hilt of my sword, I nod to her, hoping she understands I'm here if she needs me. She nods back, darting from the tent, her long black dress flowing behind her with purpose. My attention is snagged on her legs, The beauty and the shape captivating me, but a scream tears through the clearing, snapping me back to the situation unfolding before me. I follow her, ready for anything.

We make our way through the townspeople and come to none other than my idiot comrades who didn't listen to me. I followed everyone's eyes up to see Riot Blair, floating above the fire.

LOCKE

I awoke early to find Sterling gone from the tent. Riot was blindfolded in the same spot he'd been in and Kaz was still asleep. Now was my chance to get him to the town's main fire. He'd moaned when passing it and I knew he needed it in order to come back to us.

I hoisted him onto my shoulder. He was much lighter than the nights I'd carried him at Pleaides when he'd been drinking entirely too much. We would often go in the middle of the night without Vertez and just get wasted and talk about everything. I wonder if he will remember those times ever again though.

I look around to make sure Kaz didn't hear me lifting him, but when there was no movement, I left the tent swiftly. There weren't any people around as I made a beeline for the fire. It was roaring happily in the middle of the clearing.

As we got closer, the flames licked and jumped in our direction. I'd have thought I was going crazy, but the flames all leaned closer to us, burning and sending out tendrils of heat in our direction. I sat Riot down in front of the fire, as close as I could get him without the flames being able to touch him.

I watch expectantly as nothing happens.

I can hear Sterling in the tent across the way, so I have to do something, and I have to do it fast.

I pull the blindfold from Riot's eyes.

"Come on brother, I know you're in there. Please. Follow the heat or the flame or the sound of my voice."

He moans.

"That's right! Don't you remember, all the times we drank, we laughed. The planning. The girls. The fake stories we had to make up because your father told us to."

Nothing escapes his mouth, but his eyes seem to glint for a moment.

I throw the blindfold into the dirt and pull Riot to a standing position.

"Come on, Riot! Feel the flame. Hear me!" I start pleading, my voice getting louder.

Someone pokes their head out of their tent and a few others step outside to watch now.

I bring my face in close to his, looking into those dead eyes that look past me, unseeing.

"Come on, brother," I hiss.

"Come on I know you're in there."

More people pile out of their tents and into the clearing. I look around at them nervously. This has to work; I don't have another option and I refuse to let Arnoldous Blair win.

"Wake up," I whisper to him.

"Wake up, Riot Blair. You wake up right now."

My eyes dart around as the throng of people gathering thickens.

"Right now," I plead.

Riot's head flings back, his arms spread wide, and he lifts into the air, up and over the fire, the flames licking at his heels, but not touching him. The people gasped and I heard someone behind me whisper his name. I turned, looking to them all now.

"Please, please just give him a chance," I beg the crowd, trying to damage control the name.

His name.

Riot let out a scream that was guttural and not his own. Everyone in the crowd ducked, including me. I rolled into the dirt, clasping my hands over my ears, looking up at my friend. As he shouted, his head fell back, arms spread wide, blackness emerged from his open mouth.

The crowd parted and through it came Sterling, accompanied by the people's Priestess and the man from yesterday. Riot fell into the flames as they promptly went out.

I looked over my shoulder to Sterling and the person he stood there with now. They stared at Riot's crumbled body sprawled out like he'd fallen from a skyscraper, luckily, his eyes were closed now as black smoke rose from all around him, embers flying through the air and dying out.

I couldn't believe what I was seeing.
"Riley?"

RILEY

"Locke? What are you-" my words stop in their tracks as my eyes follow the gaze of everyone watching, to the boy in the center of the firepit.

A knot formed in the middle of my throat as I saw Riot fucking Blair laying where the fire once roared. A slew of emotions ravaged through me all at once, but the one I landed on was rage. I turned on the Nobelist.

"Do you have any idea who that is? Is this the fucker you were asking for my help with?" His mouth quivered like he was going to laugh, but his expression stayed stoic.

"Everyone return to your tents. Cast a shield over yourselves and do not come out until I explicitly tell you to."

The crowd stares.

"Now!" I demand and they rush to do as I said.

"Is this some kind of *joke*?" I turn on Locke now.

He stands, dirt all over him. He's looking at me like he's seeing a ghost.

"Nah, not at all... How did you get here?"

I stare at him baffled by his stupidity. The Nobelist beside me tenses.

"Take your trash and get out. I will not help you or them." I say as close to his face as I can manage. I press my anger into him and I'm pleased with myself as I feel his resistance back off. Walking back to the tent, I realize he let it back off, I didn't break through it. It was his choice to allow me that close.

I stop just outside the fabric.

Fuck.

"Nobelist," I call out.

I can feel his eyes on my back. I can almost hear him shoot a warning look at Locke, telling him not to move. Not to speak. In moments, he's next to me.

"Why didn't you tell me it was Riot Blair?" I say, not allowing the tears that stung my eyes to fall.

"I had no idea you knew him." He whispers.

"Leave. I have no interest in helping him or anyone he calls a friend."

With that, I enter the tent. Sterling doesn't follow me, and for a second, I'm alone. I suck the tears back in. After all this time, I'd thought I'd have the time to find and kill Riot Blair myself for what he's done. The fact that he was here, in the place I'd worked so hard to put together after what he did angered me.

"Priestess?" Tambo appeared in my quarters now.

"I told you not to call me that. How many times must I ask you not to call me that?" I ask, my voice quivering.

"Always once more, Riley."

I let a breath I'd been holding out, leaning my full weight on the countertop in front of me. If I turned to face Tambo now, I'd lose it completely. So much had changed since the attack on Gemini Coven a few months ago.

"Priestess, huh?" Locke's voice spanned the room.

"I told you to leave,"

"I know. I know that. I know why too. I don't blame you," he says.

I can feel his energy move closer.

"Tambo."

I can hear Tambo move to escort Locke from the tent.

"Please Riley, you don't understand!" He yells and a tear falls as I turn on him now.

"I understand perfectly well. I understood when you tried to drown me, throw me off a cliff, impale me in a park, I understand perfectly well, Locke! Get your friends and get the fuck out of here. Now!"

Tambo grabs him and pulls him from the tent as I watch. Locke's face was painted with so many things, but the thing that surprised me the most, was the fear in his eyes.

———

Later that night, I sit, mapping out Meta and the Outliers. I hadn't dared open the black book or tell anyone anything that I'd been doing. Not even Tambo.

The people here looked up to me, calling me Priestess, but I wasn't their Priestess. I refused to use any magic other than existing in the gap, looking for Arabia. I'd been looking every single day for the last few months and there hadn't been so much as a hint.

Over half of her people had died as I found out that I could cull and began using the gap to find survivors as the world crumbled in flames around me, only coming out to grab one and cull them anywhere I could that wasn't there.

We'd ended up here, and the villagers had been nice enough to offer to hide us behind the mountains so the fact they told Sterling and his *friends* we were here was completely maddening.

My mind cut to the memory of the screams of Arabia's people. The pain I'd felt in my body, the tiredness of my muscles as I loaded people both larger and smaller than myself over my shoulders. I never knew how to cull or that it was a thing, I just *did* it.

Memories of the bodies I couldn't save that were already gone as I went back and forth looking for every survivor I could haunted me day and night. I forced my nails into the palms of my hands, my heart fluttering in my chest as I heard Locke yelling through the grounds. His voice meshed with the ones from the people back at Gemini Coven. I could feel the sweat beading on my face and lower back.

I swallowed hard, trying desperately not to fall into the gap unwillingly, but its pull overtook me.

KAZ

Sterling pulled Locke, fighting and kicking into the tent, Riot's unconscious body slumped over his shoulder.

"You're an asshole!" Locke growled, spitting at Sterling's feet.

Sterling's eyes flared, but he made no move. I rushed over, taking Locke by the shoulders.

"Stop, man. Come on."

"No, man! He ruined everything!" he yells.

I look to Sterling now who avoids my gaze, placing Riot onto the couch again.

"What happened? Why is he unconscious now?" I ask, rushing to Riot's side.

I surprised even myself.

"I don't know, for that, you'll have to ask Locke."

"Fuck you!" Locke screams.

"No one told you to drag him out to the *center* of the town! *No* one told you to remove his blindfold in front of everyone! I specifically told you to stay here. You disobeyed me!" He yelled, advancing onto Locke now.

As big as Locke was, Sterling towered over him. Locke swung, but Sterling caught his fist.

"Locke!"

"I wouldn't boy," Sterling sneers.

Locke yanks his fist from Sterling's grip. His eyes ravenous, he looks at me as he walks away, slamming his door.

"I'm sorry," I say.

Sterling walks slowly around the room, hand over mouth. I could tell he was trying to hold something more than anger down.

"Sterling,"

"I didn't have to come."

I nod.

"I didn't have to come here. I didn't have to help."

"I know," I say.

He takes a deep breath, hunkering any last opinions down. Taking a seat in front of the fire, he stares at Riot.

"You need to talk to her,"

"The Priestess? There's nothing I could say, I-"

"You must. He apparently knows her."

I think about it. Locke had told me that the only known Priestess was Arabia. Why Locke couldn't talk to her now was a mystery to me.

"Is it not Arabia?"

"No, they called her Riley."

My heart jumped into my throat. There was no way she was here. I'd thought all this time she was at Pleaides.

"I'm sorry but she needs to see him."

"There's no way she will. She hates him. She won't do it, regardless of me talking to her or not."

"She doesn't have shit for mental shields Kaz. She was so close I could see there was much more there than you'd expect. She's the one we are looking for. You were right."

I reach for Amira, but she's not there. There's nothing but a swarming darkness that I assume is Riot. My heart cracks a bit, letting in a dark tinge of loneliness.

"You bargain with her, there's nothing I can do."

"Maybe Riot can make a bargain with her," he suggests.

"The devil doesn't bargain," it was Locke who answered now.

He stood in his doorway, watching us. He looked much calmer, shirtless now.

"He will never bargain with her. She won't talk to me. She won't talk to him nor Sterling now. She's not seen you. I'm sorry Kaz, but this is up to you." He says, refusing to look at us.

"Please,"

Locke hadn't spoken and looking at Sterling, neither had he. Riot's mouth was open. We all rushed to his side, sitting him up.

"Riot? Riot are you there?" Locke said, grabbing his shoulders and helping him steady his head.

"Thirst." He mumbled.

Sterling ran to grab the Silver Sap we had left while we held him in place. I noticed that his skin was much warmer than it had been now.

"Here, drink this," Sterling says offering the canister to him.

Unable to move his arms, he slowly opens his eyes. I grab the canister, lifting it to his lips and tilting it ever so slightly so the Silver Sap hits his lips. He drinks, slowly at first and then quickly as the stuff does its job.

We sit, watching him as he feathers his jaw. After a few minutes, he lifts his arms to his head and rubs his eyes.

"My head is killing me," he says, voice raspy.

Locke starts laughing and we all join in.

"I'm just happy you're fucking here right now,"

Riot sits forward, rubbing his eyes.

"I don't mean to ruin the moment, but Riot, we need to see your eyes." Sterling says cautiously.

The color returned to Riot's skin; his lips almost as pink as they normally were. The black veins were gone from what I could see past his hands.

He nodded, removing his hands and trying to stop squinting. When he opened them, Sterling dropped his head, and Riot promptly closed them again.

"We should keep the blindfold on just in case."

Riot coughs.

"What? No that's preposterous!" Locke objects.

Riots coughing turns to chuckling.

"Not a day has changed you, Locke. No, I agree. I don't feel completely here, and there's no telling what's going on." Riot says, leaning back again.

"Actually, we believe your mind has been flared by your father," Sterling offers him.

"Impossible. I have mental shields."

Locke rubs his neck with his hand, scrunching his face and looking at the ceiling.

"Yeah, well about that…"

"What?"

"When we put confusion magic on you, it scrambled you so badly, that he was able to find a way in."

Riot's jaw clenches as he processes what Locke told him. Now that he was awake, we could fill him in, get him back to speed, but it was going to be hurtful and a lot of information.

"I'll go get his blindfold," I offer.

Sterling makes knowing eyes at me as I slip out of the tent. I make my way towards the firepit. There was no one around, except a man in yellow standing where the fire once used to be.

I could make out Riley's form through the light fog that had settled over the grounds. Her arms were crossed, and she was tense.

"Riley, or.. Uhm Priestess."

She turns, her hair whipping with the power of the movement. I'd normally argue that I'd startled her, but by her pursed lips and body language, I knew she was just pissed.

"No. I've already told your pointed ear friend I'm not talking to you four. Anyone associated to that monster can kiss my ass."

"Riley," I say, softer now.

She'd started walking away, but at the sound of my plea, among all the things I wasn't saying, by some miracle. She stopped. Her hair kissed her back as she looked up at the sky.

"Tambo, leave us. Please." She sighs.

He does, but as he goes, he gives me a deathly stare. She turns, making her way back over to me, arms still crossed tightly across her chest.

She stops a few feet from me.

"Go. "

"He needs you." Is all I can think to say.

She stares at me blankly and then breaks out into a fit of uncontrollable laughter. I watch as she throws her head back, taking a deep breath in.

"Fuck you. Good luck." She says, walking off.

As she walked, I scrambled for something to say. Anything. But nothing came to me. That was it. I blew it.

"Kaz!" I heard my name and my heart exploded. Before I could even turn around, I knew who the voice belonged to.

"Amira," I breathed.

Sure enough, when I turned around, there she was, beautiful and perfect as always.

Riley stood between the two of us, confused.

"My love!" She called out.

"Amira!"

I ran past Riley and into her arms. I couldn't believe she was here. When I thought I'd have to pull away or we'd fuse together for sure, I held her face in my hands, looking into her eyes.

"What are you doing here?"

"I told you I had business,"

"You didn't say business with witches," I breathed pressing my lips to her forehead.

"You two know each other?" Riley mused approaching us now.

"He's my mate," Amira answers for both of us, not daring to break my stare.

We sat together in Riley's tent. Amira caught me up about the forest and the Centaurs movement to help the witches. It seemed like things in Meta weren't going well at all. Some of the Royalists sons had killed on another in an attempt for a leg up. By eliminating one another, they were increasing their chances at winning when they found Riot.

Luckily no one had suspected that Riot wasn't in Meta though and that was great news.

"He's here?" Amira gasped.

I nod. Riley looks at the floor. She's sat back on a chair opposite Amira and I.

"They made Riley their Priestess," she says excitedly to me.

That grabs Riley's reaction.

"I'm not their Priestess, I'm not even a witch." She objects.

"You're more than that," Amira breaths.

Riley makes eyes at her as if to say I probably shouldn't be hearing what she just admitted, but I already knew. This was just confirmation that there was more and that I had been right.

"We know," I assure the room.

Amira snaps her attention to me, gasping. Riley shifts uncomfortably, not looking away from me now. I can see on her face that she's wondering how I know Riot, how I'm involved.

"I never saw you at Pleaides."

"Because I never went."

She narrows her eyes at me now. Amira breaks the growing tension by shifting her body and clearing her throat.

"I'll hear you," she says, sitting back.

I nod and waste no time telling her everything that's happened.

After what seems like forever, I finish with how we got here and the events of the day before. I even told her stuff from before I knew Riot, making sure to make it very clear that I once hated him too. She pulled her face at that, her posture softening as I spoke.

"Oh, at least see him, Riley!" Amira said excitedly, a twinkle in her eyes.

"I still haven't found Arabia," she whispers.

"And I will help you, you have my word." Amira reminds her of a conversation I hadn't been a part of.

She looks from her friend, my mate, my universe, to me. She bounces her leg, biting her lip. Her inhale tells me she regrets the words about to come out of her mouth, but I feel like a Mantrovere when she says,

"Fine, Kaz Arnsen. I'll see him."

RILEY

I felt like I betrayed myself by telling Kaz I would see Riot. I know Arabia would probably punch me in the tit if she knew. Amira's love for Kaz was the only reason I'd agreed. I was doing it for her, not him. Not Riot.

Once I said I would see him, Kaz wasted no time in getting Sterling back to my tent. While he was gone, I decided to tell Amira the dreams I'd been having. I still was so unsure of who I could trust and I definitely wasn't going to be telling all my secrets right away. I was sure that someone had Arabia.

It wasn't like her to just leave a note and disappear. Okay, well, it was like her, but in my defense, she did it when her people were in trouble. Her people were attacked, and she just disappeared. There had to be only one explanation.

I knew Riot Blair was behind the attack, and I knew deep down he'd lied to his friends, but I planned to make sure that by the end of the night, they'd all know the truth.

"Tell me, before they come back, what you've been trying to tell me for days now," Amira asks, sitting back, smiling.

Her entire energy has changed now that Kaz was here. She had been telling me about her whole vibe being off due to losing connection to her mate and I could tell now that she had been off.

"I don't even know where to start but I hear Arabia calling to me when I try to sleep. I haven't been able to find her anywhere." I explain.

She nods thoughtfully.

"Did you guys ever share a connection?"

"Like you and Kaz?"

She nods. I burst out laughing. I was looking for Arabia purely to hand her back her coven and go back to my life. I still didn't trust her, but I had promised to care for her people no matter what. Regardless, she abandoned me. I was content learning to be a part of them and learning everything they had to teach me, but I never asked to lead them.

I have no idea what it is I'm doing. I mostly let Tambo guide me and I'm just their caring face. Besides, I'm the only one who could save them then, on the day of the attack. It was like they were hatching turtles and because I culled them here, a place I keep on reminding them I never knew existed, they saw me as some sort of leader.

"This was all completely by accident."

"Nothing is by just coincidence alone, Riley."

I narrow my eyes at her, vaguely remembering having heard that somewhere before.

"Sorry for taking a moment. We wanted to prepare," Kaz says bursting into the space, Sterling in tow.

Amira ran to him.

I stand, crossing my arms again. I have no interest in seeing Riot, but I promised Amira I would after Kaz had left. As a Centaur, she has the purest heart and she quickly mattered to me, so, if she asks me to meet him, I will.

"Are we ready?" Sterling asks the room, but he looked at me, holding my gaze in a trap with no walls.

"Riley," Amira says, leaving Kaz's side and taking my hands, lowering her voice, but I'm positive everyone hears her anyways as she speaks to me.

"Don't forget what you've done, who you are. No one can take that from you. See him. Give him a chance."

I smile tightly at her as Kaz lays a hand on my shoulder.

"Let's do this." I sigh.

We walked to the tent in silence, thankfully. The closer we drew, the more anxious I became. I didn't want to see Riot. I didn't even feel comfortable around his friends who weren't at Pleaides, how would I feel with the ones that were and worst of all, him?

As we neared the tent, the clenching in my stomach was replaced by a magnetic feeling.

"Wait," I whisper.

Everyone turns to look at me as I stop, right in front of the tents opening. I'm merely fabric away from Riot, maybe even a breath's pace. Feeling my elements flow into my palms and feet, I can feel the gap making a space for me. All I'd have to do is step backwards and-

"We didn't tell him you were the Priestess." Kaz says, snapping my attention back to the present.

"He's also blindfolded right now," Sterling says, but the uncertainty must be all over my face because takes a step towards me, smiling.

"You don't have to tell him you're there, Riley. No one has to say you are. We asked you to see him, not speak to him. If you don't want to, you don't have to."

I nod, jutting my chin towards the tent.

Kaz nods at Sterling, encouraging him to enter, Amira follows behind them. I curse at the stars who twinkle at me in response.

Fuckers.

Riot is sitting, blindfolded as promised, in the middle of the room. I round the couch and back up as far from him as I can get.

"Riot, I brought Amira to meet you."

He perks up.

"Amira is your mate, right?" He asks.

"She is." He answers as Amira takes the seat next to Riot, Kaz taking the seat on the other side.

I watch as she takes one of his hands. My stomach lurches for her. She has no idea what he's capable of. I watch as he raises a hand to her and I almost yell out, but I stop when I notice he caresses her cheek. He uses his fingertips to trace the lines of her face.

"A Centaur." He says through a perfect smile.

My heart skips a beat watching a side of Riot Blair that I never in a million years would have bet existed. My heart leapt without my permission, striking up that magnetic feeling in my chest again.

"Is there someone else here?"

I feel the color drain from my face as the room collectively turns to look at me, but no one answers him.

"I'll take that as a yes,"

"Riot, Amira is here to help, you know her." Kaz tries.

Amira squeezes Riot's hand as the others look between him and I. Sterling sits on the other side of him placing a hand on his shoulder.

"No, someone else is here. I can feel it and I'm not stupid. Is it the priestess?"

"Yes," Amira blurts.

Everyone looks to her with shocked expressions. Centaurs can't lie, and usually, I love that about her but right now, it's heading down a surefire road to disaster.

"Priestess?"

All eyes on me.

"I'm here."

The shock on everyone's faces when I answer says it all. I don't know why I did, but I don't want to be his victim. Being his victim gave him power and that's the last thing I wanted to give anyone, especially him.

"Priestess, why do you think this is happening to me?" he asks.

"We asked her to come to see you, just to see if she had any idea how we could block your father out," Kaz starts to explain.

"I asked her."

"Exactly what your friend said." It was a blunt answer.

Riot tilted his head and inhaled deeply.

"I know your voice. The priestess of this coven is Arabia Samedi. You are not her."

Maybe it was the horror on Amira's face that determined my next move. Maybe it was boldness or hatred for Riot Blair. Maybe it was hatred for Arabia. Maybe, it was the truth and maybe I'd known it all along. Either way, my heart thumped as adrenaline spiked through my body at the words I felt were true.

"Arabia Samedi is dead."

———

STERLING

The tension in the room was so thick you could cut it with a blade. Amira had let Riot know that Riley was present, but I expected as much from a Centaur. There's something else between these two. Something no one is saying. Arabia Samedi wasn't dead, that I knew for sure, being able to sense her energy on this plane.

I knew the witch of which they spoke. She'd sought me out for a spell, but not just any spell. Nobelists have access to every deity, kind of like their right hands on earth. Being a siphon, her magic dwindled the moment the tap on magic was tightened. She could only work through stealing the energy of the crystals she drained or other witches. As far as I knew, even the gods abandoned her.

She came to the Nobelists bargaining for contact to the gods and deities who'd abandoned her. How Riley knew of her was beyond me, but Samedi works for the Blairs. She can't be trusted.

The last time she came to see me, it was to strike a deal darker than any. I hadn't ever in all my time granted access to anything like it before. Now that I knew who it was for, my stomach was pitted.

"Dead?" I ask, unable to stop myself.

Riley did nothing but shake her head, her eyes telling the truth she wasn't saying. She knew Arabia wasn't dead. Nobelists don't lie but can easily withhold information, but before I have a chance to say what's on my mind, Kaz jumps in.

"I think we should-"

"I know your voice," Riot said again.

There was a sense of magnetism in the room, but I can't quite place between who until he says it.

"Riley," He whispers.

The color drains from her face and everyone around the room looks collectively between them, waiting to see what will happen.

"Yes." She answers.

At first, he sits statue still and I expect he's gone to the darkness again. The room barely breathes until

"Where's Arabia?"

"You tell me." She bites out.

"What do you mean?"

"Why do you care where she is any way? You've never spoken to us before, so you don't. Not that she would help you anyways."

Amira lets go of Riot's hand as a smirk plays out on his face.

"Is this the Gemini Coven? Is that where we are?" He asks.

Riley scoffs.

"You know damn well that it is."

"I didn't know at all."

"Well at least we had found a great hiding spot. That is until you found us again." Her voice was rising as she became more and more emotional.

Riot said nothing in return. I could feel him turning her words over in his head, thinking about what she could mean. The blindfold on his face kept his emotions hidden from everyone else, but I could see his eyes from right here, even still.

"What? No fire and brimstone this time? You thought you could just sneak in, no one knowing who you are? You thought you'd find Arabia and you got me, your plan has been successful. Run along to daddy now."

"What are you talking about?"

Riley crosses her arms and walks further into the room towards the couches.

"Don't pretend you don't know what I'm talking about! The attack on Gemini Coven? I know it was you and I know you want to kill me too!" She yells now.

"I didn't attack anyone!" Riot yells back now, jumping to his feet so quickly that Kaz has to jump up too to stop him from accidentally going into the fire.

"Disgusting liar." Riley spits.

Riot's jaw feathers as his rage builds, but I feel him quickly change gears, and his energy following his command, becoming quiet and... sad.

"Riley, Riot had nothing to do with the attack on Gemini Coven," Kaz says, standing between them now.

"Am I supposed to believe you? His best friend?"

"I'd like to think *I'm* his best friend," Locke chimes in.

"Fucking Minotaurs." Riot mumbled.

"I don't believe any of you no matter what you are to him!" She yells.

Riot just stands there, unmoving and nonverbal. The room shifted and I could finally feel Riley. Her shields went down ever so slightly, but it was enough for my Nobelist abilities to let in my darker ones.

"You two are mated." I announce and watch as Riley shoots me daggers with her eyes, the horror beneath them evident to no one in the room but me.

RILEY

"This is a disgusting idea of a joke, really." I say, turning to leave on my heel. I'm surprised when it's Amira who steps into my path, blocking my exit.

"Riley, please." She whispers.

"Please what?"

She looks over my shoulder towards the others. I'm not hearing this. I don't want Riot Blair. I don't want to ever be mated, especially to him. I have a choice and no psycho Nobelist with his band of assholes are going to take that from me.

"We need your help," Kaz finishes for her.

"I think you guys have lived out the life of this joke and I have nothing more to say."

I try to squeeze past Amira again, and she promptly blocks me.

"Move."

She shakes her head no, standing firm as the sternness in my voice surprises me.

"Riley, please just hear us out," Kaz begs.

I don't want to hear anything they have to say, so I reach for the gap.

Don't trust Riot Blair.

Embrace the gap.

I feel around for its opening, but it doesn't come. I realize it's been blocked off, like someone was holding it shut against my searching tendrils. Before Arabia had disappeared, she'd taught me a few things that acted like a key, unlocking my abilities. They'd taken on a life all of their own, and even though I don't fully understand them, they were here and they did everything I wanted and needed. Pressing them out from me, like arms that existed purely from my essence, their dark coiling wisps of black hit wall after wall behind and all around me.

I turned to see Sterling staring me down from the tops of his eyes. He's the reason the gap won't open for me.

"Stop. I'm not going to let go." Sterling confirms my suspicions that he's blocking me from the gap.

"You can feel me?"

He nods.

"Riley, you're the next host of Ophiuchus," he says, staring right through me now. I could feel his yellow eyes straight down to my soul, like a feather scraping and tickling its way through my inner being.

"Stop," I whisper.

"You're at risk and so are we. Riot needs your help. You need our help."

"Shut up," I say, louder this time.

I frantically send my dark tendrils out again, grasping and clawing for any gap I could find, fighting against invisible walls to no avail. Sterling narrows his eyes at me as I become more and more exhausted. His broad shoulders are firm and unmoving. Clearly, he wasn't nearly as tired as I was.

"You're not going anywhere," he says.

I narrow my eyes at him. At all of them.

"I don't want this," My eyes are planted on Sterling's for only one reason that I could think... he seemed like he got it. He seemed like he knew what I felt.

"There's nothing you *have* to do, Riley. We are simply asking for you to listen and to help us. I'm sure you have questions about what's going on with you and we may have the answers." Sterling answers the thoughts in my head as if he lives in there. It felt odd. Out of place.

"We have questions, too." Kaz adds.

Riot stays sitting on the couch where Kaz had sat him back down, looking as if he's not even listening. I guess if I'm being honest, he does have something different about him, but I don't trust him. Amira looks at me as if she sees all the soft places she claims I have, regardless of the fact that I've never felt them a day in my life. I was rough, out of place, and I didn't belong anywhere, ever. I feel my mouth opening while I internally kick myself.

I do have lots of questions.

"Fine." I sigh.

Immediately I feel Sterling's grip on me loosen as my already unclear future darkens more, taking a grip on my sanity. I can still feel Sterling's presence in the back of my soul, but I'm doing my best to ignore it as I sit on the couch opposite Riot.

With the fire roaring between us, the heat that was normally there was lost. The magnetic feeling is stronger than ever before and pulling in every direction. My heart felt like it was going a million miles an hour and like it was stopped dead all at the same time. I took a deep breath, pulling my darkness close to me.

"What do you want to know?"

KAZ

"Where do we begin?" I ask, taking a seat next to Riley, across from my love and my friends.

Riley's admission of Arabia's death, at the forefront of my mind. I don't just want to hop in and upset her, as she seems so fragile right now, but there's not much else I can think about. Arabia was our first plan. Her link to the deities she worked with, our best hope for the future of Meta. Riot's future, and, by design, everyone's future in this room.

"Let's start with your attack on Gemini Coven." Riley suggests, crossing her arms.

Every molecule in the room slows as we wait for someone to speak. I feel like I'm too big for the space, as the tension grows thicker.

"We don't know anything about that, Riley."

She scoffs.

"Riot Blair you never fail to live up to your true self," she mocks.

I shake my head.

"Riley, we truly have no idea what you're talking about."

Riot shifts now, leaving me to believe that's not the whole truth. Everyone watches, expectantly.

"Well,"

"I knew it." She spits.

"Let him talk," Locke interjects.

The room stills again. I fear I know what he's about to say and I try to ignore the cold growing around us that not even the dancing fire can beat. I watched Riley's brown eyes, seeing a reddening hue in them, but convince myself, it's just the reflection of the flames.

"I am being sincere when I tell you I have no idea what you're talking about when it come to the attack on Gemini Coven, but there are other things I'm not so innocent in." Riot begins.

I gauge Riley's face as a slew of emotions play out across her features. I can't quite place them. Looking around the room at the others, they too seem to be holding their breath and watching her. Riot exhales.

"Riot,"

"It's fine, Locke." Riot puts his hand up, stopping Locke from whatever it is he was about to say. A sentiment we will never know now.

"My father is a monster, but if there's anything he taught me, it's to be ruthless. Be ruthless for what you want. And if anyone gets in your way, you mow them down,"

Moments beat by.

"If I had orchestrated this attack, don't you think I'd be proud of it?" Riot questioned.

Riley's gaze snapped to where Riot's would have been had he not been blindfolded still.

"Riley, we have been running from the king for months now," Locke adds.

She looks around the room as she sits back, crossing her legs. Her eyes scrutinized everyone in the room and it was easy to see the mistrust written all over her face.

"Why? What's he done?"

"Riot had a fight with his father around the time you disappeared from Pleaides. In fact, we'd thought he'd finally gotten a hold of you…" Locke's words trail off as he notices my glare.

Too late.

His words have had an effect on Riley who's now looking from me to him, demanding more.

"What do you mean, 'got ahold of me'?"

Locke rubs the back of his strong neck with one hand, his face wincing as he mentally kicks himself for speaking at all. It's my job to clean up this mess now, I guess but Riot speaks before I can.

"Just what he said."

Everyone looks at Riot again.

"My father wants you in his grasp."

"For what?"

Riot shrugs.

"He thinks you have answers he's been looking for. He thinks you may be some sort of key or back door."

It's Sterling's turn now to clear his throat and explain.

"Have you ever heard of the thirteenth sign?" he asks.

Riley narrows her eyes at him in response and he just smiles like they are communicating in conversation no one else can hear.

"Back door to what?" Riley asks Riot, smiling at Sterling as she addresses him.

"Magic."

She looks from Sterling to Riot. Then, to me.

"And the thirteenth sign?"

Sterling stands, pulling out a bag from next to where he sat. He opened a scroll, the same one he'd been working on when I'd gone to see him that day. Using some sort of magic, he suspended it in the air where everyone could see it.

"This is Ophiuchus," he began, gesturing to the scroll.

To me, there were dots and lines and random symbols, but as Riley looked at the map, I could tell she understood something in them the rest of us could not. Her eyes followed the lines as we all watched her.

"Home," she breathed.

Sterling's eyes glistened. Riot cocked his head as if trying to hear something we couldn't, and Locke stared. A gentle pop alerted me to Simmer having culled into the space and as glad as I was to see he was still alive, the timing couldn't have been more off.

"Welcome, Simmer." Sterling offered without even looking in the disheveled man's direction. Simmer threw a look of disdain at Sterling, but quickly turned his attention back to me.

"Kaz, sir. We don't have much time."

I motion for him to follow me out of the tent, but he grabs my forearms in a death grip, forcing me to look at him in his wide, bloodshot eyes. He was terrified and it showed. The look caused me to fumble for a moment but that was all he needed. The others had gone back to their idle chatter, ignoring Simmer's presence.

They heard him anyways.

The air stopped circulating.

The room stopped moving.

The world came to a stop at the words Simmer whispered. The ones heard around the world. The ones that would change everything all at once.

They were unexpected.

They were deadly.

They were true.

My head titled in Riley's direction, horror written all over her face, as was on everyone else's faces.

"He's coming."

STERLING

"Is there any kind of backdoor to this place?" I asked Riley who was ordering Tambo and some others to gather everything they could in preparation to run.

She looked at me, her brown eyes swimming in shades I'd never seen in human eyes before. She swallowed hard, scared to offer me no answer, but doing it all the same.

"We have to cull these people out of here. I made a promise, Sterling. I *promised* her I would do anything for them." She begged me.

I couldn't help the goosebumps that kissed my neck when she begged me using my name.

'It's my nature and nothing else'. I told myself.

In lieu of a real answer, I nod. I would do anything to help friends of Kaz.

"Riley, you can cull people to Nobility,"

"Are you *insane*?" Riot yelled suddenly, jumping to his feet from his position on the couch.

Every eye in the room on him now. Even the workers of Gemini Coven stopped to stare at him.

"She can step foot in Nobility," I say carefully.

"How? She's never even been there!"

"Why do you assume I've never been there?" Riley chirps.

"Have you?" I ask, tempted by her tenacity.

Her gaze meets mine as she crosses her arms, shaking her head no, a smile playing across her lips.

"She can cull into Nobility, Riot. She can cull anywhere in the world, no problem."

Maybe it was in the way I said it, something in my voice saying that I just knew I was right, because no one questioned me. Instead, they got back to work. The coven people busied themselves with grabbing our bags, food and anything else the people needed and culled back to Nobility while Kaz talked Riot down.

I watched as she gave orders, taking people out of this place and to Nobility flawlessly. She was quick, graceful and filled with darkness that looked good on her. Like she was made from it. Normally, people ran from darkness, but not Riley.

She commanded it.

Ruled it.

Manipulated it at her every whim.

The most intriguing part was that she didn't even seem to know it. She had no idea what she was. The rarity that was her true form. On top of the way her being Ophiuchus lent it's abilities for her to manipulate the dark, her natural beauty, strong mind and independence pulled me in.

I watched her work, demanding the room. I watched the way people bent to her words, kneeling at her tongue for what she thought. It was the purest form of magic I had ever seen.

"That's it." Kaz's voice in my ear broke me from my reverie.

I clear my throat, smiling at him.

"That's all of them minus the few who can cull themselves." Kaz reiterated.

I nod, smiling as he took the space next to me.

"No issues with getting them into Nobility then?"

"None. Riot's the only one we have to worry about."

"We won't be going with them to Nobility."

Kaz looks at me, but I stare straight ahead, not daring to meet his eyes. I can feel his want to fight me on this, to tell me it isn't fair and that we owe these people now, but he doesn't.

"I know," He whispers.

"Best pack up and talk with Amira. Spend your last night with her as though you may not see her again, Kaz. You never know where things will go, but I have an intense feeling this won't go well." I say, standing and squeezing his shoulder.

He nods, silently.

I leave the tent into the clearing that was bustling with life only hours ago. The fire that once roared with life was now just a dirt ditch. I could still make out Riot's shape in the ashes. The tents gone, I can take in the natural beauty of the clearing. The trees jutting up all around us, the seasons meshing together all around us.

"I don't know what it is, but the coven likes areas where the trees cover everything but leave enough space above for the stars."

Her voice is calm. Tired, but cautious. I can smell her on the wind. Not the sweet scent everyone else can smell, but the scent of her soul. The fireball on top of the sweet. It piqued the interest of the monster within me.

I chuckle.

"The stars tell stories of the future but also of our past."

I can feel her warmth as she stops next to me, her arms crossed under her large chest, hair cascading down around her.

"Perfect then maybe you can explain to me why that drawing you had feels so familiar."

"It's never pleasantries with you," I say.

"Never."

She smiles into the silence.

"Never change." Is all I can offer her.

She laughs.

It's made of glitter and darkness. Sultry, heavy and light.

I feel it in my core.

"Funny, you're the only person who's ever told me that."

"What?"

"To never change. Lately, it seems like that's all everyone expects of me."

"Change isn't a bad thing," I counter.

"It's not. It's what got me here. Granted it's not been how I expected, but it was my goal after all. I just never thought I'd have people at every turn wanting something from me."

I glance at her from my peripheral vision. Her head is back, eyes closed, face to the stars.

"I've asked nothing of you,"

"You will."

"How can you be so sure?" I ask.

"Everyone always does, eventually. I've always been a good luck charm to others."

It was my turn to chuckle.

"What?"

"Maybe this is what I needed. I've been stuck in Nobility, looking for the next big sign, big warning or whatever it is I'm supposed to be here for so that I could go home."

"Home? Isn't that Nobility?"

I shake my head and see the questions on her face as she looks at me, but she doesn't ask them, so I let them slip away.

"I've been looking for all of the things that worries the heads of those around me. The tap, the Ophiuchus, the kings motives, the bayldonite crown. The kings of other lands have reached out to me trying to get ahead of Arnoldous Blair, but for the first time, I've had no answers."

She shifts uncomfortably like she knows what I'm about to say, so I say it faster.

"That is, until I met you."

"I'm no one."

"That's not true."

"Riley!" Locke yells, running our way.

She doesn't acknowledge him, keeping her eyes locked on mine until he stops next to her.

"What's up, Locke?"

"We need to get back to the tent. Riot's father is trying to tap into him. We blindfolded him, but I don't think it's enough."

She nods and assures him we will be there soon and he trots off back to the tent.

"It's not true and you know it," I pick back up without missing a beat.

"Listen, I'm just trying to live my life comfortably. Once I find Arabia, she can take her coven back and I can just be me again."

"That's not true either."

She shoots daggers with her eyes.

"You say you like to be alone, but that's not true. You don't really want to be alone. Don't you yearn to be more than alone or comfortable?" I ask her, hoping to break through the walls she constantly tries to hide behind.

She shrugs.

"Riley,"

"Riley! Sterling!" Locke yells from our tent, cutting off any further conversation.

She gives me a half smile and leads the way back to our people.

LOCKE

Riot started acting weird the moment Riley and Sterling left the tent, but since everyone was busy, the only person around to notice was me. At first, he craned his neck every few minutes, but then his face scrunched up and I knew he was gone again.

By the time Riley and Sterling came back, Kaz had already bound Riot's wrists in front of him with formations of his own making. Making your own formation was so extremely illegal it could land you in any of the Messiers. Probably even Messier 37, the worst one of them all. It felt good knowing we were binding the son of the king who'd made them illegal.

"So what now?" Riley asks, sizing Riot up from the tent entrance.

"Well we can't stay here tonight, it's likely his father saw where we are." I say.

"Simmer, what exactly happened?" Sterling asks the distraught man.

Simmer looks nervously from us to Riot who sat stone still, smiling on the couch.

"I can block his hearing." Sterling says and before anyone could question him, he threw a bubble of blue light over Riot's head.

"Uhm, thanks." I say, not really sure if that was completely necessary. Sterling nods and motions for Simmer to continue.

"He's gone completely wild, looking for his son. He's beyond angry, he's killing anyone who crosses him but not without torturing them first."

"Killing? That's not like him." Sterling says.

"How not?" Kaz asks a little too angrily.

"He sees death as too easy of an escape. Arnoldous Blair is notorious for torturing his victims, playing the long game. He never kills right off."

"That castle has become one of horrors. He is killing, he is torturing. I made it out because I tried to st-" Simmer choked on his words.

"It's okay, Simmer, you don't have to tell us." Riley offered, rubbing his arm and sitting next to him as tears streamed down his face.

"No, he needs to tell us, we need to know what exactly we are up against." Kaz says.

"He killed Faustus. I tried to stop him."

"Did you?" Kaz says, anger evident in his tone.

Simmer stands now, unbuttoning his black shirt and dropping it, turning his back to the room to reveal gouges to the bone.

"Holy shit." Riley gasped.

Simmer passed out into her lap.

"Well shit." I say, unable to voice anything else.

"Can you heal him, Sterling?" Kaz asked, eyeing the Nobelist.

"I can, but I'll need Riley's help."

Just then, a sonic boom echoed through the clearing. Screams from the remaining coven members reached our ears.

"Time's up!" Kaz shouted.

I jumped into action, giving into the beast the laid beneath my skin into my very core. The transition is seamless, effortless. The horns jutting from my head offer sweet relief to my skull. Once fully formed, I look at Riley who's face is a mix of awe and horror.

"You be careful, Locke." She says.

I bow to her and tear my way out of the tent, looking for my first victim and I spot him almost instantly.

Vertez stands in the clearing, scales out, in a mid-transformation. When his eyes meet mine, he smiles, water bubbling from his palms.

"Well well well, Locke. We meet again."

KAZ

Locke leapt from the tent as I hoisted Simmer's lifeless body onto my shoulder, Sterling taking up his other side. Screams echoed throughout the clearing. The tent was a wreck as everyone who could culled in and out of it, transporting people and supplies as quickly as they could. The ground rumbled beneath our feet as what I suspected were more of the kings army rolled in.

"You guys take him to Nobility, I'll stay here and make sure everyone gets out." Riley commands.

I nod.

"We will grab some of my men and come back as soon as we can." Sterling promises her.

Their eyes lock for a moment too long, and I feel something shift in the air. I reach for the gaps in time and find Nobility, but before I can pull us there, Sterling pulls us in. Within moments, we are there.

There are soldiers running about tending to the sudden influx of what's left of the Gemini Coven. I see Mordechai hunched over what looks like Tambo when he spots us and comes running over.

"Sterling, brother. Are thou alright?" He asks, placing a hand on his friend's shoulder and eyeing the still lifeless Simmer on our shoulders.

"We are. Thank you. This is Simmer. A soldier in our fight. Attacked by the king." Sterling informs him.

"I understand. I will get my best men on it."

"Have we any men to spare? We are under attack. Ophiuchus is back there, her name is Riley."

"Is she fully transformed?"

Sterling shakes his head. Mordechai's eyes widen in awe.

"We've not got much time, brother. I need every able-bodied man we can spare. She's fighting back there with Locke."

Mordechai nods and takes off into the crowd.

"Will Riley fully transform?" I ask as we pull Simmer into the castle towards the crescent room.

"No telling, honestly. We have to make sure she stays alive, first. One could only hope she will. The theory is she will be immortal if she can house it."

"You said everyone who's ever been a host has died."

Sterling nods as we approach the spiral staircase.

"I did."

We start making our way up them as quickly as possible. I don't want her to die. I'm tired of losing people I care about and honestly, aside from Amira and Locke, I didn't have anyone. Riot had come into my life but we were still in a weird place.

"We left Riot!" I exclaim suddenly remembering that no one had thought about him when the attack began.

Sterling nodded and we moved faster. Once we got Simmer to the crescent room, we were greeted by five women who took him from us effortlessly. They all were identical with long necks, black almond eyes and cascading tentacles down their backs.

"This is Simmer. Please be well with him." Sterling told the main one. She merely nodded at him, and turned to her clones, gesturing them to move quickly.

"Let's go." Sterling said, grabbing hold of me and in moments, we were back in the clearing. The tent we'd taken sanctuary in was already burned to the ground. Riot was no where in sight.

I burst through the clearing, looking for anything I could use as weaponry when Sterling handed me a Icohaber axe.

"Your father's favorite mortal weapon." Sterling added with a nod.

I took it in my grasp, feeling its power. It was no ordinary weaponry. It felt like it was carved and crafted from darkness, and it sent shivers down my spine. I'd never been one to mess with the darkness, and I wasn't about to start, but I could use all the help I could get right now. The hook and blade reflected my face in their perfectly polished surfaces.

Seeing my face reflected back at me did something to me. I never looked in mirrors because I didn't like what I saw, but this time? This time I liked the raw warrior looking back. I liked my thick brows, yellow hair and blue icy eyes. I even liked the beard hair that had grown in after all this time. It was like an ode to my true nature.

"Hey pretty boy, are you just going to admire yourself all day, or are we going to fight like men?"

Riot's voice was gruff and not his own.

"I thought you'd be man enough to face us yourself," I mock the undertone.

"I don't play games with children. The sooner you learn to bow, the easier your life will be."

It was clear this wasn't Riot, but his mind flare.

"I don't bow to those beneath me." I mock.

I turn in time to see Riot's got his blindfold off and his eyes are fully black, the irises a radioactive green. He's fuming, literally.

"Kaz!" I look past him to the voice and see Riley's horrified face.

I know instantly that she's telling me we forgot about Riot, and nod as she notices him blocking my path. Sterling pulls a sword out from his hilt that I just noticed he was wearing, and planted himself next to me, squaring up to Riot.

"We meet again."

"I won't consider it again until you're man enough to meet me face to face." Sterling says.

Riot laughed a broken laugh, shattered by the darkness within him and a vile host. I couldn't stomach it.

"That's enough, you vile fuck." I spat.

Immediately, Riot stopped laughing.

"You better hope you kill me, or you'll be begging for death." He says in a monotone voice before he lunges for me.

RILEY

Watching Riot stand in front of Sterling like that, his back hunched, his hands freakishly held open, fingers like claws. I reached for the gap and was pleasantly surprised when I felt the tendrils that had held them closed earlier were gone. I was free to move about as I pleased, but for the first time ever, I didn't feel like running away.

I used the energy around me to choke the man running towards me with a short blade with a flick of my finger and stomped towards Riot Blair's direction. He didn't notice me approaching and I took that as a good sign, catching Sterling's eye movements that indicated his approval. He stood very still, using his efforts to make it seem like he was invested in whatever Kaz and Riot were saying, signaling me along all the while.

When I was close enough to smell him, a smell I no longer recognized, I blasted him with all four elements, knocking him clean out.

"We need to get out of here." Kaz spared no time in binding Riot's arms and legs and blindfolding him once more.

"We're running? After all this?" I say, gesturing to the mess and bodies behind me. Kaz looked at them now as if he was just noticing an all out tiny war had gone on in his absence. Locke appeared next to me, back to his tatted human form and completely naked.

"Please tell me that's not your blood. It reeks." Sterling said, covering his mouth and nose.

"It's Siren blood." Locke panted.

"Siren? He's got hold of them?" Kaz stands now, admiring his work on Riot.

"No idea, but Vertez was here."

Kaz raised his brows at Locke who shook his head, lowering his eyes to the floor.

"You did what you had to." Sterling said simply. I bet that was the warrior in him.

A bunch of Nobelists appeared behind him now, ready for war. Sterling turned to greet them and give them orders. I really admired the way he worked and shut off certain parts of himself at will. Something I only hoped to master in the future.

"Riley, we need to cull out of here. Let the Nobelists to their jobs." Sterling cooed.

I nodded but had no idea where we would go from here. Where I would go.

"I need to go to the coven," I say.

"We aren't going back to Nobility." He warns.

"We need to heal Riot." Kaz interjects.

Sterling looks at Kaz as if he forgot he, Riot and Locke were standing here with us and I couldn't help but feel warmth tumble over itself into my chest. He inhales, sighing and looking like he was making a painful decision.

"Then we need Nobility, however we won't be staying long. Just long enough to right him once more."

We all nod in agreement and with that, we culled back to Nobility. Back to safety.

———

When we arrived on the crescent shaped island, efforts to save Riot were already underway. All our bloodied, bruised and broken had been carted off to the healers and the rest had been given rooms, food and water. They had traded in their colorful attires for the lilac sheen ones of Nobility, making them blend into the island even more than I thought possible.

I wished Arabia could see them. Anger flared in my core. Where is she? Why is she hiding? I thought I had been so close to finding her, but as it turns out, I was wrong again. I've tried millions of gaps. I've tried hundreds of places.

Despite Tambo's true effort at helping me locate where she could be, despite every pendulum swing, every card pull, every spirit interaction, every lead was nothing but a dead end. I walked through the cobblestone streets of Nobility, arms crossed, deep in my thoughts. I felt anything but Noble.

There had to be something I was missing. She'd had time to show me almost nothing since leaving Pleaides and yet, my powers grew every day despite my never having learned them. I felt different. Off. Like I was too much for myself. It was starting to make me consider that Ophiuchus was real and that I could be in very real danger.

There were so many things that I'd learned from Gemini Coven that didn't make sense about Ophiuchus though when applying it to me and pairing it with the possibility that I could very well be its next host.

For one, I wasn't parentless. I had a mom. No clue on the dad aspect, I just believed what my mom told me and that was that he'd died and because of that, we had to live the way we did. She told me our home in Corset Forest was built by him. She told me a lot of things I'd come to realize were lies.

"You're pacing an awful lot." A tiny voice snapped my attention back to reality. I spun around looking for the source of the voice.

Sterling stood there and in front of him was a tiny girl with pixie cut hair. Next to her, an exact match, long hair to his shoulders.

"Phae! Posh!" I exclaimed running to them.

I took them both into my arms and gave eyes I hoped read thank you and how could I ever repay you, to Sterling. I think it worked because he nodded, turned on his heel and left us alone.

"We were so worried about you, Riley. How could you just leave and not tell us anything? No way to contact you? I mean honestly, you've had us worried sick!"

Posh grabs his sister's shoulders, urging her to calm down.

"What Phae means is we love you, and yes, we've been very worried." Posh says calmly.

"I swear I didn't do it on purpose." I begin.

"What does that even mean? And no elusiveness Riley. I think we deserve to know the truth." Phaedra says, crossing her arms.

I nod because she's right. All this time I'd spent protecting Arabia and for what? I bet had I told Phae and Posh things a long time ago, I wouldn't be here now.

"Okay." I say.

Phae drops her arms and her face.

"Did she just say okay? Did Riley actually just agree to something?" She asks Posh every bit enthusiastically as it was sarcastically.

"She sure did."

I laughed and led them over to some beautiful benches surrounded by flowers in the shade of Crescent Castle.

"Arabia took me on a trip to see her home," I began.

Their eyes widened as I told them everything that had happened. Posh sat back, looking into the sky and listening to every word. Phae was on the edge of her seat next to him.

"So that sexy man is Sterling?"

I laugh.

"The man who brought you here is Sterling, yes. Which, by the way, how did that happen?"

They both shrugged.

"He just showed up at Pleaides and when we tried to ignore him, he said your name and we listened to what he had to say and here we are." Phae recalled.

"He said my name?"

"Sure did. That's the *only* thing he said." Posh confirmed.

I roll my eyes at them.

"Stop, he's just a Nobelist who's helping because of his duty to Kaz."

"Right." Phae says despite the devilish grin she has plastered to her perfect lips.

"I'm serious. Besides, you guys are better off without me. Without all of this." I gesture to the general area.

They gawked.

"What?!" Phae exclaimed.

Posh just stared at me like I'd just told him he was going to have to sacrifice his life for the king.

I nodded my head in a slow yes, placing my eyes on a flower in the grass below my feet and not daring to move them to look at my friends. I knew what their faces would say. I knew what thoughts were going through their heads. I knew that now; they didn't trust me. There was no reason for them to anymore. Anyway, once they find out I am mated to the Blair heir, I will be an enemy by default. I couldn't bear to see their faces when they found out. It was just better for them to go.

"Stop that." Posh said, his eyes planted firmly on my face.

I look down at my lap. It's crazy how connected to them I feel, even after all this time. It's like we lost nothing- no time at all.

"No way are you going to sit there and think about yourself that way."

I have no idea what they see in me. I was more than blessed to call them my friends, but to have them actually care? That was out of my wildest dreams.

"I'm not thinking anything." I protest.

Phae shoots me a knowing look.

"You're not very kind to yourself all the time."

I shrug

"Well it's a shame to let such a handsome man go to waste." Phae sighs.

"Who said I was going to let him go to waste?" I tease.

"Ahem, Riley. You're needed in the crescent tower." Mordechai said from somewhere behind us. My stomach leapt at the possibility that I'd be seeing Sterling soon, and I needed to remind myself that my teasing with the twins was just that- teasing. There was nothing between us and I still had a basilisk, a king, and the entirety of Meta's future to figure out before I could even think about sex.

Standing from the bench, I took Phae's hands, pulling her up beside me.

"What of my friends?" I ask the warrior.

"I will find them our best room if they'd like to stay in Nobility."

"Would you? Will you both stay?"

The twins look at one another and smile while nodding excitedly.

"I don't know that I want you guys on this journey, whatever it is. I'm glad you'll stay for at least a bit."

"There's no way in hell we are going to let you leave our sight again." Phae says sternly.

Mordechai crosses the tiny stone wall so that he's standing beside us now and waits patiently while we hug goodbye. It's all I can do not to run to crescent tower, giddy at the thought of seeing Sterling.

STERLING

    Of all the fantastical things in existence, not one has ever excited me. Of all the picturesque places both beautiful and haunting, not one has ever captivated me. However, right here, right now, I watched as a storm in the form of a human moved towards the crescent office. I watched her hair float on the wind around her as she walked, trapped in her own tsunami of a mind.
    She commanded the particles of life around her, devastating them. She was every element. She was every fear and every wish all in one. Her eyes land on me, standing here on the balcony and I swear I could see a hint of a smile in her eyes, but it's quickly gone away.
    When she finally makes it up the tower staircase, I've busied myself over some meaningless papers I hadn't touched in months.
    "You weren't this busy a few minutes ago," she says, walking slowly into my office. My space.
    I don't allow many into the crescent office. Mostly I meet my potential clients in the hall, but I called Riley here for privacy. I want to get to know her and see if she needs anything at all.
    "I need air every once in awhile. I can't help if you're lurking under me when I seek it."
    She rolls her eyes.
    "I have questions."
    "I'm sure you do, but I didn't call you here to talk about your questions. I called you here to talk about you." I say, my vision leaping as the forbidden words leave my lips.

If anyone found out, I'd likely be stripped of my titles, my accolades and disowned by my breed altogether.

"What about me?"

The curve of her jaw, the dip of her top lip. Her nose and her lashes. They intrigued me. I needed to touch them like I needed air, but I'm a strong man.

A warrior.

A Nobelist.

We don't allow such emotions to affect us. In fact, I never noticed these things about anyone in my very long life. Of course, no one knows my real timeline of existence, and Perdition would have my head if they ever did.

"Nothing in particular," the words I want to say are trapped within me.

"Nothing about me being on an ever accelerating path towards my untimely death?"

Her eyes are calm, her spirit wild.

"You've read the black book."

She shakes her head at me, turning her attention to the various items I have displayed on a nearby shelf.

"I wouldn't dare open that thing. Not even if you paid me."

I wait for her to say more while she turns a clear glass ball over and over in her hands. Placing it back she realizes she's lost things to feign interest in and turns towards me again, sighing.

"But it talks to me."

"Talks to you?"

She nods.

"What does it say?"

"Besides secrets I probably shouldn't have ever heard? Not much. It does particularly enjoy threatening me and letting me know I'll die though." She shrugs.

I can't say I'd ever met someone mortal who wasn't afraid of lady death, but with Riley it was different. It was somehow more than that. It was almost as if she knew death would never come for her to begin with.

"Riley,"

She throws her hand up to stop me from speaking.

"Don't. Don't tell me it won't happen if it's not true. I have been studying everything I can about Ophiuchus with the Gemini Coven and no one has any answer that ends any differently."

"If I may?" I ask.

She eyes me carefully before allowing me to continue.

"They can only see what's already happened."

"Yeah and history repeats itself, I know."

"What if it doesn't? What if it only repeated itself because of the host?"

"Are you implying it was the hosts fault?"

I nod.

"That's a different take on it, sure." She says, approaching my desk.

I try so hard not to stare at her too much or for too long in one place.

"What if you're wrong?" She snaps suddenly.

"What if I'm right?"

She smiles.

"You're not like the other people here."

"Meta is filled with all kinds of people."

"I'm not talking about Meta."

She steps forward again until she is inches away.

"I see you. I see you in the gap. I see your tendrils that look like mine."

"I don't have answers for you," I whisper, looking between her questioning eyes.

She lifts one perfectly shaped brow at me.

"I thought you had all the answers?"

"I…"

"Just tell me the truth Sterling. Tell me what I am."

I catch my breath and stare at her intentionally this time, not daring to look away from her.

"I don't have an answer."

Disappointed in me, she backs away.

"Shame. I thought you'd at least know *something* given the fact you're a literal demon."

The world stops turning at her words, and I can't help the bile that lurches itself into my throat. How could she possibly know that? I knew that she could see me back in Twin Seouls, but I had no idea how much she had or could see.

Maybe she only saw the tendrils.

"Your whole face." She says in answer, as though she can hear me.

"I can't hear your thoughts, but I know you're wondering and I'm telling you, I saw your whole real face."

Fuck.

KAZ

    Mordechai introduced me to the best warriors Nobility has to offer and then their healers. While he quickly taught me the layout of the castle, I made mental notes on every exit and entry into the main parts.

    "Thou don't need to categorize the entry points of this place." He offers, watching my face.

    "Sorry, habit." I say but keep making my notes anyways.

    I couldn't risk the possibility of Riot's father finding his way into Nobility and not having some kind of plan if he did, even though I was sure he would never find this place.

    Mordechai leads me through the various old rooms and hallways, explaining their history in great detail. The harder I try to focus on what he's saying, the more I think about Riley and Ophiuchus. Amira and her people. Gemini Coven and Arnoldous Blair. I must have lost myself in my thoughts because in no time, we are back at the front of the castle.

    Healers are bustling about tending to the last of those who need mending. Locke spots us from across the room and rushes over to us the second his healer is done placing some weird concoction and leaves to his wounds.

    "Hey, have you guys seen Riley? I have questions about Riot."

    "I know you do, and he's fine. He's here, but just unconscious."

    Mordechai shoots me a look like I've said too much and should keep my mouth shut, but it's Locke. Locke who cares so much about Riot and his other friends. I shot Mordechai a look.

    "How is he here if he can't see Nobility?"

    "He's under formations."

    "So what you're saying is he's unconscious again and therefore completely susceptible to his father's power."

I look between Locke and Mordechai. Mordechai's face is stern but friendly. He wins out over Locke who ends up just shaking his head in disappointment.

"I'm sorry, Locke. I wish I could tell you more. This is how it has to be. It's the only way to help him right now."

"I get it, I'm just sick of hearing it."

Sterling and Riley enter the chambers and I'm relieved, hoping they will offer new discussion. I apologize to Locke again as they join us, Riley looking exhausted as ever and Sterling matching her energy.

"Any news?" Sterling asks despite his face giving away that he already knew we hadn't made much headway on anything.

"We have healed mostly all the injured from Gemini Coven. Riot is still under formations. Not much has changed."

"I might have something," Locke pipes up.

We all look at him expectantly.

"I'm sorry I'm waiting until now, but I wanted us all to be together and I think this right here is the most together we are going to ever be probably for a while."

"What is it, Locke?" Riley sighs.

"Well, I was talking to someone at Twin Seouls while you were all running around figuring shit out. She's here now, but she's one of the injured. She tells me that there are more coven members in hiding."

"Like we need to go back?" I ask.

He shakes his head.

"No, like within Meta. For one, there's the Madame who's not been seen since the first attack on the coven. But there are members within Meta who weren't there."

I search Riley's face at the news, and I'm not really surprised when it doesn't show much more than apathy.

"More. There are more?" I stammer.

Locke just nods.

"Did she give names?" I ask.

"A couple."

"Would one of them happen to be Elliot Mantrovere?" Riley sighs and even those hustling around us stopped to look at her.

No one dares speak about the Mantrovere family, even in Nobility.

Locke doesn't answer, he just stares at the floor.

"I'll take that as a yes," Sterling chimes in.

"That's a death sentence and a wild accusation."

"It's not an accusation." Riley snaps.

I narrow my eyes in disbelief at her.

"When I lived in the Outliers... I was a spice runner."

We all just stare. I can't say that I'm shocked by the news, but I'm also somewhat intrigued by it. I know she's not straight edged, but I didn't think she was one to ride below the law, especially not intentionally.

"Wow." Locke looked at Riley with an odd expression on his face like he was suddenly in love.

"Don't even think about it." Sterling hissed.

Riley's face went pink, but she continued with her sentiments.

"We decided that we were going to do one last job. It was all I needed to get out here and we needed a newer, bigger target. Elliot just happened to fall into our laps one night while we were scoping out a club and after months of stalking that vile man, I can promise you, it's not an accusation."

We all just stared at her.

"He gave me money for a job I never completed. The job led me to Pleaides and now here we are."

"I think you were set up." Sterling says.

Riley nods.

"Well do we have any idea by who?" Locke asks, looking around at all of us.

"I think so, but what they didn't know, was that the truth would set me free."

RILEY

"We need to talk," Sterling grabbed my arm in a firm hold that probably would have left a bruise months ago, but I wasn't weak anymore. I yank it from his grasp, channeling heat into it hoping it would leave a burn in its wake.

"Remarkable," he gasped.

"I don't want to talk." I snap.

"Too bad. We're going to talk. You can't just run off every time you feel overwhelmed."

I narrow my eyes at him and slip into the first gap I find. It's thin and I sigh deeply as the castle and shrubbery around me turn violet. My aura thrums within it. What does Sterling know anyways? Dropping details about my life before Pantheon isn't exactly easy and admitting out loud that I'm some weird host and probably going to die before I'm thirty doesn't make for a fun pow wow.

I ran after dropping the bomb on them because as much as they want to work together, we are all truly alone. I, even more so than them. After all of this, they would have their friends and their families and everyone they loved, and I would be gone. Nothing.

That is... if they don't die because of me first.

I inhale the misty air deep into my strengthening lungs. If black had a scent, this place would be it. I back away from the place I left behind in front of the castle and scream when I hit something solid.

Sterling.

"You can't hide from me, love." He chuckles.

"Who said I was hiding?"

"Come on now Riley. Let's not play coy. I'll chase you to the end of the universe, there's nowhere you can hide."

"I think that's a little stalkerish don't you?" I tease even though his words warm me.

He smiles, slowly, devilishly.

"Not even a little."

I roll my eyes at him, desperate to not show any kind of emotion other than boredom. He's an ass.

"What do you want to know?" Our voices echoed as though we were in a cave.

"You give up that easily?"

"For all intents and purposes, I don't want to get stalked the rest of my probably short life."

"Ah, so it's existential crisis."

I roll my eyes.

"No."

"No?"

"No." I stare him down. Being this close to his body, I could feel electricity between us. It's a nice change from the constant magnetic pull Riots presence often pains me with.

His smile widens.

"Do you feel that, star girl?"

Before I could answer him, he had me wrapped in black smoke and a kaleidoscope of stars. The air collapsed in and out of my lungs until no more was left and something within me took over. I was no longer breathing but somehow alive.

We soared on for what seemed like forever but ended all too soon the electricity between us held us together. I was all too aware of his hand on my lower back, just above my ass and the other which held me to him.

When my hair settled in a floating pool of stars and dust, I forced myself to look up at him. His eyes were fully silver now, the yellow gone from them. His face.

His *real* face.

Even in the darkness, I could see it here.

His Noble face was beautiful, but this one, even more so. It was dark and light all in one. The strong nose was lost in the stars that made up his skin, his silver eyes became moons that commanded them all.

"Riley," he whispered my name like it was a secret of all his own.

Like *I* was his secret and he intended to keep it.

My mouth is so dry I can't speak, so I just look, taking him in like I'll never see him again. In his arms I didn't feel the anger that usually racked my insides, nor the sadness that occupied my mind. In his arms, I'm a calm black ocean.

"Turn," he said, and I did.

Behind me and all around us are galaxies of every color. Ones I'd seen and ones I could've never imagined existing.

"These are all yours." He whispers in my ear.

"Mine?"

"Yes. If you want them. If you try and work with me so that I can save you-"

"Save me?" I should have known this was what it was.

His eyes widened in horror as he realized what he'd said.

"I don't mean-"

"Yes you do. You want me to *sacrifice* my life, *my* sanity to host Ophiuchus!" I accuse.

He was still holding me in his firm grip, but I felt it loosen.

"No, Riley, I-"

"Did you think about asking me what I want? If I even want to host it?"

"No, I didn't ask you."

A tear escapes down my cheek, and I'm surprised when he grabs it. There on his finger is a single tear in the shape of a droplet, completely crystalized. Completely black. Completely me.

It changed nothing.

"What if I'm okay with dying?"

He looked like I wounded him in a totally immortal way.

"What if I'm not?" he whispered.

"You don't get to make that choice." I whisper back.

With not much more to say, I feel him pulling us back to Nobility. I take one last look at the surrounding galaxies as they dissipate into the black smoke that's us.

'*Help*' I think to myself.

They continue to disappear, none of them making any sacrificial moves for their sacrificial lamb.

I don't deserve their beauty.
And *they* don't deserve my darkness.

STERLING

I messed up. I thought showing Riley what she could have would change her mind and soften her up. I should have known that she's not that type of woman. Even with not knowing her for long, I could see parts of her life in her eyes, the parts she let slip through the cracks or the ones I stole from her while she slept.

I know it's wrong, but I can't stop.

She felt so heavy in my arms as I pulled us back to Nobility. I didn't dare take us from the gap though because I still had questions.

"Riley, tell me what happened while you were with Arabia."

"You're not really in the position to demand things from me."

The safety of the gap was quickly beginning to feel like a trap. She didn't try to run, she just stared at me and as hard as I tried to dip my tendrils into her mind, I was blocked. I'm not used to being matched in power.

"If you're not willing to host Ophiuchus, then at least help us while we have you. Don't damn your friends."

She turned away from me, her arms wrapped around herself. I could tell that truly, deep down inside, she wasn't ready to die. She thinks so, but she's not.

Fuck, I hope she's not.

When she finally turns around, her face is stoic.

"I'll do what I can, but don't expect it to be much. Nothing happened that was Earth shattering when I was with Arabia and the Coven."

"I find that hard to believe. You were whisked away by someone we are looking for to a coven formerly believed to be dead and spent real time with them. You were the only one present when a huge attack happened, even though they had been previously so well hidden the entire *world* assumed them dead. That's not nothing, Riley."

She stares at me, her eyes wild.

"Are you insinuating I am the reason they were attacked? That Arabia is gone?"

"Not at all."

"Then what?"

"Just that you were the last to see them. Last to see Arabia. I'm not entirely sure you know this, but Arabia is the Voodoo Priestess of a dead coven. That means something."

"It means a lot." She sneers.

"For someone burned by the witch, you sure are protective over her."

"She's my friend."

"I thought you didn't have friends?"

Her eyes narrowed on me.

"I said I would help. Why are you doing this?"

"You won't tell me willingly, so I have to assume then. I'm merely giving light to what my thoughts are and in turn, am giving you time to deny or accept those facts."

"Fine. It was horrible and magical all at once. I was uncomfortable. They did their best to make me feel welcome. Then, one night, I was talking to Arabia, and I could see for the first time, how truly she loved these people. *Her* people."

"You think she loved them?"

"I know that she did."

"Interesting."

She rolls her eyes and continues on.

"She taught me acceptance. She taught me to look closer. Above all else, she taught me not to trust *anyone*."

That hit harder than I thought it would.

"What about magic?"

"No. She never did what she said she would. She never taught me a thing. The Madame was the only one who answered my questions and even then, it's questionable if she helped me at all."

She stares at the floor now, remembering something. I don't respond.

"She's the reason I got out on the day of the attack. She shoved that book into my arms and I ran into the gap."

"Was that the first time you entered the gap?"

"No, it was right before. At the start of the attack. It was an accident. It was terrifying but felt so right all at once. I didn't know it was a thing until later."

"Who taught you?"

"No one," She says.

Then, "There are times when I feel different. I'm not who I was when I first came to Pleaides, but I'm also not who I thought I'd be. I feel stronger at times."

"It's Ophiuchus." I say, almost regretting that I had to.

"I know."

"Are you afraid?"

"No. It feels natural. Sometimes it feels like I'm losing myself. My essence, I guess."

"It will. For a bit."

"How long have you been studying this thing?"

"Since I was assigned but I was assigned because I was interested my whole existence."

"How long do I have?"

"No telling. It's always been different."

She closed her eyes tightly. I don't want this for her. I have time to convince her to stay. There *has* to be a way to help her contain Ophiuchus.

"You're holding the power well, though." I offer.

"It doesn't feel like I've changed much. I just feel like I'm always on, like I'm buzzing or something."

I nod. A strange notion, sure, but it made sense.

"It makes sense. Ophiuchus is the purest form of power. Actually, it's the purest form of life, Riley."

"Why? Why me though?"

"I wish I could tell you. What I do know is that usually the host is chosen by someone closely related to Death."

"I've almost died numerous times," she whispers.

"Ophiuchus chooses very wisely. It's just that no one has taken the time to learn to house its power. This doesn't have to be over, Riley."

She looks up at me now, her face still emotionless, but her eyes showed a glimmer of hope.

LOCKE

Riley ran from the hall, Sterling chasing after her after nodding to Kaz, leaving us behind.

"What was that all about?" I ask, looking between Mordechai and Kaz.

Kaz shrugs but it's not very convincing. I think he knows that I can see through the act because he sighs, furrowing his brow and leading me from the hall. Mordechai does a tight bow and shoots Kaz a look that says more than I think he intended it to.

"Locke, a lot of things are happening and are about to happen," He begins, leading me by my elbow to a covered walkway with tall gothic archways.

"I know that. I've told you all I'm here, no matter what."

Kaz chuckles.

"It's not that anyone is questioning what side you're on, it's that we want you to realize the sacrifice you're making. You'll never have a normal life again."

I shake my head.

"I *know* that Kaz. It's never *been* normal. I don't care. I know where and what I stand for."

Kaz pulls his mouth taught, nodding as he does.

"The things that happen in war... the things you'll see..."

I clap my hands onto his shoulders, looking him dead in his ice blue eyes.

"I know, Kaz." I assure him again.

"Right, well. We better find our friends. There's lots to do." he says, accepting my answer for what it was.

There wasn't anything I'd rather be doing than helping. I'm a Minotaur for fucks sake, war is in my *blood*. I walk swiftly next to Kaz as he leads the way through various corridors and gardens looking for Riley and Sterling who are no where to be found,

We find ourselves outside the healers' chambers in no time and with still no sign of Riley or Sterling, Kaz leads us inside. The chambers are gorgeous with cathedral ceilings and tall windows. The gothic architecture of the entire island of Nobility was magical in and of itself.

"Kaz, what are we doing?" I whisper, so as not to disturb any of the bed ridden patients lining the corridors.

"Giving you what you want." He huffed.

We walked on silently until we reached a stone staircase that spiraled upwards. We took the steps one by one, nothing but the soft shuffling of our feet scraping the steps surface to comfort us. When we reached the top floor, most of the place was deserted. We walked, passing corridor after empty corridor until we came to a dead end walled by glass panes.

The ones that separated us from the outside were kissed with dew droplets, fogged so much they almost looked frosted. The wall of glass in front of us provided the perfect view of our friend laid out on a grey bed. He was under glass, machines pumping into the chamber the glass created.

"What's that for?"

"It's keeping him spelled."

I watch as the healers work around Riot, hooking him up to various machines that looked foreign from anything I'd witnessed in Meta. It was all so technically advanced. There were no walls lined with shelves of various specimens, herbs and the like; although, there were plenty of plants providing ambience to the space.

The healers all looked like clones of the one next to it. Pasty lavender skin, long necks and large black eyes. They wore long veils and matching outfits. Long smocks in grey and overcoats in white.

"They all look so sterile and move so slow." I whisper in awe.

"They are ancient people," Kaz explains, holding back a laugh. The braids that usually lined the sides of his head have been let out, letting his hair hang long and free over his broad shoulders.

"Yeah." I agree.

"Mister Arnsen? We have a report for you." One of the clone healers stuck her long neck out from around the glass wall. We could see her body just inside, pressed against the pane of glass she now leaned on.

"Thank you, Moira. We will be right in."

She nodded her head once, then retreated back inside.

"Locke, you're kind of... for lack of better words... a bull in a China shop? This place is made of glass and has very expensive equipment." He says softly.

"Yeah. I know. I'll be careful!" I chuckled.

I followed behind him, letting him lead the way to what felt like doom; but we didn't go into the room.

Instead, we were led to a very dark, very cold stone office- a direct contrast from Riot's room. There was nothing on the walls. No floor coverings. Nothing to make it warm or homey except a single desk, two chairs and a small light barely able to light the desk beneath its base, much less the whole room.

Kaz takes a seat in one of the uncomfortable looking chairs while I elect to stand, not knowing what we could be about to come up against. Within in moments, the healer I assume was Moira and another one wearing all black entered the small space.

"Thank you both for making your way to us today. We were getting wary of whom we would speak to about the young Blair."

"Thank you. I'm Kaz Arnsen, this is my friend, Locke Montoya." Kaz announces, bowing his head to them.

"Yes, the son of the greatest wolf warrior of all time. We know the Arnsen name well. It is because of your name that Nobility holds you so dearly, regardless of your refusal to wear the status bar. Any friend of yours is a friend of ours."

"Thank you." He says, and it's the most genuine thing I've heard him say all day. You could hear how proud he was.

The ladies bow their heads to him.

"How long has your friend been battling darkness?"

I look at Kaz who's already searching my face for answers. Turns out, neither of us have one. I never considered Riot that way. I thought he was just rough around the edges.

"Tsk, tsk. Such shame it is to lose a good heart to the darkness."

"Lose? Is...is he dying?" I stammer.

"No, not quite. His soul is somehow pulling out into another state of existence when his body is being controlled by his mind flare."

"So his mind is flared then? That's what we were afraid of."

They bow their heads.

"Anything new on the report?"

"Other than the mind flare, no. We don't know how you'll save him, Warrior. We just know you better do it soon. His stay here in Nobility should end sooner rather than later. The longer he's out of his mind, the more his father can take it over. We wouldn't be surprised if you're harboring a ticking time bomb tied directly to the king."

"Right. Well, can his father see we are here?"

"No. However, the longer you stay, the deeper their connection will become, and it could take over even his hearing. It wouldn't be long until he figured it out."

"We would never want to put you at risk. If there's nothing else, we would like to see him." Kaz says, standing.

"Of course. You may go in at any time." Moira says, gesturing towards the door.

I held my breath as we exited the room, waiting for someone to say something else, but no one did.

KAZ

We rushed from the healers as quickly as we could, looking for Sterling and Riley, but they were nowhere to be found. We searched the entire castle for what felt like hours until we ran into Posh and Phaedra in the gardens.

"Kaz! Locke!" Phae yells, running over to us. Posh, hot on her heels.

They wore matching outfits, and I couldn't help but smile. Even here, they matched. Today was some sort of green number. Phaedra in a dress and Posh in slacks, a cream shirt and matching green vest. Along the edges were intricate floral and greenery detailing that sparkled in the daylight.

"I'm so happy you guys are still here." I say, smiling as they reach us.

"We aren't going anywhere. Riley seems to think we will be returning to Meta, not helping."

I nod.

"We won't stop you from joining us. I'm sure Riley could use some real friends around here. She's never been too keen on the friends Riot keeps, even though we are good people." Kaz chuckles.

"Well, *you* weren't at Pleaides," Phae huffs, eyeing Locke.

"You don't know what *they* did to her."

"We were wrong! I can admit that." Locke chuckles, throwing his hands up in surrender.

"Yeah, it's Riley you need to explain it to. Not us." Posh admits.

"We will want to be there though, because I need to hear the excuse myself." Phae adds, elbowing him in the ribs.

"I promise we will. Right now, we need to find Riley and Sterling and get Riot out of here."

The twins nod simultaneously.

"Just tell us what to do." Posh offers.

"We've searched the whole castle, they aren't here."

Phae looks at her brother and juts her head our way. Posh shook his head no relentlessly.

"If you think there's something that you can tell us that's going to help, please divulge it."

Phaedra stares her twin down, her eyes round. I can see she's begging him to say something, but he doesn't give in. Instead, he adjusts his pocket watch and sniffles at her.

"Fine. I'll do it myself." She says, putting her nose in the air.

"Back at Pleaides, after Riot and his band of wild oafs humiliated her, Riley disappeared. For weeks on end. If I'm not mistaken, it was almost months. When Arabia finally found her, she was on her bed and the place looked like she'd been there the whole time. When Arabia asked her where she had been, she said right there. The whole time."

"Woah what the fuck?" Locke breathed.

Phaedra nodded, eyes glistening like she was about to cry at any moment.

"Yeah, so we didn't find her like that though. Arabia did. I hate saying it, but I think we all know Arabia isn't the most trustworthy person around." Posh admitted.

"I understand. However, this time, I think she was telling the truth. I've never seen it for myself, but I've heard many times that something called a gap exists."

"A gap?" they all asked in unison.

"Yes. The gap has only ever been talked about in theory but is quite interesting. Essentially, it's a pocket or a rip in reality where one could exist between timelines, but yet still in tandem with their original one."

They all look at me, perplexed and with questions brewing in their minds. I could practically see the wheels of thought turning in their eyes.

"Could Riley really be in the gap?" Locke asks.

"Not without knowing it, Locke." Phae snaps.

"Actually, she very well could." I interrupt.

Phae and Posh both look gob smacked.

"Tell me, twins. What special talents do butterflies possess?"

PHAEDRA

Before Riley disappeared, she'd come to Posh and I. She warned us. She told us that if she disappeared to come looking. She didn't show up in our rooms, but we both had the same dream. When I ran to Posh, he had the same look embedded in his face that I did. I just knew.

Call it twins, call it just divine knowing. Posh and I have always depended on one another. For everything. We make up where the other lacks. I would be nothing without him, so when he asks me for help, I help.

We met in our garden haven and decided to go. Finding her in Nobility wasn't luck. It was one of the many gifts of our shift. Growing up, it was always hard knowing if people liked us because we both have the gift of entrancement. Butterflies all have some kind of special gift unique to the person, but we *all* have entrancement.

The powder of our wings, when used purposefully, causes a state of in-between. The person we use it on becomes left in a world of their own peace. We typically only do this if we are in extreme danger or if they are beyond help and are dying. It soothes the pain. It distracts from the pain. It's a beautiful and sad gift.

When Sterling found us lurking outside of Nobility, he already knew why we had come. We fluttered to him, landing on his shoulder. The entrancement hadn't worked on him though. He just spoke to us like we were standing there in front of him. He somehow just knew what we were asking. Posh had been extremely thankful to Sterling once he'd given us permission to step foot here.

Now, standing here in front of Riot Blair's friends and thinking about helping them, I couldn't feel more unsure. I didn't want to hurt Riley, but something about Kaz kept me had me trusting him.

"Tell me twins, what special talents do butterflies possess?" he asks, the corners of his mouth tipping up in a smile that made my insides explode.

Kaz Arnsen was handsome, sure. However, the sparks had nothing to do with his looks and everything to do with him seeing my shift as more than just a bug. An insect.

All our lives people have disregarded Posh and I as being nothing more than fragile, delicate and quite frankly, boring. I am over it. Kaz's blatant question made me more over it. It's our time to shine.

I smile back at him, feeling my air element perk up, the wind whipping around my face carrying the scent of Jasmine on its back.

"Something tells me you already know, Kaz Arnsen." I smile, grabbing Posh's arm and linking it with mine.

"Entrancement could really help us, twins. If you're willing."

"For Riley." Posh confirms.

Kaz nods, accepting our answer and takes off towards the healers' quarters again. I excitedly skip along with them. The warriors walk with such definition and purpose as I glide along beside them, my feet barely touching the ground. Being amongst them made me feel just as powerful as I should.

In no time, we stood in front of a glass room, Riot lay inside on a bed. He was in a glass tube, sleeping. I wanted to go in there and punch him right in his perfect asshole of a mouth. Laying there, he looked galaxies away from the kid who'd torn a body in half in front of everyone the first day at Pleaides. He looked quite different.

Laying there, helpless, his green eyes shut, I could almost believe he was a good guy. Someone I needed to help. I preferred to think of him this way instead of the guy who's the son of the terrible king who has ruled my home since I was little. Sure, Pantheon has been a blessing to my family, but the reign of Blair has been a terror on many.

"I can do this," I reassure myself out loud.

"You sure can." Kaz said, appearing next to me.

I shoot him a look of doubt.

"I think you give me more credit than is due."

"I've seen your shift work. I know the beautifully treacherous things you can do. I also know the beautifully noble things you can do as well. It's up to you, Phaedra, the kind of person you want to be."

"I want to be a good friend. I want to be a good sister. Honestly, I want to be the hero." I said and meant it.

"I think if you want to be the hero, then that's exactly what you should be." Kaz leans on the glass, looking at me like he sees the world in my eyes.

"Don't you do that, Kaz Arnsen. Don't you put the weight of this on me. I still may fail."

"I didn't even have to tell you my thoughts, and you knew exactly what I thought about. What I needed from you, and then you offered it without question. You are a hero today and every day that you follow your heart. I think you're going to be more than successful." He said, watching my face.

I nod, willing myself not to cry and square my tiny frame and shoulders to the massive wolf.

"What's the plan?"

Posh and Locke appear next to me, awaiting Kaz's next words. We listened as he filled us in with what the healers said about getting Riot out of Nobility and what happened before Riley and Sterling disappeared.

"So, we need to get him out, but since Riley and Sterling are missing, the only place they could be is within the gap. I don't know that they are stuck, but you guys are going to pull them out."

"Pull them out?" Posh gasps from beside me. I shoved him in the ribs with my elbow again.

"Butterflies can do that?" Locke says looking from Kaz to me and then to Posh.

"More or less," I offer.

Kaz shakes his head.

"It's complicated but basically, only someone with emotional ties to the person in the gap who has entrancement could pull this off."

"Someone like me and Posh. I'm going to do this alone though." I say. I half expected Posh to fight me on this, demanding I should let him help or even just let him.

Instead, he just nodded.

"Thank you." I whisper and he just nods back.

"Alright, let's do this." Locke claps his hands together and we get to work.

Kaz takes care of ending Riot's care with the healers, explaining to the them that we are leaving Nobility. Although their faces remain pretty expressionless, I swear I can see the wave of relief wash over their features simultaneously.

Posh assists with some air magic so we don't have to carry Riot's limp body through the winding staircases and corridors. When we finally get outside again, Kaz leads us to a space in the garden where Posh can set Riot down.

"I don't know where in the gap they could be, but it shouldn't be too hard to find them once you're in."

"I don't know what that means. I have to warn you all, I've only ever used this power once, when my grandfather passed in front of me." I whisper.

Suddenly, I'm terrified to let them down. I look around at them all as I admit my truth out loud.

"Phaedra, you don't have to do anything other than your best." Kaz assures me.

I nod, hoping he's right. Taking a deep breath, I steady myself. My heart races in my chest, but I can feel my element and my shift at my fingertips. Air wraps and weaves itself between my fingers, curling around my wrists and swimming up to my elbows. I shut my eyes tightly, letting it find its place within me. My heartbeat slows and finds a matching rhythm to my element.

I open my eyes, seeing all theirs on me.

"I'm ready."

"We're ready when you are." Kaz reassures.

"Won't she need some kind of anchor or something?" Locke asks Kaz. I assume he was trying not to let me hear as he leaned over and whispered it, but we have great hearing.

"She has me." Posh answers, confidently.

I nod in agreement.

"Okay. We're here for you." Kaz says, giving me the floor.

They all back away as I square my shoulders, walking a few paces from them to the other side of the garden space. There are bubbling fountains and wisteria lining the cobblestone path. At the end is a stone fence and as I turn back towards them, I can feel air kissing my cheeks softly.

I breathe in, rolling my arms like bubbling water from my core until they are up over my head. Air grows excited, urging me on as it builds in my palms, encouraging me to reach for its aid.

I find the part of me that I love the most, reaching deep into the space around me, but it's not enough. There's nothing but the gardens near me. This can't be happening. I can do this.

I can do *this*.

I snap my eyes shut tightly, forcing them that way until it feels like my lids are going to curl over on one another, and force the focus into the space around me. I can feel the spirit of the trees, hear the buzzing of the bees around me, doing their work.

My shoulders sag as I open my eyes again and see their expectant faces. I've not failed, but I don't know how to make it work either. There's something missing. Stomping my way back over to them, I gear up to speak but Kaz beats me to it.

"You need someone more connected to her."

"Yeah, I think so." I agree.

"Would her mate be enough?"

I stare at Locke like he just told me magic isn't real.

"I'm sorry, her *what*?"

Kaz looks at Locke with fire in his eyes and a scowl on his face.

"What? She's going to find out eventually." He answers him.

"You two can not be suggesting that this scum *Blair*, could actually be Riley's *mate*?" My words are laced with poison as I spit them at these... these... I don't even know what they are to me, except for right now, I feel like they are traitors.

"We don't have time-"

"I know that, Posh. I know. Fuck I know." I say, trying to wrap my head around their words.

"Later. Later, you *will* explain this to me." I demand of all of them.

When they all nod simultaneously, gesture for Posh to raise Riot up.

"I'm doing this for Riley, you pompous ass." I whispered in Riot's calm face. He really is gorgeous. He's also really an idiot.

"Okay guys. Let's get this over with. The sooner we can get them out, the sooner we can wake this asshole up, the sooner I can have words with him."

I take my stance again, this time, face to face with my enemy, sending out a final hope to the gods and praying they have all but abandoned me.

KAZ

Telling Phaedra that Riot and Riley were mated probably wasn't the best option, but it was for a just cause. I needed Phaedra to find it within herself to summon whatever she needed in order to pull Riley and Sterling from the gap. Watching her square her shoulders, eyes shut and her lips moving to an incantation only she knew, I prayed I was right about the gap.

I watched alongside Locke and Posh as she brought her hands, palm to palm, rotating them like a babbling brook. She started low, near her stomach, and brought them up over her head for the second time as we all watched.

At first, nothing happened. She looked peaceful as her lips moved in time with silent words. Then, suddenly, I could see it. A glittering wave that flowed like a soft breeze wrapped itself around her wrists. She was glowing in gold, her long white hair swirling around her on rivers of air element that we couldn't see.

Her small feet lifted inches from the ground as she tilted her head back, floating in front of Riot now as he knelt before her, head bowed, eyes still shut. His arms were limp at his sides. If you didn't know any better, you'd think he was maybe kneeling to her.

The glittering streams of gold swirled slowly as if they were in water, speeding up slowly and then all at once. After some time, she brought her hands down in front of her, palms facing Riot. She pulled them apart slowly and as she did, Riot's head tilted back.

Everything silenced, then, with a boom, golden wings, intricate and lacey made of gold glitter exploded from Phaedra's back. They jutted four feet behind her. The hind wings curled down in billows to the ground like sheer satin in the wind. From them, a glittery dust billowed. Once it settled like a fog around her, Phae guided it towards Riot.

As the dust obeyed her command, behind Riot, a golden line began to form. It started about eight feet above his head, traveling downward towards the ground. It trickled, crackling along, sparking glitter and gold in all different directions, but the line stayed straight, perfect. We watched in total awe as she glowed and sparkled.

Once the line was formed, it began to crack, the sounds of winds filling our ears. Thousands of voices on the winds of time filled the air around us. Phae let out a scream as she started pulling her hands apart. As she did so, the golden line pulled apart.

Beams of violet light shot out from different positions in the line as it tore open. Louder and louder, they screamed. The light shot out from more and more places until violet light blocked out the sun. The whole sky was violet, but still, no sign of Riley or Sterling.

"Phaedra!" I yelled over the deafening winds, but she couldn't hear me.

"Kaz! She needs to rip further or turn!" Locke shouted.

"I know!"

He threw an arm up to shield his face as bits of flowers whipped past us, ripped from their stems in the strengthening winds. Locke turned from me, looking through his fingers at Phaedra who was floating higher now, widening the tear.

"Riley!" he called.

I looked around for her but couldn't see her.

"Call for her, man! Maybe they will hear us!" He shouted.

I nodded and ran so that I was facing the tear now. From this side of it, I could see gaping black and cosmos; something I couldn't see from where I stood before.

From here, I could also see Riot's arms. His fingers were turning black. I watched as the darkness snaked around his fingers, traveling up, stopping midway to his elbows. They stopped screaming as black wisps flew from the tear and into the sky. Black lines branched off from the dark glove-like marks, running up towards his shoulders at all kinds of intervals, fire leading the way like a lit fuse.

Suddenly, everything stopped, coming to a complete standstill. The glitter trails exploded like galaxies and floated around us. I could see every speck individually as it floated around our heads. I found Locke, who was now on the other side of Riot, on his knees. Whatever he was doing was interrupted now as he too, took in the glitter and black wisps frozen in the air, like they were painted there.

"Phaedra?" Riley stepped through the tear, eyes wide.

"What's going on here?" Sterling asked, stepping through after her.

"We've been looking for you two,"

"The gap. It's real!" I breathe, cutting Locke off.

"It is." Sterling assured me.

"What's happening? Make her stop!" Riley exclaimed, running up to Phaedra who was still floating there.

"Posh! Pull her out!" I yelled at him.

He nods, taking a stance behind his sister. Lifting his hands, he placed them palm out towards her. He levitated to her height, swirling around her. When he was in front of her, he lifted his hand over her, a silver light forming in his palm. It wasn't glittery like Phaedra's, instead, it was glowing and bright.

As he worked, she tilted her head forward again as Riot's fell and the golden gap started to close behind him. The wisps sucked back into the gap as it formed together flawlessly, disappearing completely behind Riot as Phaedra landed on the floor. The gap closed, just like that, it was gone as though it was never there.

"Phae!" Riley exclaimed, running into her arms.

"Don't ever make me do that again." Phae breathed, returning the hug.

"*Why* did you do that? What's going on?"

"We couldn't find you. We have to leave Nobility right now," I interrupt.

Sterling nods and promptly binds Riot's hands with green light formations.

"Let's go. You can tell us everything on the way."

RILEY

Sterling doesn't understand what it's like to be told you're going to die. He has no idea what I'm feeling and that for whatever reason, doesn't anger me even though I know it should.

The moment we were pulled from the gap, I could have sworn he wanted to kiss me, like it would make me change my mind. I have to admit, Sterling was something else entirely. Even though we didn't do anything other than speak, I felt exposed and guilty standing here in front of my friends.

My friends.

Holy shit.

We left Nobility without saying a word further. Apparently, they'd wasted hours looking for us. If it weren't for Kaz's knowledge, they probably would have left us. Mordechai was the one to lower the gates as we took off, closing the people of Nobility and Gemini Coven inside.

I had to admit that leaving them behind sparked tightness in my chest. I was worried. I didn't want to abandon them, but I had a choice to make. I stood on the edge of Nobility, not feeling very Noble.

"Riley? Are you coming?" Phae asked as the others prepared to cull away from this place for gods knew how long.

I looked back at the pearl gates. Their beauty never ceased to amaze me as they glinted in the sunlight. I had a choice to make right here, right now just as I did when I was back at Pleaides.

How do I always end up having to make choices like this? Why is my life always at a crossroads? My stomach clenched as I made my decision, but Arabia abandoned them first. She abandoned *me*. I did my part. They were safe now.

"Yeah. I'm coming." I say, turning back on the gates, on Gemini Coven, and joining them.

Without another glance, I put my hand in the middle as we all grabbed onto one another. Sterling and I shared the weight of the cull. We didn't have to say where we were going, we just kind of knew. There was nowhere else for us to go except to what I knew.

"Ew where are we?" Posh said, crinkling his nose.

"The Outliers. This used to be my home, so thanks for that." I joke, even though I too, crinkled my nose at the smell.

"Well, well, well. What *do* we have here?"

A slender man with big shoulders, and equally big hands sneers at us from somewhere behind me. We turn collectively, Riot still on the floor behind us. There are three men, all who look weirdly similar but with different features. The talking one had freckles on his cheeks and a black line the started above his strong brows and ended in line with his nostrils over each eye.

"Looks like that chase we were looking for and something to do just fell right into our laps, Kodjo." The white haired one sneered to his leader.

Kodjo, as we learned his name was, nodded to the white-haired boy, his golden eyes fixed on mine.

"Indeed, it does, Rori. Tell us, where are you lot headed?"

"How about you turn around and walk away?" Locke squared up to Kodjo.

"Locke!" Kaz snaps.

The three boys laugh out loud.

"Yeah, Locke. Better listen to your master." The other boy says. His skin is like bark with rings and patches in other hues of golds and browns. His golden eyes blazing with the chase he thinks he's about to have, but I'm not about to give it to him.

"Shut up, Jira!" Kodjo sneers.

"Oh, so *you* actually have a master? That's rich." I smile.

"Shut up, whore! That's the way of the Panthera, you have no idea what you're talking about." Kodjo turns his anger on me.

I can see now his canines are thick and sharp. Sizing them up, I can see they would be a bitch to fight. However, I'm in the mood.

"Panthera? You're *cats*?"

They roar at me in unison, taking a stance like they are ready to pounce when Sterling steps in front of me. Almost instantly, they back off.

"I wouldn't do that if I were you." His voice is calm, but firm.

"This bitch doesn't know her place." He growls.

"I would subside from the name calling as well, as this *woman* may be the key that saves everyone. Including you."

"Why would we care?" Jira sneers, his lip quivering like he could barely contain his excitement.

Kodjo slaps a hand to Jira's chest and like they had some kind of telepathy, I watched them all look behind our legs. The wheel of understanding plays across their faces.

"We care because we got more than a chase, Jira. We care because we got the chance, at the crown." Kodjo sneered.

As the word left his lips, I learned very quickly why they called them Panthera. The three of them simultaneously shifted into their respective big cats. Kodjo, a tiger. Rori, a snow leopard and Jira, a Jaguar. They're massive, their paws deadly weapons alone.

"Fuck." Was all I heard as Kaz erupted into a wolf beside me.

Thankfully, he was larger than the three of them. They entered a standoff, Kaz snarling as he paced back and forth in front of us. Sterling straightens his back, and I can feel him pulling the energy around us to him.

"You don't want to do this Kodjo," I say, warning the tiger that stood in front of me. Even with Kaz's massive frame pacing back and forth, I could still see the Panthera trio. Their eyes were glowing with the possibility of a better life, the hairs on their backs raised as their tails flicked behind them in warning.

"He's not worth it. King Blair will *never* give you that crown, even if you did kill him, and even then, you'd have to also kill all of us." I try, but he's not listening, his eyes planted directly on Riot's unconscious body.

"He's not listening, Riley!" I hear Phaedra call out.

"Then let's do this!" Locke yells, erupting into a towering Minotaur. Normally, Locke was massive. This was massiveness on a whole other level.

With his declaration, the Panthera trio pounced, Jira going right for Locke. Kodjo took on Kaz and Rori circled us.

"Come on, Rori. I don't want to do this, but if you're going to make me, then I will." I say, low enough that only he can hear. I can see in his eyes that maybe he doesn't really want to fight, but he continues to circle us anyways.

I can feel Sterling as he approaches us. Phae, Posh and I all stood, protecting Riot. I was grateful for him making his way over to us. Rori looked like he realized that he was outnumbered, but before I could say or do anything, Sterling hit him with a formation that sent him flying.

"No!" I screamed, but it was too late and in seconds, Kaz and Kodjo were pressing into us, lost in a whirl of teeth and blood. Their snarls and growls echoing around us.

"Why did you do that?" I yelled at Sterling.

"He wasn't touching you. That's my job, Riley, to protect you."

Kaz tore into Kodjo and sent him tumbling across the grass. He paced again until Kodjo got up, then took off, charging him.

"I don't care! I don't need you to fight my battles for me, Sterling!" I yell.

"Um, guys?"

I can hear Posh, but I don't pay him any mind as I lay into Sterling more.

"I'm not useless. I'm not fragile!"

"I know that, star girl, I-"

"Stop calling me that!"

"Guys," Posh tries again.

"It's a nickname."

"My name is Riley." I demand.

"Okay, star girl, I'll try and remember that." Sterling seethes.

"Are you joking?"

"Guys,"

"Not even a little."

I have to physically stop myself from punching him in his smug, beautifully stupid face.

"Guys!"

"What?" We snap in unison.

"Now probably isn't the time- duck!" Posh yells and we all hit the ground as rock goes flying past us.

"What the fuck?" I yell, covering my head.

Kaz and Kodjo are shifted again, Kaz on top of him, naked, pounding

Kodjo's face in. I watch for a moment in horror before I can get up.

"Kaz!"

"Riley, stop!" Phae exclaims, grabbing for my ankles as I manage to get away.

"Kaz stop, you'll kill him!" I scream, pulling at his massive, sweaty shoulders.

He doesn't stop, though. Instead, he thrusts out a hand towards me, blasting me with a heavy stream of water. I sputter, trying to catch my breath and push back against it.

"Kaz!" I yell when he finally stops and goes back to punching Kodjo.

"Riley!" Phae calls out again.

I don't stop to see where she is or if she's rushing towards me before I throw a dome of energy over us to keep everyone away. I pulled at him again, to no avail.

"Fine! You chose this, you mongrel!" I scream, blasting energy into him. He flew into the air, hitting my dome and falling to the floor.

"I'm sorry." I apologized to him as I rushed to Kodjo's side.

"You should have let me, Riley! He was getting what he deserved!" He screamed.

"You killing him isn't what *you* deserve, Kaz! Do you really want to live with that?"

"I don't care! I made promises!"

"I know you did, so did I! Mindless killing is off the table. You want me to help you, then agree." I demand.

His hair was dirty and a mess. I could visibly see the knots. It was a stark contrast to the way he usually looked. His body was slick with sweat, dirt and blood as he heaved, thinking of my words.

"You're something else."

"Agree."

"Fine, I agree. But I can't promise not to protect you guys. I'll always do what I have to."

"What you have to is one thing. Blurring those lines and going haywire until you kill someone, is something else entirely."

"You're not what I expected, Riley."

"Good. Now, help me." I say, kneeling next to Kodjo.

He passed out long ago and his face is barely recognizable. He looks almost nice when his face isn't laced with the excitement of a hunt. There are multiple bite marks and gashes from Kaz's claws along his body, but I can still make out shallow yet steady breaths.

"He's alive." I confirm, lowering the shield as Posh, Phae and Sterling rush to my side.

"I've got this." Phae promises as she and Posh immediately get to work, placing their hands over his wounds. I watch as golden glitter forms under Phae's hands and silver under Posh's.

"Where's Locke?" I asked Sterling, suddenly realizing he's not joined us yet. His eyes widened in horror, and we ran back towards where the fight started.

Sure enough, Locke was there, standing over Jira.

"I'm sorry, he was going to kill me." Locke wipes blood from his face, his voice quivering.

"It's fine, don't worry." I say, kneeling to check Jira's lifeless body.

He was long gone. Sterling led Locke away, back towards the others as I spotted Riot, still unconscious. I hadn't had a moment alone with him since that night in the club, I realized as I approached him. A night, I forced myself not to think about as much as possible. Looking over my shoulder, I half expected Sterling to be marching his way back over to me to stop me or mediate the interaction, but he wasn't.

Clearly, he was occupied with something else and that was my cue to proceed. Keeling down next to Riot, I sensed his breathing picking up pace. I hadn't touched him since that night either, and I was half surprised at how badly my hand was shaking as it hovered over his bicep, waiting for my brain to command it to meet his skin.

I could feel the magnetism of our connection swirling with the electricity of Sterling inside me, creating a supercharged feeling.

'Touch him.' I command my brain.

Before I could, Riot sat up straight, gasping for air.

STERLING

I felt him wake like a boulder slamming into my gut. The twins were busy not only saving Kodjo's life, but also calming Locke as I searched for Rori when I felt Riot wake.

It took everything in my body to not go running to Riley, and to bite down the jealousy like bile as I felt their connection rekindle like a pilot light.

Was it jealousy?

Never having felt something like that before, I couldn't be too sure. What I *am* sure of is that the longer I stay here on this sentence, the longer I am becoming like them. Feeling what they feel. I've not sent word home in months, nor have they checked. The stars still whisper to me, so I'm not worried, but I'm concerned no one has reached out.

Being abandoned by them would be devastating, but it's happened before. I can't think about it now, though because all I can feel is her connection to *him* and I can't stand it. Maybe I shouldn't have said they were mated, but it flew out of my mouth before I could help it. I always tell the truth, say what's on my mind.

I don't find Rori, but I could care less. To give her more time, I check on the others first, which proves to be a mistake as well.

"Sterling! We can't stay here much longer. Kodjo's awake and he's warned us that more are coming. The hunt for Riot is on and everyone is hungry for blood." Phae says, leading me away from the others.

"Phaedra, they've been after him for months now. We've not died yet." I say, trying not to sound annoyed.

"I know, I remember the announcement."

"Announcement?" I ask. She shakes her head at me, her big eyes focused.

"Yes. He came to Pleaides and made the announcement in front of the whole school. He came three times, each time bargaining a new prize. First, it was money. Then he opened it to all of Meta and offered the crown."

"And the last announcement?" I ask, fearing the answer.

"He just added money to the pot." She lied. I could feel it.

"Phaedra Poplin, I know you're not lying to a Nobelist." I eye her.

"Okay he offered the money, and something called a Bayldonite crown."

My heart lurches into my throat. I haven't heard those words in centuries. Bayldonite was the bane of my existence at one point. Aene and his selfishness almost cost us everything.

"You're sure he said *Bayldonite*?" I ask, unable to let it go. My mind is slipping on the word.

"I'm sure. I've never heard another word like it. I wouldn't forget it." She promises.

I nodded, keeping my face unemotional as my stomach found its home in my throat. Blair couldn't possibly have Bayldonite anything. The last time it was destroyed, its pieces were hidden and only a few people knew of their hiding places. This was done to keep them safe and away from the mortals.

He's bluffing. He wants Riot dead, but why? What's his endgame? Before I had time to question Phaedra any further, a rumbling sound filled the air. Motorcycles pulled up to the clearing as far as the eye could see.

"Phaedra, get to the others." I demand her. She obeys, eyes wide and face pale.

Nervously, I look around for Riley and Riot and see that he's standing now, talking to her, but my view of them is quickly obscured by the throng of heavily armored men in front of me.

"We heard the heir is back. Where is he?" their leader boomed in my face.

He and his clan of misfits all wore dark leathers, carrying weapons I hadn't seen in Meta in ages.

"I suppose you think you're going to all get a piece of the crown?" I sneer, turning my attention back to them.

He laughs and it booms across the clearing as Phae, Posh and Locke appear somewhere behind me. I can sense the Panthera not far off behind them, but even if they would stand in this fight on our side, they were in no position to do so. Having just been healed from near death will have them weak.

"None of your business. Look, you can throw the heir to us, and we will be on our way, or, you can fight us, die and then we will take him by force. The choice is yours, but we don't have all day. It's a one-time offer, so hurry up and decide." He spits.

With what was going on between Riot and Riley, it would be in my best interest to throw him to this pack of hyenas, as I confirmed they were by the patches each one of them wore on their person, and leave. Run away with Riley and get her the help she needs.

She would never forgive me, though. Even if it *were* Riot Blair. I would never forgive myself, if I'm being honest. I inhale sharply and force myself to chuckle with them. When the leaders' eyes are on me again, I pull him in, dragging his mind with me to the depths of a hell specially curated for him, by him. The images I was granted access to as I delved deeper and deeper into his mind became ammunition for the hell he was seeing himself in. I'd driven many men to madness this way, effectively causing them to do the job for me, but this one tasted so much better than those.

"Stop! What are you doing to him?" His right hand called out as his leader dropped to the floor, foaming at the mouth.

Terror lived all over his face and quickly spread like a pandemic to the others, but instead of fleeing they drew their weapons and took a fighting stance.

"For Isaiah!" the friend yelled.

At his words, they moved to charge me, but before they could, my wings burst from their holds, blasting them back like twigs in a tornado. I hoisted myself into the air, looking over the mass of tumbling bodies for Riley, but she'd already found me and was staring, mouth wide open as bodies landed around her.

RILEY

After Riot finally caught his breath, the bikers pulled up and before we can even react, they're threatening our peace. Sterling blasted the bikers away from him, sending them bruised and angry over Riot and I. New abilities show up for me almost weekly at this point, so I'm not really all that surprised when a blast of air propels me up and away from the men being tossed our way. I search the grounds for Sterling, and when I find him, he looks the way I've only ever seen him in the gap.

His eyes are fully silver, fully on me, his wings spread wide. They had to be at least six feet. His skin mimicked the stars, his beauty unmatchable. When our eyes met, it was like everything slowed down, frozen in time.

"Riley!" Riot shouted.

I don't think I've ever heard him actually use my name before, but hearing it now made that magnetic feeling explode. I looked down at him, his expression confused as I floated down to meet him.

"Riot, I-" I'm cut off by one of the bikers shouting as he swings a bat with nails poking out of it over his head at us. I grab Riot without thinking, pushing him behind me as I blast the guy with my other hand.

Water and rock slam into him, sending him back, as more of his men come forward, aiming for Riot. I blasted them quickly, one after the other, away from us. Until they are so far across the clearing, I have time to speak between each attack.

"Move towards Sterling, let's go!" I shout, this time blasting fire then air at a man wielding an axe. They had to be a gang from the Outliers. Not one was attacking back with magic.

"What do we do?" I shouted at Sterling once we reached him. He had just blasted four men away, his powerful wings splayed out around him. He tucked them in and opened his mouth to say something, but the voice that answered wasn't his own.

"We fight."

I turn in the direction of the voice and am surprised when I see it's Tambo. Behind him, Gemini Coven, only there were more. People I'd never met and faces of all kinds. Words escaped me.

"We left you in Nobility," Phae breathed.

"Indeed, you did. However, our coven is one of permanence. We help each other." Tambo said plainly.

"We can talk about this later. Right now, we have a fight." He smiled. I nodded in agreement. We needed him and the coven and if they were here to help, I was in no place to question it.

With that, Tambo gave orders to his people. They acted immediately as we took on the men using magic, formations and pure strength. In minutes the fight that would have taken us hours was over and we made our way through the tangled sprawl of corpses strewn about, assessing the damage.

Sterling stood over one in particular, shaking his head. His arms were crossed over his broad chest, one hand on his chin as he stared.

"Sterling? Are you okay?" I asked, suddenly very aware that at any moment, more could show up.

"I'm fine. He's not." he says, gesturing towards the mangled body on the floor.

I roll my eyes as the others chuckle uncomfortably in varying tones. Without Gemini Coven we would still be fighting. I look around as everyone gathers around us. It looks like everyone is here. Tambo must see the questions on my face because he smiles and holds out a closed fist to me.

I place my palm under it and into it, he drops the ring I got the first day at Pleaides. There are still holes where stones should be, but the metal is cool against my skin. Tambo's eyes are plastered to me as he watches me recognize what he's given me as I turn it around in my hands.

"This ring brought us to you." He says.

I feel like a bug under a magnifying glass as I realize that everyone around us is watching and listening. Including Riot Blair.

"I don't understand," was about all I could manage.

"It's okay. You don't have to, but you will begin to. When you decided in your heart that you were going to try, the ring woke up. It knows you, Riley. Knows your spirit."

"How is that possible?"

"It was made entirely for you, by the universe. You are the chosen host of Ophiuchus. Not because you've gotten so close to Death herself, or because you were always destined to be alone, but because you've overcome those things. Because you were given an impossible life and no matter what, you have *always* overcome the task."

I run my thumb over the gilded edges, and notice something pooling into the bottom of one of the holes along one of the vines. It fills slowly, a deep blue taking the place of the dark silver that once was there. When it finishes, a beautiful blue stone sits there. As it catches the light, a white star is formed. I twist and turn it, watching in awe as the star follows the light.

"Star Sapphire." Tambo says, watching in awe himself.

"What's that mean?"

"It's the stone of destiny." He whispers, but somehow, everyone can still hear him. I can feel them pressing in, waiting to hear what either of us will say next, but I don't have words.

I just continue to turn the stone this way and that, taking in its beauty.

What now?

What's next?

I said I'd help all my friends and the coven, but what I didn't consider was how. I don't have answers or steps and I've never been relied on so heavily before. These people are looking for answers. For a leader. I raise my eyes to Tambo's smiling face.

"You're the leader we're looking for. Nothing happens by mistake. He assures me as if he could hear my thoughts.

"Okay. I'll do it. Whatever it takes. I'll do it."

Tambo smiles, his eyes glistening. It was like I had just given him the key to his whole existence. All of them, collectively shifted, as though I'd saved all of them, even though I felt like I'd just condemned myself.

The movement was slight, but enough to shift the energy that Sterling, the twins, Locke, Kaz and even Riot looked around at the faces that surrounded us. Every member of the coven clasped their hands together, standing as one around us. A symbol of unity.

One.

STERLING

As the coven gathered around us, the feeling of hopelessness left the space. I watched as Riley turned in place, taking in the faces around her. Cataloging them in her mind. There had to be somewhere to keep all of these people safe while I figure out how to proceed in all of this. Riot's father was actively looking for us and no doubt someone would have heard the fights we just overcame.

We are tired. We are bruised. We need a place to call home, even if it's temporary. There's a place I was promised eons ago by my home, Perdition. A place where all history comes to a head for Meta. Pleaides is more than a university to hone abilities beyond your wildest dreams, it's a piece of history. A place of pure magic.

"I have a place that would serve us. It was promised to me eons ago. I know for a fact they will be willing to serve and help."

"How could you possibly know that for a fact if it was so long ago?" Phae demanded.

"Because it's a place where they would want Ophiuchus to survive."

Riley surveys my face, searching for the answer.

"Take us there. At this point, I don't care where it is. It just needs to house all of us and it needs to be able to be protected." She stands tall, shoulders back, waiting to see if I'll do as she says or not.

I bow slightly to her, promising her everything within the small gesture. Even though she couldn't read my mind, I felt her warmth of understanding flood through me. It was to soon to know for sure, but I felt like we understood each other, and in our own way, had our own connection.

"I wouldn't do it any other way."

I grabbed onto Locke and Kaz, feeling the members of the coven placing hands on my shoulders. When they were all touching, ending with Riley, I culled us. Her eyes never left mine, even in the gaps as they all swirled around us.

We landed hard in the middle of bright green grass, the smell of apples and sweet honeysuckle filling our noses.

"Pleaides?" Locke sounded exasperated.

"Yes. Regardless of what you think of it, it has been promised to Perdition whenever the time of Ophiuchus was prevalent."

He rolls his eyes. I'd have thought him rude if it weren't for the smirk on his face. Riley stepped out of the circle of us, looking around as if she was seeing Pleaides for the first time.

"It's... different." She whispers.

"Let's head in, the Archetypes should be waiting for us." I lead them all towards the main castle. Gasps of appreciation and awe fill the air as those who've never seen this place take it all in. Riley walks by my side, head up, shoulders squared. Riot, on her other side. His eyes meet mine as we both look at her, but she's unphased by us.

Pleaides is quiet, all of its attendees having gone home for the summer now. The Archetypes should be in their wing, watching over the grounds. A few of the staff remained.

"I'll go with you." Riley offered.

I nod, knowing there's no point in arguing with her. Locke and Kaz have already busied themselves with Tambo and figuring out accommodations for everyone. I figure Riley escorting me to see the Archetypes shouldn't be a problem. We head off towards the main castle without saying a word, enjoying the silence. The various stairs and archways providing beautiful scenery as we go.

"Tell me something," she mumbled, startling me out of my thoughts.

"Anything."

"Why would the Archetypes hand this place over?"

I sighed, not wanting to lurch into the long winded explanation of the past. It was full of lies, deceit and promises unkept.

"It's a long story."

She sighed.

"What I will tell you now is that long ago, amiss all that crap, were the

Archetypes. Back then, Pleaides was the central hub of the Zodiacs. This main castle housed the Cardinal signs. The night the betrayal happened, was the night the Archetypes were called forward by the cardinals. Statler was the name of the Capricorn Lord. He feared that nothing would be left."

We reached the top of the main stairs, stopping on the landing. The wind blew Riley's long hair around her face. She looked at me with inquisitive eyes.

"He was the one who started the war?"

"Not exactly. It's said that Marcella, the Scorpio Lordess and Statler shook on opposing views, thus launching us into this war."

"I've had this feeling that the war never ended."

"It hasn't. It's merely gone dormant as the people learned how to live again. How to just keep to their own."

"And the division of Meta?"

I shrug. I don't really have an answer for her.

"The kings. They thought of the humans as scum. Diseased and below them. They of course, branched into their own mindset of who was better. There were many fights and displays of power to decide who belonged in their new world."

"In Pantheon?"

I nod.

She nodded in tandem as the huge oak doors swung open. The Archetypes stood before us, wide eyed. It was clearly written on their faces that they knew why we stood here now.

"Sterling. Welcome back, Riley."

"Thank you. You know why I'm here."

They bow their heads serenely.

"It is yours. We knew this time would come. We are just happy it's a promising student."

"Promising?" Riley practically spat the words at them. I felt my eyes widen at her display. No one ever questioned the Archetypes and her blatant disrespect sent shivers up my spine. I think I love her.

"You never once visited me or answered a single question I had while I was here. In fact, I doubt you even knew I left the grounds with Arabia that day. It's been months."

The Archetypes looked between her and I, gauging whether or not I agreed with her. I kept my face as puzzled as it probably was when Riley started speaking.

"We don't need to babysit you, Riley. You were talked about relentlessly by your peers."

She scoffed, rolling her eyes.

"Yeah, about being trash right?"

"Actually, no. Quite the opposite. They adored you. When you went missing, many of them offered to help, despite the king's announcements and offers of luxury."

"Those announcements were for his son, Riot. Not for me."

"If they were for Riot, they were equally for you."

Riley just stared. I couldn't tell if she wanted to laugh or cry, but her energy was pulsing, flooding with every emotion until it landed on something that tasted like a cross between disbelief and uncertainty.

"Archetypes, you said that they were willing to help Riley. Where are the ones who expressed such sentiments now?"

The Archetypes look relieved to have a subject change presented to them. They bow their heads in thanks before answering.

"Most of them are home, but we can gather them."

I nod.

"Thank you. That will be most helpful. In the meantime, past your departure, I'll be shielding this place. You'll need to present yourselves and your elemental signature to get back in."

They nod, accepting the instructions.

"We will leave right away."

With that, they walked past us, making their way out of the castle. Locke and Kaz run up the stairs, staring at each other as the Archetypes pass them by.

"What was that all about?" Kaz asks, glistening in sweat.

"Why are you sweaty?" Riley counters.

"The Archetypes just handed over Pleaides."

"Good shit. You guys wanna come train with us? Kaz spent time a few months back teaching us connection formations and Riot never got his shot at him so they are gonna fight now." Locke said, jumping from foot to foot in place.

"I'd pay money to watch Kaz hand Riot's ass to him on a platter." Riley chortles.

"I wouldn't be so sure, Star Girl. Riot is pretty mighty when he's at his fullest potential." I reassured her.

Locke boomed a laugh as he stopped jumping.

"Star Girl?"

"Watch it, Minotaur." Riley snapped.

"Hey, easy! I'm just saying it suits you." Locke defended.

"Lighten up a bit, will you? We're all on the same side."

I watch as Riley's features soften into understanding. It looked like it was the first time she had ever considered that people were on her side.

"Right. Okay, I'm down."

"Cool, let's go." Locke said, hopping from foot to foot again before he took off down the stairs.

"You coming?" She asked as Kaz took off after Locke.

"Yeah, I'm going to cull there though, unless you're up for a run?"

She laughed, for real this time. I couldn't help taking her into my arms and staring right into her brown eyes that mimicked the soil as I culled us to the clearing.

RILEY

Sterling grabbed me by the waist so unexpectedly I didn't have time to react. When we landed in the clearing, Locke and Kaz were arriving and everyone was looking as I pushed away from Sterling. Riot leaned against a rock, his arms crossed, joint in hand. Smoke clouded around his face, his green eyes plastered on Sterling and I.

Kaz rounded the clearing that I now recognized was the grassy area just outside of Glistening Cove. My stomach lurched as the memory of the water flooding my lungs that night returned with a vengeance. I shook my head, needing to move and walked abruptly over to where Locke stood. He was the furthest from the coves entrance and at least he wasn't Riot.

"Hey Chica! Oh sorry, do you prefer star girl now?"

I glared at him and he raised his hands in surrender as if to say sorry just as Kaz took a stance in front of Riot. I turned my attention to him, wanting nothing more than for Locke to forget he ever heard Sterling's nick name for me.

"I didn't get to do this back in the arena, but I'm ready now." Riot taunted.

"Are you? It's merely for practice, but I think you're taking it as more serious." Kaz laughed.

"I'll show you how serious I am. Let's do this."

"I think since we are doing this, we might as well make it educational, no?"

"No." Riot chortled, flinging out a hand towards Kaz.

We all waited but nothing happened. Something that kind of looked like a mirage flowed out of Riot's palm, but no elements. Shocked, he pulled his hand back, inspecting it.

"What the fuck?" He exclaimed.

"Seems like you're not so ready after all. Your father's mind flare has weakened you, leaving you defenseless and without magic."

"I am *not* weak." Riot countered, his voice gruff and angry.

"Aren't you though? Only someone so weak wouldn't notice the presence of someone else in their most intimate of spaces; their own minds."

Kaz was surprisingly good at taunting the beast within Riot. Even I felt a bit triggered at his words. I don't know why they bothered me, other than what Sterling had said about us being mated. I shuddered at just the thought of something like that.

"Shut up." Riot breathed.

A sickening smile crossed Kaz's face.

"What's wrong Riot? Feeling a little weak?" Kaz teased.

Riot screamed, thrusting his hands into a formation this time, relying on the energy around him. Again nothing happened as he thrust them in front of himself. Everyone shifted uncomfortably. I could sense that no one had seen Riot not get what he wanted when he wanted it. Part of me wanted to rejoice at knowing that he had now felt the way he'd made so many feel before.

However, my chest pinged with sorrow for him. It was sad to watch him struggle. Part of me wanted to help him. Before I knew what I was doing, my feet were carrying me across the field and away from my safe spot next to Locke.

Kaz looked as confused as the others. Sterling sat up straight from the lounging position he'd been in on a nearby boulder. The twins clasped hands, watching and holding their breaths.

"What are you doing?" Riot glowered.

I didn't have an answer for him. It was my gut fueling my actions, not my mind because everything in my head told me to stop. To walk back over to Locke and sit my happy ass down.

I didn't budge.

Instead, I turned shoulder to shoulder with him, lacing my fingers between his. When our palms met, it was magnetic. Like nothing in this universe could pull us apart. I swallowed hard, trying to ignore the stares and gaping mouths just as much as I tried to ignore the heat building between our touching shoulders.

"Try again." I managed to shout out to Kaz, despite my throat being dry.

He shut his mouth, nodding. This time, he didn't speak. He made a formation, one I recognized. It was a simple one we'd learned on the first day of formations class. He brought his palms together, like he was praying. Then, he turned them outwards towards us. The simple motion should send a blast of air towards us; a perfect warning.

I willed Riot to throw his free hand out, making a shield and did the same with mine. Simultaneously, he did it and I watched in awe as Kaz's simple attack bounced off our invisible barrier making energy waves as it did so.

Sterling's mouth gaped open.

"No fucking way." Kaz breathed.

I had no idea this would work, but it did. Riot turned to me, his green eyes looking down on me. I never noticed he was so much taller. So much broader. He was a predator and I, his prey. That smell of coffee and bourbon infiltrated my nostrils, burning their way to my inner self along a path they carved out long ago.

From the corners of my eyes, I could see everyone rushing in towards us, their faces looking odd and not quite the way they had moments ago. Was it horror? Was it something else? Before I could look at them though, I was sucked into darkness. I can't see anything around me, but I can feel Riot's hand still in mine.

With my other hand, I feel for his arm, but there's nothing there. I can smell him, *feel* him. My heart starts racing and I concentrate on my breathing. I'm not afraid of darkness.

"Riot?" My voice echoes.

"Riley." He answers back.

"Wh-what's going on? I can't see anything." I sound pathetic even to myself.

"This is who you are." He says.

"It's not."

"It is. Why don't you just say how you really feel?"

"I-I don't know what you mean."

Although I can't see him, I can feel his sneer. See his perfect teeth in my mind. I can sense him looking me up and down. I want him to stop, to walk away like he did that day in elementals, but I also didn't want to let go of his hand. I clenched down tighter. I would bet anything my fingertips were stark white against his olive skin.

"Sure you do. It's the reason you're clutching to me so hard right now."

I loosen my grip.

He chuckles.

"Think about it Riley. It's always creeping in the corners of your mind. It's always there, lurking. You want it."

"No, I don't."

He laughs again. It's a laugh filled with knowing and confidence.

"Yes, you do. You think about it all of the time. You don't give in, but you keep it there on the edge of your tendrils. Enough that you can taste it, but far enough away that you can convince yourself-"

"I'm a good person, Riot and that's all I want to be!" I cut him off.

"Why do you think that having darkness makes you not a good person?"

"Look at you. Look at your father. I don't want that." I cry.

"My father is pathetic and evil. Darkness has nothing to do with that."

I thought for a moment. He stumped me. Darkness *is* different than being evil. We were taught that magic is neutral with Classique. That it was the intention of the wielder that made magic what it was, but I am *nothing* like him.

"How do you know all of this?"

I swear I can feel his breath on my neck.

"Because I have it too. Because we are the same. Because ever since the day in that club, I haven't been able to stop thinking about you. Something happened that night. Something that changed everything."

I have to admit even to myself that yes, everything changed that night; for me too.

"Darkness sits in the corners of your mind."

"I don't want it to." I whisper, unable to deny it any longer. He's in my head. He knows as well as I do that what he's saying is true. I come undone, feeling the heat build behind my eyes.

"It always has. Those feelings you have of always being alone is darkness."

"It's not. It's depression."

"What's the difference?"

He stumped me again. My eyes dart around trying to make out any object I can, to put myself in a location. The knot in my throat growing tighter. I've been stupid. Trusting Arabia and Elliot. Coming to Pantheon. Being a spice runner. I've been careless. Reckless. There's not a word for what I've truly been. With my free hand, I feel out into the abyss, the fingers of my free hand grasping at the darkness.

"I don't want to play your games, Riot. Let me out of here."

"It's not me doing this. It's you."

"I'm not doing anything. Stop it *now*." I demand him.

This time, I feel his grip tighten on *me*. For some reason, it calms me immediately, offering comfort. Offering stability.

"I promise you, it's not me. You brought me here. You figure out why."

I think on it. If this really was me, I wouldn't be surprised. In my head, I always feel like I'm losing control. Like my grip on reality was becoming more and more blurred with visions of a life I've never lived, pieces of me falling apart. Maybe I'll *never* live the lives I've seen in glimpses of Ophiuchus. In visions that could be.

"What's the truth, Riley?"

Maybe I'd really brought us here. Maybe I'd brought us here to show Riot something. What exactly, though, I'm not sure. I know deep down that all I've ever wanted was someone to love me. To be enough for someone. To be the one someone fights for.

To fight for us?

Definitely to fight for me.

"What did you come here to show me?"

It is time. Maybe Riot Blair wasn't the one I thought I'd be vulnerable with, but maybe it *is* time. Maybe I should take a chance. Maybe he would care. Perhaps, he *does* know what it's like to go through this. I've pushed everyone away who dared get too close.

"The truth is..." I start, my voice small.

He clenches my hand and I clench back, the comfort allowing me the courage to say my truth.

"The truth is...I'm scared, Riot. It's dark. *I'm* dark..."

There it was. Big bold and loud. The truth. I'm dark. I'm afraid of the dark and not in a childish kind of way. I'm afraid of *my* dark. I don't want to be alone. I don't want to be a bad person. Hosting Ophiuchus gives me both hope for the future and fear of becoming something I'm not even sure I'm capable of being.

The thoughts started swirling in my mind, creating a whole new branch of darkness. I feel it tip up and away from me, towards a cluster of stars I could see in my minds eye. As I try to focus on them, the vision disappears. A whole new storm of madness. I want to clasp my hands over my ears as voices flood them, taking place of the vision. There were so many. Voices of those before and those to come. Pain seared through my head but the darkness didn't subside.

I don't want to be stuck.

I can be dark, and good.

"Stars can't shine without darkness, Riley."

As if Riot Blair had spoken words that were my remedy, the voices disappeared with a boom. Time stood still when he spoke and I felt myself fold into him, our souls rolling one over the other. We meshed in a way that made us into one giant pool of cosmos and elements, but at the same time, staying wholly ourselves.

There's magic in being able to mesh with someone so fully and without boundaries but still remaining who you are. Here, we are stripped of the things that separate us in reality. No race, no time, no Ophiuchus. No one expecting me to save them or give them answers I don't have. Just him. Just me.

Without words, without gestures, it was like our souls had made the divine commitment to one another, without any permission. Without any witnesses. Here, there was nothing stopping us. All that our past was made of didn't exist. Images from lives we'd lived before and had yet to live invaded my mind, pushing the darkness out more and more until all I could see was white.

It's blinding light showed promises of a life right now. A life of *happiness*.

I want *you*.

Without warning, we were thrown onto the wet grass. The sun was asleep and the moon was out, singing her curses. There I laid, next to Riot fucking Blair. On our backs, looking up at the stars.

Our friends faces, looking down at us.

RIOT

I'm laying on the dirty ground, next to her.
Her.
The stars in front of us like they were clusters of everything we *could* be. Lives in sparkling, fiery versions of uncertainty and hope. Everything I'd ever worked to be is gone from my mind.

I don't care if I'm powerful or the king.
I don't care that my father is out to kill me.

The only thing I care about is her; the fire of what I just felt more fulfilling and powerful than *anything* I've ever felt in my entire life. This kind of power is different, though. Somehow, it's not the power I'd come to know and crave all my life. This was power in a new form; a form I could get *high* off of.

I sigh, a stupid smile crossing my lips. I don't even care that my back is getting more and more damp the longer I lay here. I don't care that anyone could see me here with her. It's bliss.

"Riot? Riley? Are you guys okay?" I can hear a voice off in the distance, but I can't quite make out who's talking.

"I think they are tranced." That's Locke. I would know his stupid voice anywhere.

"We aren't tranced." Riley. I would know *her* voice anywhere.

I feel her move beside me. Her hair brushing my arm as she gets up. I want to tell her no, fight her for just a few more stolen moments as I feel her grab my hands, pulling me to my feet.

"Riot, snap out of it." She demands.

I can feel the haze in my head clear away at her command instantly. The haze is different from the fog my father causes. It's more clear. I feel level headed. Normally, I'm chasing this type of clarity with fae shrooms, but here, with her? She does that for me.

Kaz's question from before replays in my head.

What do you feel, Riot?

For the first time in my life, I have an answer to that question, and the first person I want to tell it to, is Riley.

"I'm here." I say. I looked at her, taking in her face. It was different somehow. Not quite the way it had been before, but I can't quite put my finger on it.

"What the fuck just happened?" Riley was looking past me at Sterling, demanding answers even though her face registered fear and knowing. I can almost sense her energy, frantic and erratic.

I turned around to see he too, looked different to me. Sterling shrugged, his face shallow and filled with Melancholy.

"Divine Connection."

Fuck.

STERLING

A Divine Connection is the worst possible outcome for me when it comes to Riley and Riot's relationship. It's a rare occurrence. So rare in fact, that I've only seen one ever in all my time, although many have happened.

Divine Connections are chosen by the universe itself. It's more than being mated. It's more than a marriage. It's more than love. It's the end of my world. She's not mine. It's the worst type of rejection I think I could ever have felt. It's not because we don't mesh or we tried to be together and couldn't, it's because the universe made her perfectly. For him.

For *him.*

Not me.

The evidence of betrayal by my own was made evident on Riot's face. Thin black lines in the shape of a crescent moon starting above his thick brow on the right and curling itself around, ending below his eye. The lines kissed with tiny stars along specific intervals. Her star cluster, Aries. It's over. I can't even look at her, the fear of knowing what I'll find thrumming inside my chest. A matching tattoo from the universe, a permanent mark that can't be undone. His cluster.

I sneak a glance at her, searching her temples as she talks to Phae, but there's nothing on either side of her face. Maybe there is hope. I know it's not her fault. I know it wasn't even her choice, but the hole carving itself out in my chest, shattering, exposing the blackness within proved this didn't bother me in the least.

At least, that's what I'm telling myself.

"Sterling?" Phaedra's warm hand lightly touched my arm, making me jump.

A cold crystal slid down my cheek. I assume it was the equivalent to a human tear. Pathetic. I am becoming pathetic. I am a demon of Perdition. A superior galaxy to this one. A cluster so profound and beautiful that the colors there alone don't even exist within this galaxy.

Of all my time, of all my wars and trials and tribulations, a mere human girl would be my undoing? No. Riley is a grain of sand in the hourglass of time. She wouldn't be the grain to break *me*. Even as I'm thinking it though, my chest pangs back at me, searing me with every word. I know that it's the opposite, but for now, I'm going to pretend it's the truth.

"Sterling?"

I smile at Phaedra Poplin. When I look at her, I see hope. I see purity. I see potential.

"I'm fine, my friend." I say, and mean it. I am fine. I'm never anything other than fine.

She smiles at me. I notice now that everyone else has walked off, leaving me alone with her. The imprints of Riley and Riot still pressed into the grass at our feet.

"I see the way you look at her."

"At the next host of Ophiuchus?"

"At *Riley*." She corrects.

I smile.

"I think any *one* of my species would look at the host of Ophiuchus the way I do. The world has been waiting for this for eons."

She scrunched her nose at me.

"Okay, demon boy. But I know what I see."

"*Demon boy?*" I snarl. Riley must've told her.

She shrugs her shoulders, skipping away from me as Tambo joins us. He's wearing his coven's colors and traditional dressings once more. I envied him, longing to be back in my traditional wear and skin, but I could only get a taste of that in the gap.

Suddenly, I craved the gap.

"Goeie more."

"I don't speak the filthy languages of *witches*."

Tambo raises his brow at me.

"No? I thought demons didn't pick and choose anything, much less languages?" He questions.

I pull my face at him. The word is spreading fast about my species. I guess Tambo was somewhat right. It isn't really of great importance if people find out. I am what I am and no amount of time in this cluster is going to change it. I might as well accept it.

"What do you want?"

"Nothing more than to help."

"Don't you think your coven has done enough when it comes to helping? You're the reason this is all happening."

Tambo let out a laugh that came straight from his midsection.

"Not all is what it seems, I would think you of all people would know that. Riley has her first stone, it's time to train her."

"Her ascension isn't due for quite some time."

Tambo clicks his tongue at me.

"Time waits for no one. You should know that better than anyone as well. Why do you think nothing but the proximity of Riley to Riot was enough to pull him from his mind flare?"

I hadn't even thought to question it then. The mere proximity of her was enough to make Riot whole again. Strong enough to fight off his father. The answer had been right in front of me all along. I make to storm off, leaving Tambo where he stood, but as I turn my back to him, he grabs my arm.

"I'll lead you to Elliot Mantrovere, but first, there's something you should know."

KAZ

We walked with Riley excitedly down towards Glistening Cove. Everyone was bubbling from the events that had just happened. I've always heard about Divine Connections, but most of the world revered them like tales of the faeries.

I don't even think my grandparents had ever seen one happen or anyone who bore the marks of the universe. The air was electric with excitement. Phaedra and Posh draped themselves over Riley, each having an arm slung around her shoulders as we sunk into the white sands.

"Can you tell us what it was like?" Phae exclaimed excitedly.

I watched Riley as she eyed the crystal clear waters that shone like glass, reflecting the moon on its surface.

"I don't really remember." She mumbles, avoiding everyone's eyes as she turns her back to the glassy surface.

"Oh Riley, it was beautiful for us. No one and I mean *no* one has ever seen a Divine Connection in our entire generation." Phae swooned.

"Come on Phae, you have no clue if that's true." Locke challenged.

"Sure I do."

"Just because you're a hopeless romantic doesn't mean you can attest to every person's experiences. I'm sure there have been some. They're *rare*, not impossible."

Sterling stormed onto the beach, his shoulders squared and jaw tight.

"There's Sterling now. Why don't you ask *him* if there have been any in the last, oh I don't know... hundred years?"

"Don't ask me shit." Sterling bit out.

Phae gave him a forlorn look, turning her attention back to Riley.

"Anyways, Riley. You and Riot looked at one another, and it was like the stars exploded."

"Yeah, into literal blackness." Locke scoffed.

"Still, it was amazing." She sighed, widening her eyes at him before turning back to her friend and continuing her recount of the connection.

"I knew what was happening the moment it went dark. Your elements emerged from your back like giant wings. The five of them tumbling about as one. Then, fire took over, exploding behind you!"

Riley looked up in horror.

"It was honestly the coolest thing I've ever seen." Locke reassures her.

Riley gives him a half smile, before looking down at her hands again, her hair covering her face.

"Sterling, what's the problem?" I ask. Riley mouths a secret thanks from under her lashes as everyone turns their attention onto the Nobelist.

Tambo silently joins us as we sit, waiting on Sterling to say something. He has his hands thrust into his pockets as he leans against a tree trunk.

"Well?" Locke leads him.

"Tell them Tambo." He says, closing his eyes.

Everyone looks at Tambo expectantly. He smiles slowly, understanding what Sterling has just done. He's made *him* the bad guy.

"As you wish, Sterling. I know where Elliot Mantrovere is located. He has the location of Arabia Samedi."

The group shares confused looks.

"I thought you said Arabia was *dead*?" Locke snaps at Riley.

Riley doesn't answer him, still hiding behind her hair. Phaedra flings her arm over Riley's shoulders, as if she's protecting her from Locke's sharp tongue.

"Don't yell at her. This has been traumatic for Riley enough as it is."

Riley mumbles something from under her hair, but I can't quite make out what it is.

"Tell them the truth." Sterling sneers from the tree.

"That is the truth." Tambo chides.

"None of this makes sense, Riley. You can't just say one thing and then change it later." Locke continues yelling at her.

Posh stands now to defend his twin and before I know what's

happening, everyone is yelling. Posh and Phaedra are yelling at Locke, who's throwing his arms around animatedly and shouting over them. Tambo abides by his covens conservative ways, but continues speaking, drawing out the vowels of his words, over Sterling who's speaking another language entirely.

"I said I can speak for myself!" Riley yells, standing.

Everyone stops to look at her.

"Riley?" Phae whimpers.

"No, I've had enough! I can speak for myself. I'm not broken, I'm *dying*. I don't want to spend the time I have left, listening to everyone fight."

Riot approaches her, reaching for her elbow, with his still blackened hand. Her hands are plastered to the sides of her head like if she lets go, it'll explode. She yanks her arm out of his reach just in time, and backs away from him.

"I can decide for myself, I can speak for myself." She directs at him.

"Riley, Please."

"Sterling. This connection shit... will I die or something if I'm not next to him?" Riley asks, ignoring Riot's plea.

"No."

Riley turns on her heel, facing the whole of the group.

"I'm dying. I need you all to help me help you to fix this before then."

"You don't know that you're dying." Phae whispers.

"No one who's ever housed Ophiuchus has lived for very long." Riley admitted.

There it was, a secret uncovered. Out in the open where it's most vulnerable.

"Riley, you really need to hear what Tambo's about to say." Sterling pushes off the tree, moving into the lot of us. He eyes Tambo who's still standing a few feet away.

"Sterling, I-"

"Tambo. The floor is yours." Sterling cuts her off.

Tambo adjusts his yellow vest, and walks into the center of the space, eyeing us all.

"As I was saying, Arabia Samedi is not dead. Elliot Mantrovere knows where she is and how to find her."

"Doesn't that mean *you* know how to find her? After all this time of me being here?"

"Let him finish, Riley." Sterling interrupts her, his jaw feathering.
"Arabia is hiding because she has safeguarded her life."
He turned now, facing Riley head on.
"With yours."

GEMINI COVEN

RILEY

"What the *fuck* does that mean?"

Tambo stands firm as I take a step towards him. There's only one thing keeping me from punching him in his smug mouth.

Respect.

I don't know if it's respect for Arabia or the coven; maybe it's for Tambo alone, but I just can't do it. The corner of his mouth tips up, like he knows what I'm thinking. When he answers, his voice is low, soft.

"Just what I said."

"So what you're saying is that Arabia pretended to be Riley's friend- all of our friends, just to use Riley's life?" Phae demands, exasperation in her tone.

Tambo nods, letting out a chuckle.

"I don't see what's so funny about this?" Posh says, coming up from my right, next to his sister.

"The snake knows."

His words slip out so effortlessly between his pearly teeth. It takes me a second to register what he means, but when I do, I round on Riot *fucking* Blair. He throws his hands up in front of himself, blocking my fists as I drive them madly into him. I land a couple of good hits to his chest and arms.

"Riley!" Multiple sets of hands pull me back from him, holding me in place, but I'm seeing red.

"What did you do?" I scream.

"Nothing!"

"Liar!"

Sterling somehow put himself between us before I even saw him. Probably using the gap, but right now all I wanted was for him to move so I could punch Riot. It's unfair how even with the dirt on the side of his face, he's gorgeous.

"Tell me the truth, Riot Blair!" I yell, my chest heaving as I stop fighting the hands holding me steady.

He swallows hard looking around at all of us, his gaze moving from Locke to Kaz, and finally, to me.

"Arabia... Arabia was working for my dad." He lets out.

"No!" Phae screams.

"You *knew* that? You knew that and you never told me. Is this some sick fucking joke to you all?" I yell, thrashing to get away from whomever was holding me in place.

"I didn't have any part in this!" Phae yelled.

"Not you, *him*" I snarl, pointing a finger at Riot.

"I didn't have any part in it Riley, I swear!" Riot takes a step towards me, like he's trying to catch the pieces of me as they shattered, but I move away.

"*Don't touch me!*" I hiss.

"Riley, I think you should hear the rest." Sterling interjects.

I face my body towards Tambo, my back to Riot. As I wait, my heart slams on the other side of my chest. My emotions were out of control and I could feel something changing within me. Something right now was toppling over the edge and into unchartered lands. A feeling I'd come to know as Ophiuchus making a move.

"I can get you, all of you, to Elliot. However, none of you are ready to face him." Tambo continues.

I stare at him blankly despite the storm brewing inside of me. His words becoming my undoing. Ophiuchus pushing on the underside of my skin, threatening to break loose. Promising to protect me. I try giving in just a little to see what will happen, but nothing does.

"Riley, I think you should know that Arabia's actions to save her life over yours, they can't be undone. Whether she did it with ill intention or not, the fact remains that if Arabia Samedi dies, you will too."

I don't move.

I don't yell.

After everything. After all that time with Arabia at Pleaides and

Gemini Coven. After introducing me to her people. After eating with them, learning about them. I even danced with ferns. I wore their clothes and accepted their traditions.

I *must* have meant something to her.

To *them*.

"Riley," Phae's voice is light, just barely above a whisper.

I don't move. I'm as still as a statue, halfway hoping that if I'm still enough, I'll disappear into the gap. Into nothingness. What's the point of existing at all if everyone just wants to hurt me?

"Riley." Sterling whispers.

I feel him graze my arm as my body succumbs to numbness. My chest burns like I'm drowning and I realize I'm not breathing. Losing my balance, I flail my arm out and Sterling catches me on my right just as Riot catches my left. They ease me to the ground.

Sterling tucks some hair behind my right ear, the foot of his palm grazing my cheek as he does. A cool sparkling sensation poses between his skin and mine, causing my eyes to dart to his. When I find his silver eyes, his face is full of disbelief.

STERLING

Riley stopped breathing. I could feel her heart thumping wildly in her chest as her lungs screamed for air. She was holding her breath as her eyes darted around wildly. Riot shoots me a sideways glance and we both move quickly to grab her, easing her down to the sand.

"I will take you to Elliot," Tambo says again.

"Now is not the time, Tambo."

Phaedra elbows her way between Riot and I, falling to her knees in front of Riley.

"Her marks are…different…" I whisper, not caring who heard me.

"What? What marks?" Phae asked, looking over her shoulder at me.

I can't take my eyes off Riley's face, and Phae follows my gaze to Riley's right temple. She shuts her eyes solemnly as Phae and I stare. Riot kneels beside me, the moon our only source of light. He stares at my profile intently. I can feel from his energy that he doesn't want to look.

"Please tell me she has the marks…" he whispers to me.

I don't answer. I don't budge. I don't even dare to blink. I can see from my peripheral vision that he swallows hard before looking at her. He narrows his eyes, leaning in.

"Why are they scarred?"

"They're white." Phae hisses.

"No matter what they are, they are different than other marks. Traditionally, they have always been black."

Phaedra signals Posh to come look as Riley squeezes her eyes together tightly. A single tear rolls down her cheek. I know she's confused, but I'm not stupid. I know that regardless of how she may have felt about Riot before, she most likely didn't now. I also know that based on the timing of her tear, it was most likely for me.

It's not crazy to think we have something between us. We shared too many intimate moments for us to just be friends. Battle partners. We had a connection I could feel in my soul the moment I first saw her. I mean, I felt it when she was moments away, before I could even physically see her. That's not something you come across every single day.

Although we are ethereal, demons abide by the same rules the universe sets forth for everyone. You can't undo a Divine Connection and you might as well not even try because the punishment for that is even greater than watching someone you love connected to someone who's not you.

But I don't care.

I'm going to try.

Perdition help me, because I don't even care that warmth billows within my core like a wildfire every single time I think about her, growing and igniting over and over again.

"I'm fine. Tambo?" She chokes out.

Tambo moves forward, kneeling down before Riley. He could have stood where he had been. He could have spoken from his place in the circle. Witches have notoriously *never* bowed to anyone. Yet here he was, bowing to her.

"Yes, Priestess?" The word left his mouth but it wasn't said as a position or a title. It was said as a *name*. A name for her.

I think it fit perfectly.

"Please lead us to Elliot. I'll do anything it takes to be ready to face him."

"It's not him I worry about you facing. It's Arabia."

"I'll find Arabia."

He smiles, taking Riley's hands in his.

"I know you will, Priestess. When you do, I know you will find a way to combat this. I know you'll find a way to take this life as your own."

Riley smiles at him, nodding her head.

"So, what now?" Phaedra asks.

I help pull Riley to her feet before answering her.

"Now? Now, we get ready for a fight. Death is approaching, and she's taking someone with her."

TAMBO

    The day my father introduced me to the Samedi family was the worst day of my life. My father's loyalty to the coven drove my mother crazy. She wanted us out of the coven and safe, living independently of them. He said no and she left. His loyalty to the Priest outweighed his sorrows for her absence, and I was quickly thrust into a position of serving him and the Priest.

    Samedi wasn't just dark, he was evil. Using me for things children should never be subjected to. His only mercy came after he had his one and only daughter, Arabia. Of course, I was already eighteen by then. My life path had always been to leave the coven once I was able, but Arabia's birth changed everything.

    When she was just six, Samedi fell to his own demise, leaving me in charge of her. It's wrong to hate children, but I sure did. I did right by her, and eventually, respected her. That is, until she was handed the coven.

    Arabia Samedi is not one to mess with. She is a powerful siphon witch, fully using her powers and her zodiac to overpower many. The real change was the day she was summoned by King Blair to do his bidding. I don't know what he threatened her with, but I can only imagine.

    Arabia has always been stoic towards us, but she left us to fend for ourselves from our secret hiding place, upheld entirely by magic. For the first time in over twenty years, we were at peace. Her time away at Pleaides was a blessing. Then, one day, she brought the next host of

Ophiuchus to us. Right to me.

Everything the Samedi Priests had done, had been to find Ophiuchus. Finding and controlling the host meant possible transfer of Ophiuchus from them to the Priest, granting the coven immortality and untapped power. What the Priest didn't realize was that no one had been able to successfully host it. Not ever.

So, they worked, concocting spells and incantations meant to entrance and trap Ophiuchus, hopefully allowing them to transfer it to one of their own. They think they've found the way, but I know better.

Arabia answered the king's call a little too excitedly for my liking. When she disclosed what spells she had done from the coven's black book, I knew that Riley needed to be protected. My moves to make sure Riley had ample time with Madam Devereux were not by accident.

The attack was unforeseen, however it landed us right where we needed to be. Here.

I started training Riley and her friends to siphon magic only days ago and their progress has been astounding. We moved into siphoning from harder things like the elements around us. I circle around them now, as they stand in the same clearing I destroyed Riley's fondness for Arabia in. Their independent work was blossoming.

"I can't do this!" Phae yells, picking up dirt and throwing it, blasting it with air onto Locke.

"Dirt has no energy!"

"Everything has energy, Phae." I say. For a butterfly, she was fiery.

"So you throw it at me?" Locke says, wiping the dirt from his white tank.

"I could throw something else, if you prefer?"

"Phaedra, finding energy is hard. You have to open yourself up to the area. Close your eyes."

She closes them, her entire demeanor becoming soft again, the way we knew her. Her hair long and whipping around in the wind. Posh approached us, ready to help. His own long hair was pulled up into a neat bun on the crown of his head. Everyone had been on edge these past few days, the twins being no exception.

"I find connection between my wings. Where they attach to my back." He offers her.

She shoots him a sidelong look, crossing her arms.

"I can do it myself and find my own connection, Posh."

"Alright, I'm just trying to help,"

"I'm not a baby. In fact, I'm older than you."

I know that, Phaedra, I'm just trying to help." He takes a step back.

"I think tension is running high and perhaps we should stop for now?" The suggestion disperses the group and I watch as Riley runs off after Phae.

"I think we're coming along just fine." Sterling says, stopping beside me.

His wings were out, glistening against the sun. His shirtless body, slicked with sweat from helping Kaz and Locke. I nodded slowly as I watched Riley until she was out of sight. Witches don't mingle with those who hail from Perdition, but Sterling was hard not to like.

He took care of everyone around him, making sure they had everything they needed. He even cared for the coven, something he didn't have to do.

"Yeah."

"Listen Tambo," he starts. I busy myself picking up the staffs and crystals left behind from the days' work.

"We need to go find Elliot. We've been here for days. We've trained. I have them, I can take care of them."

I don't answer. Leading them to Elliot was giving them a death sentence. Ever since that day, I wished I hadn't offered it.

"I don't want to tell you, if I'm being honest." I shrug.

"*What?*" He snarls.

I stack the staffs on a nearby boulder, and turn to face him.

"Just what I said."

Before I know it, he's got me in his clutches, his eyes daring to pull me into my own personal hell. I'm not stupid, I know what he's capable of, but the closer I get to having to lead them to him, the more I feel like Death is my only friend.

"You'll tell me now. We are going today." He whispers.

"Sterling!" I hear Riley screech from somewhere behind him. Even though I know he could easily torture me, I keep my eyes fixed on his.

"Stop! Stop now!" She yells, pulling at Sterling's large frame.

"I'm not doing shit. He's backing out of his promise."

Riley scrunches her nose up, narrowing her eyes. She looks between us, waiting for Sterling to let me go. When he does, he pushes off me and I have to fight to stay upright.

"You'll give us Elliot, Tambo." Her voice is even. Firm.

"It's a death sentence."

She scoffs, "I have several of those already. What's one more?"

She has a point. I drop my shoulders in defeat. I couldn't stop this even if I wanted to. It was over. They were going to see him whether I gave him to them or not.

Unless I lie. Unless I truly believe he's somewhere he's not. Anything is worth trying at this point. I don't want any more blood on my hands.

Sterling backed up, a sickening smile crossing his face.

"He's going to lie. I can see it."

"Tambo?" Riley questions me.

"It's fine Riley. In his lies, I saw where he really was. He was trying to convince himself that Elliot was somewhere else, but in doing that, he's shown me Elliot's exact location." He sneered.

I lower my head, shaking it.

"I thought you were a friend, at least to Riley. You're nothing but a pathetic coward. Just like your father." He sneers at me.

Riley crosses her arms. I can see disappointment written all over her face. It's nothing compared to the disappointment I feel in myself, although it's not for the same reasons that Riley and her friends feel.

I've failed my father. I've failed my coven.

"The truth is.. Elliot controls Gemini Coven. If he says to do something, we must do it. He's not just a promiscuous drunk."

"What do you mean *controls* Gemini Coven?" Sterling demands, taking a step towards me.

"Control your peasant or I'll stop talking."

Sterling grabs me by the throat, squeezing hard. He stopped just enough that air could make it through, but it was uncomfortable. My heart rate increased suddenly, catching up with what my body's experiencing, giving me a sudden head rush.

"Careful, *witch*."

"Sterling." Riley snaps.

"Tambo, please. If you cared about Arabia at all. About this coven. About *me*. Please just tell us what Elliot's plans are, what control he has over this coven."

My eyes left hers, Sterling's grip loosening on my throat as they noticed the coven members surrounding us.

"Let him go." The Madame Devereux spoke.

RILEY

The Madame stood before us, dressed in all white. Her dress flowed to the ground, her hair, pulled back into a high bun. Her head was adorned with jewels and chains. The coven stood behind her, all of their eyes on me.

"Madame." I breathed.

"Riley. I'm not sure what's going on here, but it's time to dismiss Tambo."

"Thank you, Madame." Tambo said, grateful.

"From this coven."

"Wh-What?" Tambo stammered. Chatter and whispers broke out all around us.

"Madame?" I couldn't believe what she was suggesting.

"Tambo, you have revealed secrets of this coven,"

"For the betterment of those he cares for!" I cut her off.

"He doesn't care about anyone. He's not even a witch."

Her tone is even, and very matter of fact. Back in the Gemini Coven hideout, she was never like this. She was helpful and kind. Full of magic and truths. So very different from how she's here now.

"Does it matter? He's been a part of this coven all of his life."

Defending Tambo wasn't on my list of things I wanted to be doing, but I couldn't just let them just kick him out. For one, I knew if he was, he would most likely follow us and I didn't want to risk him betraying any of us again.

"You're sticking up for him?" She asks, perplexed.

I look around at the coven people who stood behind her. Their faces neutral to the situation that was rapidly unfolding before us. The twins, Locke and Kaz must've heard the commotion, because they were now headed this way with Riot in tow.

My heart rate quickened at seeing him behind them, rushing to get to us. To me. Elation and warmth spread through me and at the same time, I'm mentally kicking myself for it.

"I guess I am." I say, straightening my back.

She nods slowly. The trees that surround us seem to even hold their winds in lieu of missing a single word. I stare at her, waiting for whatever's next. My elements tingling in my palms, swirling around one another, letting me know they are there. I can feel Ophiuchus, stroking the corners of my mind.

If there was anything Riot was right about, it was about the darkness that lurked there, always. Ever since I could remember, it's been there. I may not have known at the time what it was, but I know now.

I had another choice to accept it or not, even though I don't believe Ophiuchus will give me that choice fully. I need to learn more. All I know is what I feel.

"Riley, we can help you, but not if you stand against us." Madame warned.

"I'm not standing against you. I'm standing for what's right. It's inhumane to throw Tambo out of his home, regardless of how he has acted."

"Don't you guys have a punishment system or something?" Locke piped up from next to Riot.

Everyone's eyes darted to Locke and Riot, who stood beside him. Some murmured aloud, whispers of *Blair* and *traitor* filled the air.

"As a matter of fact," Madame began, raising her right hand.

The world stilled, but before I could react, she shot a shard of white light towards Tambo that shattered into thirteen shards, and sent them flying towards the covens advisor.

"No!" I screamed, rushing forward, flinging my body in front of his, but I was too late.

I could feel the air rushing past me, as I turned to Tambo who was still standing. His eyes were on the Madame, a smile across his face.

"As you wish, Madame." He whispered, falling to the ground.

"Tambo!" I screamed so loudly, that the coven and Madame were blown back from it.

Pulling Tambo's limp body onto my lap, I could see blood starting to seep through his bright yellow dashiki. Its fine embroidery warping from bright greens and colorful flowers to bright red.

"Tambo?" I whisper.

His eyes meet mine, a single tear escaping down his cheek.

"I'm sorry priestess." He whispers.

I place a hand to his cheek.

"You have nothing to be sorry for. Nothing."

He smiles.

"You can do this, Priestess. You are so much more than they know."

"Shhhh." I caress his cheek, mildly aware that the Madame is yelling something in the distance.

"Go." He whispers.

"Riley," Riot's voice is soft, but urgent.

I throw a shield over us to buy more time. Any ounce of time.

"I'm not leaving you."

"Riley, we have to go." Phaedra tries.

I can see Riot touch her shoulder out of my peripherals as Tambo nods slowly.

"I'm with you Priestess. Long live, Riley."

With that, he was gone. My chest heaved, my heart shattering in my ears. I can't leave him here. Once we cull away, who knows what she will do to him.

"Riley," Riot tries again.

"We take him." I say, looking up at them all, despite the tears streaming down my face.

"What?" Riot's confusion is clear.

The Madame and coven members are on their feet now, rushing towards us. I look over my shoulder and all around us as their magic bounces off my shield, no match for its power.

"Riley, we can't take Tambo."

They're right. What am I going to do with his body? The next place we cull to, Elliot will be there. He very well could be prepared for a fight.

"I need time to think." I whisper.

"We don't have time." Locke says taking up a fighting stance.

"Yes we do." Riot stands up, readying himself next to Locke.

"We do?"

"You've frozen your surroundings before, can you do it again?"

I did that out of fear that day in the park. I have no clue how I did it, either. Up until now, all of my powers have emerged out of a situation I couldn't control. I look at Tambo's peaceful face, still so young. You could believe he was sleeping.

Control.

"Riley," Riot calls out, his voice cracking as he braces for impact.

All of their backs are to me as each one of them take a fighting stance around Tambo and I. My shield cracking in various places under the pressure of the coven.

"Riley!" Phae yells.

Tambo's head is heavy as I pick it up, and gently move him aside, resting his head on the soft ground next to me. If this didn't work, we would be surrounded by the coven and I felt cracked and broken already. It was a fight I didn't want to have.

"Riley! Now!" Kaz called out just as my shield gave way.

I can do this.

I can *do* this.

Arms spread out, I welcome in the darkness that's going stir crazy at the edges of my mind, letting my control of it go. My mind races, looking for a feeling to land on, but for once, I didn't have one. I usually land on anger. On hatred and survival.

This time, those thoughts were meshed with something else. Of course all I could vision were green eyes, a storm of emotions paired with them. Those eyes have given me stress, hell, intimacy, fear and more since the day they landed on me in that club.

My mind races through the events of that night, and locks in on him from across the room. The first smile he ever shot my way. That's it. That's my control. I let that emotion roll through my core like an avalanche. Within seconds, Ophiuchus greets me, matching my soul at its core. I can see the auras of everyone around me and grab onto my people, throwing us into time itself. The space around us responds immediately. The coven members freeze, elements and formations in mid flight, stopped now.

"Holy shit!" Locke exclaims, looking around.

Phaedra runs from her position over to me.

"We have to hurry, I have no idea how long I can hold this." I tell her, motioning to Tambo. She nods, stooping down beside him.

"Hang on, I can help." Locke says, rushing over to help. " I can move the Earth easily and quickly. Where do you want him?"

I look around at the space we have under my shield. There's no way we are going to be able to get through the coven frozen in place, but this is the perfect spot. Across from the cove were some Lilly gardens. My favorite ones of the whole school.

"Over there." I say, gesturing towards them.

Posh makes busy floating Tambo's body with us to the short iron gate that led to the normally peaceful setting. There are two bushes that are blooming colors as bright as Tambo's meticulous embroidery on his many dashikis.

"Here. Here is perfect." I say, sniffling.

The boys quickly get to work, moving the soil and various rocks out of the way. When they are done, Kaz uses his water magic to wash the blood from Tambo's linens, making them look new. He washes the dirt from his back, hands and face, and then steps aside as Phae uses formations to bloom a flower, leaving it floating in the air next to her.

She pulls out a small knife and gathers her long hair in one hand. Without taking her eyes off Tambo, she slices it right at her collar bone. Posh cries out then lets out a welp as Kaz elbows him in the ribs to shut him up. She curls the strands around her fist, and lays it in a circle over his heart, the flower in it and steps away. A sign of respect, love and goodbye from a butterfly.

It's my turn to say goodbye within minutes and I'm not ready. Riot and Sterling take a place on either side of me, making Ophiuchus purr within me like an idling engine.

I square my shoulders and step forward to his side.

"Goodbye, my friend. May Death greet you as the friend you always said her to be."

With that, Posh lowered him into the grave Locke had created. When he was settled, I turned my back to him for the last time. I have never been good at goodbyes and now wasn't any different. This wasn't the way I wanted to leave him but we didn't have a choice.

"Let's go." I whisper. Sterling and Riot gently place their hands on either of my shoulders. The others join them and I launch into the cull, bringing us to none other than the Pub Girl Club, where I met him for the very first time almost a year ago.

RIOT

We landed at a seedy club in the middle of none other than the fucking Outliers. *Again.* The music boomed from inside the club, rattling its cheap windows. The parking lot filled with vehicles you'd never find in Pantheon for the simple fact that they weren't high class.

"Okay, this time, I *know* it's the Outliers, but what is this place?" Locke asked, looking around at the various cars. Even with the clubs attempts to light this place, it was dingy and dull like the rest of the Outliers.

"Riley?" An unknown voice came from somewhere behind us. I turned to see Riley running into the arms of a tiny girl with hair that ended by her ears in all different colors.

"Chains!"

"I can see why they call her *that*." I scoff to Locke who laughs.

I wish someone would have told me Riley being Ophiuchus meant that she now had supersonic hearing because she shot me a look that made my gut churn. Normally, I probably would have loved getting that kind of reaction out of anyone, especially her. Now, it was different.

Call it whatever you want, but maybe there are perks to Divine Connections after all. I'd heard about them growing up, but it was never meant for me, or so I thought.

"How are you? Where the fuck have you been and...and who are those guys?" Her raspy voice carried over us.

For someone so small she was so loud. She wiggled her brows at us from over Riley's shoulder as Riley laughed. Locke flexed, wiggling his eyebrows at her.

"I'll introduce you, although I'm sure Locke will do that himself." She laughed.

"Indeed I will! My name's Locke as Star girl said- I'm a minotaur."

I don't hear the rest of their conversation because as Locke leans on the hood of a random car, Sterling nudges my arm, pointing to a blonde haired man staring at us from across the lot.

"That's him."

"Why is he watching us?" I question, looking *the* Elliot Mantrovere up and down.

I'd seen him growing up in Pantheon weekly magazines and on advertisements, but in person, there was something different about him. He was riddled with darkness and secrets. Something was so familiar about him, but I couldn't put my finger on it.

Of all the high end advisors, kings from other lands, famous shifters, authors and millionaires, my father had never managed to get a Mantrovere to come to Stone Castle. Not to a single party or Loyalist meeting, even though the Mantrovere family were known supporters of the Blair reign.

"Riley, our appointment is about to pass." I call over my shoulder to her, not bothering to take my eyes of him.

I hear her saying her goodbyes to her friend and make a mental note to ask her more about Chains and her life here in pantheon as soon as we have time.

Elliot matches my stare, not daring to take his eyes off me, as he smokes a cigarette. The embers light the left half of his face that's hidden in the shadows of the club beside him. His white tee shirt is pulled on his muscles so that I can see his body is chiseled. His black pants so tight, I'm not sure they won't rip at the seams and fall off if he tries walking towards us.

Riley leads the way towards Elliot, all of us marching behind her like an army. Elliot smirks, revealing perfect teeth. His blue eyes set on Riley. He drank her in like she was the best meal he'd ever had and it made my insides boil. I felt fire awaken, roaring through my veins.

"Elliot." Riley started, coming to a stop in front of him.

"Spice runner! So nice to see you again." He says, flicking his cigarette to the ground and stepping on it. His pants didn't rip after all.

" I see you've made new friends in lieu of your old ones. Didn't even care to check on them after the fate you left them with."

I feel a pang of guilt that must belong to Riley under the heat of my element, because the feeling definitely isn't mine and I sure as fuck don't like the way it feels.

"I-I..."

"You what? Got new friends and forgot about your old ones. It's that simple. Just say what it is." He hunched over and stretched back, shoving his hands into his pockets as he chuckled.

"That's not true."

"Isn't it?"

"I just saw Chains. I know they aren't dead." Riley bit out.

Elliot laughed a hearty laugh. It echoed off the alleyway, obviously laced with saccharine. When he got the gist of it out, he stopped abruptly, meeting Riley's eyes again.

"Who said I was going to kill them?"

"You did."

"I didn't. Or did I?" Elliot tilted his head, making a show of trying to remember a conversation they apparently had at some point.

"Stop the games, Elliot."

"Stop lying to these people, Riley. Pretending to be something you're not."

He smiled again.

"What? You think I didn't follow your whereabouts? You went off to Pleaides with more money you'd ever seen in your life. You met Arabia and from there, the moment you crossed into Pleaides, you forgot about them. And apparently, you made such an impression to the universe that you've been bestowed the rare gift of a Divine Connection. "

"What did you do to the others?" She asked, ignoring him.

"*Do* to them? I didn't *do* anything. They made their choice and their choice was that they didn't really like being forced into the position of a sacrificial lamb." He shrugged.

As he spoke, two men and two women stepped out from the shadows. Riley backed up a couple of steps, her eyes wide with recognition.

"Snake, Fang.. Chains?" She gasped.

"You see Riley, you light the match, the bridge burns." Elliot chimed.

"You can't have everything without losing anything. You want to be special and powerful. You want someone to love you, but what sacrifice have *you* made, Riley?"

"Hey, man. That's my Divine you're taunting." I say stepping in front of her.

"Riot Blair. Word on the street is your life is worth an awful lot these days. What's stopping me from cashing in on that prize?"

"Nothing, motherfucker, so sign on the dotted line."

RILEY

I have to admit, Riot standing up for me, going after the elusive and admittedly handsome Elliot Mantrovere, had my emotions tied up in a confusing way. Maybe having Riot Blair stick up for you wasn't so bad after all. What was truly nice though, was not being the subject of Riot's anger.

"Riot, I can handle this." I try.

"Sssh." Sterling shushed me, stepping back with me as Riot took up the space between them and us.

"Tell us where Arabia Samedi is." Riot demands.

Elliot laughs. I take the time while they're talking to look over at my crew. They look like themselves, but different. Something is off about them as they stand there, motionless and staring at me. Something familiar, but foreign all the same.

As I watched, it was like they weren't even seeing me. I just spoke to Chains moments ago. She recognized me and seemed like her typical self, just with her normal pixie cut growing out. I remember her always cutting it off because she couldn't stand the way it felt, but people change their hair all the time. They didn't *all* look different based on just her haircut.

There was something else.

"Riot," I warn.

He's getting awfully close to Elliot and I don't want them to touch. I'm sensing something new. I can almost bet it's Ophiuchus trying to tell me something, but I can't quite put my finger on it. As Elliot makes small advances towards Riot, I can see that my crew is mimicking the movements, closing in on us.

"Elliot, what's going on. You weren't like this the last time we met." I say, trying to distract him while I think of a plan.

"You see Riley, I'm really sick of having to chase down what I want."

"Chase it down? You're a *Mantrovere*, Elliot. Surely you have everything you need?'

I motion to Sterling that we should grab him and cull, but he's already on it, making small strides away from the group to try and position himself behind Elliot.

"Of course I have everything I need, Riley. What kind of question is that?"

"Not one meant to taunt you, of course. I'm just asking. You seemed like you really cared about me and what I needed." I lied.

Sterling motioned for me to move forward at the same pace he was. My heart thumped and I hoped Elliot couldn't sense it. We made our first advancement undetected. Even with my heart betraying me, he was still going.

"I don't have what I *want*, Riley. There's a difference."

"Oh yeah? And what is it that you could possibly want that you don't already have, Elliot?"

He lets out a loud laugh that booms off the strip club wall. Elliot's moves are laced with spirits. He'd clearly already had a few and was slightly drunk, which was helping Sterling and I as we took another step closer. Riot kept pace with me, making it look like we weren't really moving at all.

"You know Riley, I know you don't really want to know what it is that I want, but I'm going to tell you anyways."

Another step closer.

"I want to be rich and not riche because of my name. I want to be rich for what I do."

Another step.

"I want to live in Pantheon, on the throne I *deserve*."

Another step.

"I want to eat lots of food and get really fat and then siphon all that stored energy, using it to lull Ophiuchus out from hiding inside your body, and use these spells we've been generating for over a hundred years to trap it."

Another step.

We were right on him now.

"I guess what I'm saying is, I want *you* Riley."

Before I saw it coming, he reached out, grabbing onto Riot and I just as Sterling reached his back. I had time to see him throw out his hands but everything happened too quickly to be sure whether or not he came with us. We spun over and between one another until we landed in a huge ballroom with black marble floors and high ceilings.

I look around, trying to place the room in my mind. My eyes darted around the room until I landed on green eyes, slicked back hair, the smell of burning flesh infiltrating my nose.

I tore my eyes away, the rolling feeling of doom creeping up my spine. The next thing my eyes saw, took my break away. A naked Arabia, on her knees, wearing an iron collar with a chain protruding from the middle. The chain looked thick and heavy. I could see multiple cuts around Arabia's neck and shoulders, some still bleeding.

My eyes followed the chain as it coiled and circled around itself on the floor, until it disappeared behind a black cloak. I met the gaze of the familiar green eyes again. I'd seen them before, but these ones were much older, clouded with the fog of disapproval, and something adding to them that I couldn't quite place.

"Welcome, Riley. To Stone Castle."

Coming Soon...

A ZODIAC RISING NOVEL

GODS & BEASTS

SEVEN

Made in the USA
Columbia, SC
09 February 2023